Don Carlos and
Giovanni

MASTERWORKS OF FICTION

Our advisory board

Douglas Messerli, *Publisher*

THORVALD STEEN

Don Carlos *and* Giovanni

Translated from the Norwegian by James Anderson

MASTERWORKS OF FICTION
(1993 / 1995)

GREEN INTEGER
KØBENHAVN & LOS ANGELES
2004

GREEN INTEGER BOOKS
Edited by Per Bregne
København / Los Angeles

Distributed in the United States by Consortium Book Sales and Distribution
1045 Westgate Drive, Suite 90, Saint Paul, Minnesota 55114-1065
Distributed in England and throughout Europe by
Turnaround Publisher Services
Unit 3, Olympia Trading Estate
Coburg Road, Wood Green, London N22 6TZ
44 (0)20 88293009

(323) 857-1115 / http://www.greeninteger.com

First Green Integer Edition 2004
English language copyright ©2004, 1997 by James Anderson
These fictions were first published in Norway as
Don Carlos (Oslo: Tiden Norsk Forlag, 1993) and
Giovanni (Oslo: Tiden Norsk Forlag, 1995)
Published by agreement with Tiden Norsk Forlag
Don Carlos was previously published in English
by Sun & Moon Press (Los Angeles, 1997)
Back cover copy ©2004 by Green Integer
All rights reserved.

The translation of these books was made possible, in part,
through grants from NORLA (Norwegian Literature Abroad)
for which we thank that organization.

Design: Per Bregne
Typography & Cover: Trudy Fisher
Cover Photograph of Thorvald Steen ©John Petter Reinertsen/Samfoto

LIBRARY OF CONGRESS CATALOGING IN PUBLICATION DATA
Thorvald Steen [1954]
Don Carlos and *Giovanni*
ISBN: 1-931243-79-4
p. cm — Green Integer 137
I. Title II. Series III. Translator

Green Integer books are published for Douglas Messerli
Printed in the United States of America on acid-free paper.

BOOKS BY THORVALD STEEN

Hemmeligstemplete roser (1983)
Gjerrige fallskjermer (1985)
Neonulvene (1987)
Månekisten (1988)
Tungen (1991)
Ilden (1992)
Don Carlos (1993)
Giovanni (1995)
En fallskjerm til folket (1995)
Jungel. Essays om litteratur og politikk (1996)
Kongen av Sahara (1997)
De tålmodige (1997)
Konstantinopel (1999)
Den lille hesten (2002)
Historier om Istanbul (2003)
Fra Reykholt til Bosporus (2003)

Don Carlos

Buenos Ayres, 23rd September 1833

Dear Roberto!

Outside I can hear intermittent gunfire. The clouds seem to drift nowhere today. They will soon gather. The sky is pregnant with rain. Thank you for your long letter. When I woke up I felt sure I would spend the whole day writing to you. As soon as I picked up the pen I was struck by the thought: what is my real purpose in this world? I took a nap. I thought I might find an explanation.

Sleep released me. The walls embrace my bed.

Sometimes I find myself wishing that you'd done something really bad. I believe you might have been closer to me had you committed some terrible or indecent act. Perhaps then I'd have felt some devotion and concern.

Do you remember the last time we saw each other? I lied to you. It was on the quayside in Genoa. We were leaving. The schooner was to weigh anchor for Buenos Ayres next day. We'd said goodbye to mother three days before. We'd hugged her for a long time and cried. I'd arranged berths for us both aboard the Santa Maria. In my pocket were the tickets I'd been given earlier that day. I said nothing about them to you. We stood on the quay ready to embark in a few hours. A wicked thought possessed me. I begrudged you the pleasure of coming with me. I asked you to look after the baggage and said I was going to collect the tickets which were in my name. I went behind the warehouse shed and tore up your ticket. When I returned I said there wasn't any room for you aboard. I comforted you by saying that you'd surely have another chance. You accepted all I said without a single murmur. We embraced each other. I wept. You went back home. What would have happened if we'd made the crossing together and been forced to take to the lifeboats? If there'd been room for just one of us, would I have given that place to you?

I think of the last years we lived together. You and mother prayed for me in vain. The first few years I felt like a traitor. Can anything be worse than disappointing your family? You consoled yourselves in the knowledge that luckily father never knew anything about it. I expect you think my moral standards have shrunk from the size of an orange to that of a pea after I renounced my childhood faith. Your opinion can hardly have been altered by what I've written here. Before you deliver your final verdict, I ask you to call to mind the pious Father Razio. Do you remember how he tied you to a tree, after pulling off your breeches? I heard your shouts for help and came to your aid. No one was in any doubt about what he'd been planning to do. Nor was there any doubt amongst us then that he was a true believer with intense moral strength. Give me a chance, Roberto! Believe me when I say that God still tempts me. I can't tell if it's in my flesh, my spirit or my words, but — he tempts me. I can't accept that he exists, but when I brush him aside, I feel remorse. He's the part of me that won't let itself be fobbed off by the poor creature that I am. He transforms himself each time I try to seize hold of him. Father used to say: God was interrupted by man.

My relations with women are the same as before. I shall waste no more words on childhood and women, merely learn to forget. Send my greetings to your wife and to your two children whom I would so dearly love to embrace and toss into the air. I wish all four of you every happiness.

Governor Balcarce has lost control of the government troops. General Rosas' supporters have begun opening fire in the city itself. The president stands for the French ideals of freedom. He's hamstrung. The gaucho's leader is against everything European: "Our church and our cattle industry will be ruined." Rosas pledges allegiance to the memory of José de San Martín, the hero of Argentine independence; the academic Balcarce to Diderot and Voltaire. He doesn't look as if he's ever sat on a horse. At any rate, he's no warrior. Rosas is the patriot, the *Argentine*, and sceptical of industrialization. It's only a matter of time before Rosas takes Buenos Ayres. It's civil war. Rosas can put up an effective blockade if he wants to. The city is surrounded. People are killed every day. My tall frame has become gaunt since last you saw me. A few white hairs streak my dark mane. My appearance interests me less and less.

There's an animal skull on the stool in the corner. It was given to me by an Englishman. An odd fellow. He's told me everything about his short life. He thinks it's possible to reconcile religion and science. He really means it! His name is Charles Robert Darwin. Here he is known simply as Don Carlos. He's no older than you. Twenty-four. A whippersnapper. A new hand.

It's raining.

Outside it smells of dust, gunpowder and garbage. The sewer is open to the street. The houses here on the southern side of the city are built of driftwood and any other materials that come to hand. Nearer the city center there are whitewashed brick bungalows with roof gardens. At present their windows are barred and shuttered. Further north is the most important plaza in the city and the country, Plaza de la Victoria. Public buildings several stories high surround the plaza. The buildings and the avenues that radiate from the plaza are wide and imposing. This fast-growing city wishes to surpass its European models in size and splendor. Delusions of grandeur. The rich live around the Plaza de la Victoria or in the northernmost parts of the city in Palermo or Recoleta. Buenos Ayres has Spanish, English and French quarters. An Italian quarter is springing up here in Boca. The Indians aren't allowed to settle in the city, but they may sell their wares in the market. The blacks are either slaves or servants of the rich. The city stretches like an elongated dragon by the Río de la Plata. And here, in the bowels of this troubled beast, I live!

I've forgotten what you looked like, Roberto. It makes it easier to write.

I met Don Carlos between two of the twelve Corinthian columns outside the Metropolitan Cathedral, the biggest church in the city. I was just about to go in when I heard a voice say, in rather broken Spanish:

"What a marvelous building. I take it the pillars represent the twelve apostles?"

I turned and saw a tall man, maybe six foot high. His hair was long and blonde and he had a receding hairline. The powerful features were framed by a large beard. The beard didn't make him look at all bad. I mean that without a face he looked quite pleasant. His forehead sloped down to his eyebrows. They were strong and bushy. His eyes lay in shadow. Were they brown? After a while I noticed that they had an expression of total calm. Peaceful and extrovert. An observer. His head reminded me of one of the earliest human crania ever found: homo primigenius. Sunlight streamed from a rift in the overcast sky. I glanced in through the cathedral's open doors. That floor! I never tire of looking at it. Flowers. Red, white, green, yellow and blue in Venetian mosaic!

"Yes," I answered in English.

He grasped a light, wide-brimmed felt hat in his right hand. The beard had fooled me. It made him look older. He gazed at me in astonishment and said:

"You're not English, are you?"

As the lover of an Englishwoman here in the city,

I'd picked up a few words of the language. He continued:

"I'm passing through."

"And English?" I said.

"Yes."

I became loquacious:

"My name is Giovanni Graciani. I was born at Varazze, a small town twenty miles west of Genoa. Two years ago I settled in Boca, or Little Liguria as we Genoese call it. We live by the harbor. There are also a few Andalusians, Balts and Croats. Some of us wish to move closer to the center of the city because of the tides. It's so muddy where we live. The tides are so huge. We fear the spring tide when there's an on-shore wind."

"I disembarked there. Is that why the houses are built on piles?"

I nodded. He was still speaking Spanish. He used the odd word of English when he got stuck.

"I live in the Calle de la Ribera. I emigrated when I lost my job at the shipyard back home. I heard that it was possible to find employment in Buenos Ayres, because trade with Europe is growing."

A group of men whistled at the women walking across the plaza. An elegant and manifestly well-to-do woman passed between us with her maid. No sooner had they stepped into the cathedral, than they knelt side by side. The chorus of whistlers was made up of sailors. They'd been standing close to the square obelisk in the middle of the Plaza de la Victoria. The sailors took courage and approached. Two of them came right up to us. The taller had plainly met the Englishman before:

"El Naturalista! Aren't these the most elegant women in the world?"

"In all my twenty-four years I've never seen their like," replied Don Carlos.

The sailor whooped with joy and relayed the message to his less adventurous brethren. I was struck by their youth.

"I have another question," the sailor continued. "Are there women in any other part of the world that have such large combs?"

"No," replied El Naturalista loudly, clearly keen to amuse his audience.

The sailors laughed and disappeared.

We stood amongst the elegant columns that carried the triangular tympanum above the porch of the cathedral, just as the apostles had carried the gospel of the Holy Trinity. We were content looking into the cathedral. Outside the sky was peach-colored and mottled with sun.

There was gunfire close by. Don Carlos stocked up in the market. I told him I had contacts in the highest places, if he needed any help.

"Most interesting, thank you," said Don Carlos.

Why did I deceive him?

We arranged to meet the following day.

Darkness had fallen, and the night was starry. He was staying nearby with Mr and Mrs Lumb, an English couple. I walked home and thought: what did he say his name was? The name one is given is a matter of pure chance, just like being born, a hazard, a ludicrous accident, but no sooner has one lost sight of this fact than one starts behaving as if it were of great significance, essential to the progress and equilibrium of the planet. One becomes as conceited as the town flower that bursts into bloom in the springtime, in the belief that it, and it alone, drives the seasons forward.

A couple of days ago a stray bullet struck me in the foot. I must tend the wound which is still weeping. I was hit on the only day I wasn't carrying my pistol in my belt. I won't get feverish I hope! The pistol is under my pillow.

I am prepared. Say nothing to mother about my injury.

It's been a glorious day! The peaceful noises of the house were made of gold. I was floating. Was someone praying for me? If someone had told me a civil war was raging I should have said: lies!

The window was open. I caught the scent of the jacaranda tree outside. Don Carlos wasn't to be found anywhere. I didn't get it wrong. Something may have happened. I'll give him another chance. Am I soft-hearted?

Roberto, this letter is longer than I expected. Bear with me!

Buenos Ayres is a greyish-brown crust on the pampas. Do you know how this city was founded? I've been to the National Library. I read just as much as ever.

Everything has its origins: Juan Díaz de Solís was a member of Captain Pinzón's crew in 1493. They were to find a western passage to India. They made land in Honduras and sailed southward along the coast, before turning back for Spain. De Solís wanted to try again.

In 1508 he sailed out from Cadiz, the master of his own ship. They stepped ashore at Río de Janeiro, before continuing south to the Río Colorado. From the deck they could see the river carving deeply into the flesh of the landscape. They gave up.

When de Solís returned home he was made chief pilot. In 1515 he set out on his third attempt to find India. This time he discovered the wide estuary of the Río de la Plata. He steered towards it under full sail. At last! At the bow the sun sank like a red wheel into the sea. Astern, the moon rode high in the heavens. The water changed from the brown of the silty bottom, to copper with the setting sun. Then, as the moon was left alone to reign in the sky, to silver. They landed on a small island in the estuary. They had to bury one of the crew. This done, they sailed to the mainland. They dropped anchor. De Solís ordered a rowing boat out. He took six men with him. As he waded ashore he noticed that the water tasted almost fresh. The area looked like an endless plain, a swamp. Here the town was to be situated, and it would be called Buenos Ayres, good air. They were attacked by the Indians, and killed and eaten. The crew stood watching from the deck. They might as well have been in India.

I don't know why Don Carlos didn't turn up. I ought to have seen it as an omen and kept away from that rich man's son! I walked home. I turned the key in the lock. The key sealed my loneliness in that small first floor room. I plunged into a mire of blackness, before I found the bed. I lay down. One can ponder eternity in a prostrate position. Sleep wouldn't come. The wind got up. The walls shuddered. Later in the night the wind dropped. A tavern in the direction of Calle de Reconquista was still open. Threats, screams and shouts. They stopped at three o'clock. There was silence, utter silence.

The dogs in the neighborhood noticed it immediately. They must have sensed some indefinable anxiety deep in their entrails. At first a pricking, succeeded by small jabs, until the heart felt itself encircled by an army of malignant muscles. The alarm sought refuge in the cranium, in the brain, that sacristy serving so many thoughts. And the thought that reached it was: this silence all around me, is it death? The uncertainty must have made their coats itch. The cranium is a dark cathedral. <u>To find out if one is alive, one must bark.</u>

Barking came from all the neighboring houses. The mangy cur that belongs to the Alborellos on the ground floor was no exception. These household gods, invoked to divert man's faculty for love! Some of these creatures even occupy a place in the amours of women, while others lie hour after hour on the doorstep, soaking up the sun, while their lords and masters have to fuss and fawn to get a lazy, grudging wag of that highly venerated tail, followed by a lethargic glance of recognition.

I couldn't sleep. I sat up. I got out of bed. I looked out of the window. Three dogs were outside. I got the pistol. I changed my mind. I found the wash basin, tore down two cups, knocked over the chair, poured in some water, opened the window and threw it at them. I was met with indifference. On the ground floor everyone was asleep. The dogs wagged their entire bodies. The motion of the serpent.

When the deluge had ended, the night called off its hounds. I went back to bed and tried to consider eternity more fervently. I fell asleep:

I was walking through the city, only dogs could be seen, some walking on one side of the street, some on the other, while over their backs were slung bags made from human skin, I pressed myself up against the wall. I awoke, turned over and slept again.

Year after year Aunt Florentina walked her little dog in the park in Varazze, they exchanged glances, becoming more and more alike, until finally they were both walking on all fours, the dog putting more and more weight on its back legs, she on her hands.

There was a loud knocking at my door. I started up. It was Signóra Alborello.

"What is it?"

She banged louder.

"Well, what's the matter?"

"Did you kick my lovely Bobo?"

"But my dear Signóra Alborello, I've been lying here asleep. Is he still alive?"

Two days later I bumped into Don Carlos behind the Cabildo, the city hall. I asked him what had happened.

"What do you mean?" he replied.

Even then I didn't react! Without showing a trace of resentment or irritation I let him carry on. It was as if I knew this would turn out to be a fateful meeting. Earlier that day he had been rushing about trying to get a visa for Santa Fe. Mr Lumb and Mr Gore, the British chargé-d'affaires, had tried to help him.

"If they don't succeed, we can try an acquaintance of mine in the printing firm of Bacle & Co. Bacle is a countryman of yours, and his wife's maiden name was Pellegrini. She is from Genoa."

"I believe it'll be all right," he said. "Can I meet you tomorrow if I don't get one?"

"Yes," I said.

He became calmer. He mentioned that it was now almost exactly two years since he'd been given the unique opportunity of setting out on his great voyage.

Roberto! The man believes he is one of the chosen!

"The 5th of September 1831 will always be a memorable day for me. It was on that day I met Robert FitzRoy."

"Yes, coincidences are often momentous, aren't they?" I said.

Dear brother, I am trying to relate the conversation word for word so that you can build up a picture of him for yourself.

"Just what I was about to say. I remember the room we sat in. It was extremely formal. We greeted each other conventionally. We seated ourselves. Would he like me? I had never attended such an interview before. How should one behave in order to succeed? These thoughts revolved in my head as he told me the objective of the voyage. For me, travelling from Shrewsbury to London had been an adventure in itself. HMS Beagle's task was to compile comprehensive navigational charts for the southernmost part of South America and make a survey of the coastal flora and fauna. This was where I came in. FitzRoy had written to Sir Francis Beaufort, our leading hydrographer, suggesting that the Beagle needed a geologist and naturalist. Beaufort got in touch with the astronomer, Professor George Peacock, who in turn consulted my teacher, John Henslow, clergyman and professor of botany at Cambridge University. Why did he recommend me? I was by no means his best student. Perhaps he liked me? I'm to be ordained and am very keen on botany and zoology. Geology too. Just before I left I had been on a journey to Wales to study rock and stone formations. Henslow held a number of informal gatherings at which teachers and students met on Friday afternoons. We would go on excursions and discuss various topics related to botany and zoology. Perhaps he fell for my story about the beetles? Once, quite by chance, I came across some beetles. Three really magnificent beetles! You should have seen them. Can you imagine my dilemma?" exclaimed Don Carlos waving his hat at me. "What was I to do? I put one in each pocket, one in my mouth, and walked home. FitzRoy sat facing me across the table. Actually, I'd heard a little about him beforehand. He was posted captain of the Beagle at the age of twenty-three. You realize it's the name of a bloodhound?" Don Carlos went on speaking.

"The Admiralty sent the Beagle to South America as long ago as '25 to explore the southern coast. FitzRoy was flag-lieutenant. The captain committed suicide off Tierra del Fuego during a deep bout of depression. Admiral Ottway promoted FitzRoy to captain. He'd been sent to the Royal Naval College at the age of fourteen. Do you see?"

As he said it, Roberto, he looked at me and I thought: this puppy doesn't even know he's been born!

"It was an honor to be in the same room as FitzRoy. Of course I admire my teachers at Cambridge, but he, though young, had achieved so much. He was tall and slim. His presence exuded authority. He spoke rapidly: the Beagle was 242 tons, 90 feet long, had a crew of 74 and two guns. People often said the vessel looked like a coffin. I started when he insisted I procure a brace of pistols. 'That's an order,' he added without smiling. He is a true captain. When I realized the man might have some liking for me, I relaxed a little. I was able to observe more: the way he paced the room, sat down, his eyes, his fingers. When he began to speak of his own background, I felt I had a chance. Robert FitzRoy is the grandson of the Duke of Grafton. An aristocrat. A Tory. A conservative of style and rare courage. Perhaps he liked my naïveté or my enthusiasm? I looked at a letter tray on the table between us. He said that we would be sharing a cabin for two to three years. If we quarrelled or couldn't get on, I would have to move out.

"'Naturally, you are the captain.' I didn't say this to please. I said it because I liked him. My Whig background didn't seem to alarm him. 'I'm a doctor's son from a Liberal family,' I said.

"'Indeed, I know that. Wasn't your grandfather a doctor too?' he asked.

"'Yes.'

"'You should know that I don't much care for those verses of his, those poems he wrote about evolution,' he said.

"'No?' I said. 'I haven't read them.'

"'Really?'

"'No, indeed I haven't, but from what I've heard he was a respected doctor.'

"'Quite so. May I take it as understood, then, that you'll vacate the cabin when I wish to be alone?'

"I remember how I leapt up from my chair.

"'We are not aboard yet, sir.' He smiled. 'You're to put up five hundred pounds for victuals and remember that any finds you may make must be studied in the light of the Bible.'

"I'll never forget that scene as long as I live. FitzRoy has a profound faith in the Bible, and I'm — a Christian."

I looked at Don Carlos' belt with its two pistols.

"I take it he persuaded you to buy the pistols?"

"Yes, I bought them in Plymouth the following day. I've needed them several times. On our first visit to Buenos Ayres, after we'd been at sea for twenty-eight days — dear Lord, how seasick I was — we were about to sail up the Río de la Plata. Montevideo was behind us, the penguins left a phosphorescence in their wake and we saw St. Elmo's fire in the sky: everything was on fire, even the masts were covered in blue flames, a strange, blue incandescence. Dolphins and whales swam at our side. Suddenly a cannonball whistled over the mast. Was it a warning shot? The next one wasn't. It missed us by a whisker. FitzRoy would not be threatened. He sailed straight towards the Argentine vessel and shouted that he would sink her if they fired again. Inwardly, I wished they had! Our guns are first rate.

"We returned to Montevideo where the British frigate, Druid, lay. The plan was for the frigate to accompany us to the harbor at Buenos Ayres. We wanted a personal apology from the Governor. Then, of all things, there was a sudden uprising in Montevideo. Don't ask me what for or against. The captain ordered me and fifty-three of the crew ashore to bring down the rebels. Just imagine it. We marched through the main streets of Montevideo towards the fort. I had my two pistols and the sabre FitzRoy had handed me. The rebellion was over before we reached the fort. If we'd come face to face with them, I would have fired. That same day Druid sailed to the Governor. He made us an unreserved apology. The miscreant was arrested."

Roberto! Where does he get his vitality from? The following day a victory celebration was held at the town's theatre. The arias of Rossini delighted the public. I was on the point of asking Don Carlos if he didn't consider that Argentina, as a young nation eager to defend its newly won independence, had an excuse for blunders of this sort. I decided against it, there was something about the moment, about his enthusiastic and frankly spirited account. I wanted to hear more. It didn't occur to me to ask him what he knew of pain and loneliness. I inquired:

"Has the captain no faults?"

It took him a long time to reply. He would be any captain's blue-eyed boy, I thought.

"His devotion to the Bible can lead us into some quite heated discussions, but he always apologizes afterwards. And for that matter, some of the crew are scared of him. When he's had one of his outbursts, they'll often ask me before his daily round of inspection 'if much hot coffee was spilled this morning?' But then a captain must exercise control. The crew respects him."

Don Carlos' loyalty, his rather ingenuous piety, reminded me that, behind the beard, a young man stood before me.

"Wasn't it hard for your parents to send you away?" I asked kindly.

"Mother died when I was eight. Father is a really big, powerful man. At first he refused to allow me to go. My dear Uncle Jos Wedgwood persuaded him. I'll always be grateful to my uncle for that. When I was here in Buenos Ayres for the first time last November, I had dinner at the Hughes' house. When the soup tureen was brought in, I thought there was something familiar about it. I turned my plate over. There, as I'd suspected, was the Wedgwood mark. Jos owns it all. But I was telling you about my interview. After I'd begun to feel more and more at ease and he, becoming increasingly forthright, had in reality already made up his mind to engage me, I began to realize that he was studying my appearance. I tried to pretend I didn't notice. For fairly obvious reasons it was my face that claimed his rapt attention. When we'd shared a cabin for a few months he told me the reason for it. 'Your nose is very special, very special, you must have been told that before. It's a nose one either likes or dislikes. For some reason I decided to take to it. It was decisive, quite decisive.'"

Don Carlos fell silent. We looked at one another. He looked away. He thought. He hesitated. He drew breath. I looked in another direction. He asked: "Would you consider joining an expedition to the south?"

He asked me to think it over. I tried to stand naturally. He must never suspect there was anything wrong with me. *This* was my chance to get away. But why could I not answer?

Dear brother, I hope you will be patient with my crossings out and smudges. After every few words the paralyzing power of reflection grips me. The nib's scratching gradually subsides and the ink bleeds across the page. When the letters are deformed, is it conscience or contemplation that makes my right hand numb?

★

A month has passed since that stray bullet entered my right foot. I was riding through Palermo. Where the shot came from, I have no idea. I bound up the wound with my neckerchief. It hasn't healed.

Far from it. Occasionally I reach a threshold of pain reminiscent of the moment that anyone who has climbed a cliff will be familiar with: one lets go voluntarily because of cramp in one's fingers. Don't fret. Everything is under control. After a few days' pause I have begun writing again. By coincidence I met the Norwegian and Swedish consul, John Tarras, outside the National Library. He'll be journeying from Montevideo to Hamburg in a month's time. He's promised to take this letter. My faith that it can reach you has been rekindled.

I heard there was a job going at the shipyard. I hadn't the money to visit a doctor. The morning I went to the shipyard, I couldn't bring myself to rip off the kerchief. It had grown into the wound. The foreman recognized me. He gave me a heartening glance. I inquired about work.

"I know you to be a capable craftsman," he said, without sounding ingratiating. There were plenty of men after the job. I have reasons for believing he meant it. He described the new ship orders and what he thought my work would consist of and so forth. I nodded. I heard myself saying:

"Of course I can work into the evenings. Money isn't everything. I can start immediately. What about tonight?"

"You seem to be limping," he put in.

"No," I said. I knew my answer had been too pat.

"Have you been injured?" he asked.

"Not in the least," I said and walked up and down in front of him, determination banishing all pain. Where to, I don't know. I paraded before him, my face betraying nothing of my condition, as far as I could tell. When I stopped, he looked me up and down. He looked out of the window saying:

"Don't you think it'll get worse?"

I didn't look down at my foot. I met his gaze as he turned to me and said:

"You're not such a fool as to imagine I can't ask you to turn up your trouser-leg."

"No!" I said.

"Can I stand on your right foot, then?"

"Yes!"

"Right now?"

"Yes!"

He raised his left leg, looked at me and brought his foot down hard on the floor. I looked him in the eyes.

"You're hired. For a week!"

I lost my job after three days. No explanation. I got my money after brandishing a knife. I was livid. I was going to get the foreman the next day. That afternoon, Rico Trappatoni knocked at my door and asked if I'd go hunting with him and his brother. The offer could scarcely have come at a better time. I was penniless. I needed food for the next few days. They lent me their father's horse. They'd invited me because I'm a good shot. Dear brother, there are at least a few things I can still do.

Next morning, I rode north-westwards with the Trappatoni brothers, past Córdoba, towards the Andes. The sky was a tumult of black and meat-colored clouds. High mountains on the horizon. Ahead of us we spied a throng of women and children. When we got nearer, we saw a dead man lying under a tetipuana tree. It resembles an enormous acacia. Its branches are almost thirty yards long. The women and children had been attacked by itinerant Indians. Their men had given chase. Using hands and sticks the women had tried to dig a grave by the side of the road. The ground was too stony. They had given up and were sitting side by side a couple of yards from the corpse, with its upturned beard. A small boy, a native, or criollo as they call them here, scratched and clawed and finally managed to dislodge a stone. He crouched on his haunches. The vertebrae of his thin, sensitive neck stood out plainly.

What a sight for a hangman! With loud surprise and delight he watched as a colony of ants streamed in all directions about their various tasks. In the midst of the swarm lay hundreds of white eggs. Carefully he replaced the stone. A few minutes later he lifted the stone up again. The eggs and the ants had gone. We sat on our horses uncertain which way to go. I rode to the top of a small knoll to get a better view. Not far off I spotted three birds of prey I had previously only seen in illustrations. Andean condors. Two of them were eating the carcass of a wild llama. The third circled above them. The birds' voraciousness sickened me. Even though one could say they were doing nothing worse than the grazing llama, in principle. I was about to ride back to the others. All at once I noticed the condor that had not been feeding. It circled higher and higher, before plummeting vertically into a steep slope. I rode closer. The two others took off and flew after their fellow. I watched all three in the rock crevice below me. The pair began to poke at the dead one with their beaks. No sign of life. They raised their beaks, hacked, tore, ate. I rode back to the others. The condor's suicide ritual reminded me of the bullet's rotating passage through the bore.

Our bag consisted of three llamas. When we got

back to Buenos Ayres and were about to go our separate ways, it was time to divide the spoil. My dear Roberto, I wouldn't have believed that these rapacious knaves, having cut up the carcasses, ordered me off my horse. They presented me with a haunch and thanked me for my company! I was three or four miles from home. They expected me to walk back with that damned joint on my shoulder. I thought it was a joke at first. But before I knew it, they'd remounted and were leading their father's horse away with them. I raised my pistol and then lowered it. I couldn't have dealt with both of them.

"Thieves! May you both burn in hell!" I screamed after them.

I tear my enemies to shreds in my mind every evening. But I always leave their skeletons. Mercy makes a coward of me. I normally dream of angels afterwards. The more I dream, the clearer they appear. The ever-sharpening outlines of these angels tell me I'm no longer of this world.

Roberto! Perhaps it wasn't selfishness that made me lie to you. Perhaps I simply felt responsible for you? I was sailing away, leaving my homeland, my family, my old religion. You were a boy! Why should you be torn from the bosom of your family? I had nothing to lose. Don Carlos, posing his question in all its ingenuousness, has caused me to shudder. Am I writing to justify myself?

A few days after the hunting trip I met Don Carlos in the market, which had been closed for several days because of an attack by Rosas' forces. He gave me a friendly smile when he saw me and said:

"You needn't hurry with your answer."

I started. I said nothing.

On both sides of the Recovan, a building some one hundred and fifty yards by twenty, there is a mass of shops of a more or less temporary sort. The ladies never go into the market. Their husbands only rarely. But rather their servants, or a trustworthy slave. The market is situated in the northern part of the Plaza de la Victoria. On the opposite side of the plaza some of Balcarce's men had strung flags and banners over the balcony railings of the Cabildo. The silken material fluttered in the wind in vivid colors. The flags were spoil from Rosas' army. The jail in the Town Hall cellar was crammed with prisoners. Don Carlos and I heard the screams and curses of the inmates as we walked amongst the stalls. We searched for shoes for Don Carlos. With stout soles. Four pairs, preferably. We saw beef in every guise, fish, carp, a beetle in a box. It was a beetle he recognized from tropical Brazil. A beetle that changes color to resemble a poisonous berry. We saw stuffed flamingos, blue Morpho butterflies from Bahía, silver maté straws from Paraguay, pepper, camphor, red and green parrots, a lion in a cage, cakes, the Virgin Mary, oranges, melons, Jesus, meat of every description, pears, cherries, coal from England, watermelons, wine from Medoza, liquor, butter, milk, live hens, a consignment of armadillos delivered by two Indians, eggs, bread, roses, marguerites, weapons and hemp.

"I want shoes!" Don Carlos said.

"What are you complaining about?" said a beggar who was sitting on the ground rolling cockroaches in flour and frying them over a tiny fire. A fly settled on the beggar's brow. The fly has plagued mankind for thousands of years without being exterminated. The fly has remained totally unaffected. The cat, on the other hand, has sold itself to mankind and feigned tameness. The fly settled itself comfortably in the man's eye. From whose salt tears it took its daily nourishment.

"You can have my shoes. I've worn them out," said the beggar. A Negro, clearly a trustworthy slave, approached us carrying two baskets full of fruit and meat. The slave stopped and began to scold the beggar for addressing a gentleman.

"That's rich coming from you, you nigger!" the beggar rapped. Don Carlos was embarrassed. I laughed. The beggar stood up and made as if to hit the slave. The Negro walked faster, fearful of losing any of his valuable load. Don Carlos and I were startled. Shots could be heard coming from the harbor. We thought the town was about to be taken. The people about us seemed unconcerned. The market stalls were shut up. A salute sounded from the governor's house. Birds on strings were released from the windows round the square. The church bells began to toll. Into the square came a procession of Franciscan monks. These were closely followed by a regiment of the army. Two soldiers carried yellow and purple cushions of medals. After that came Jesus on the cross, and the city's elite in their finery. There was the scent of perfume. The men wore their decorations. The soldiers fired into the air. Yet another regiment arrived, and yet more monks and priests bearing relics. The birds, fastened to the branches by long strings, flew terrified in all directions. Flowers were thrown from the balconies. The procession included a line of lions, tigers, wolves and dogs in cages. Baskets decked with blue and white ribbons were hung out of the windows. The baskets contained flour and rye. When the procession arrived at the cathedral, a salute rang out from the fort.

"What are they celebrating?" Don Carlos asked.

"Victory over the English in 1807," the beggar shouted above the din.

"I've no idea," I said.

The beggar stood by the side of us. He swatted flies and tried to tidy his clothes so that he wouldn't attract the attention of the soldiers. His face was gaunt. Mulatto. Black hair and beard. He looked at us. For some reason I noticed his eyes were green. Was I expecting them to be brown? I can't remember. We were both surprised to find the beggar knowledgeable and extremely talkative.

"The English were hunted from street to street," the beggar told us. "Captain Brookman was shot outside the church of St Domingo. He managed to shout: 'We are betrayed! Forward, Britannia! Forward!' The survivors of the 38th regiment were gripped by greed and mortal fear. One sergeant led the English soldiers into the church. It was surrounded by the 71st Argentine regiment. They had hidden on the roofs of the low houses in San Telmo. The sergeant discovered the gold coin in the treasury of the Virgin Mary by the sacristy. The others obeyed his shouts of command. They grabbed what they could. As they came out of the church, the sergeant was shot through the head. Coins rolled in all directions. Eighteen of the nearest soldiers ran after the gold. They were shot. A hundred English soldiers were taken prisoner. The Argentine general shouted to them that if they returned all the booty, they'd be arrested and later handed back. Everything was accounted for. Except one crucifix. 'Line them up,' shouted the Argentine commanding officer. 'Load your rifles!' The crucifix slipped from an anonymous English tunic onto the cobblestones. The rifles were lowered.

"Isn't that a fine story?" the beggar asked.

"Very fine," said Don Carlos.

The beggar brushed away a persistent fly.

"Insects want to take over the world," he said. "I've tried cooperating with flies. It just doesn't work!" said the beggar and swatted again.

Two ostriches were led into the market place. Don Carlos went straight across to the owner and had a few words with him. I walked slowly after Don Carlos. He seated himself on one of the ostriches. We looked at each other. The ostrich yawned. Don Carlos adjusted his hat. The wind ruffled the ostrich's feathers. The light was beautiful. Don Carlos smiled.

The ostrich careered off amongst the stalls with its rider clinging fast to the animal's neck. The owner laughed. The ride lasted nearly fifty yards before Don Carlos was thrown off. The ostrich was captured with a bola. Don Carlos dusted his felt hat. He was uninjured. Don Carlos told me what had happened:

"I told the owner I'd always wanted to ride an ostrich, but I was afraid it wouldn't be able to bear my weight. So the owner said 'Go ahead, try it.'"

Roberto! It was then that Don Carlos told me the story about the Land of Fire. Has it occurred to you that men are prepared to sacrifice everything for an idea, providing it's not completely clear to them. He talked, leaving me to wallow in my own anxieties.

When HMS Beagle set sail from Plymouth on 27th December, 1831, it carried three passengers, York Minster, Jemmy Button and Fuegia Basket, plus a crew of seventy-four. York Minster was twenty-eight, the other two sixteen and eleven respectively. Fuegia was the only female aboard.

She was York Minster's sweetheart. These three were to be put ashore in the southernmost country in the world, Tierra del Fuego, the Land of Fire, which they had left the year before.

When FitzRoy had assumed command during the Beagle's first journey, he'd brought four natives from the Land of Fire away with him. Boat Memory was the fourth. Don Carlos gathered that he'd become ill and died in England. They had been christened by the crew of the first Beagle expedition. Jemmy Button was so named because he'd been bought for a button. FitzRoy had paid for their entire stay in England.

On the eve of their return they were invited to the palace by King William IV and Queen Adelaide. The King made a number of interesting inquiries. Suddenly the Queen left the room. The King couldn't explain why. She returned with a lovely hat for Fuegia. It was one of her own. Fuegia was also given a ring and some money to buy clothes with. The King was impressed with their command of English. FitzRoy spoke of how rapidly they had come on. When they arrived in England, York Minster had been terrified of passing animal statues. "An interesting characteristic is that these natives have better eyes than us, Your Majesty. They can sight land and other objects at sea long before we can," FitzRoy had explained. The King was most attentive.

In addition to studying English, clothes and table

manners, they had been given daily Bible instruction. The two younger ones learnt fast. York Minster was a bit duller. He even seemed a bit apathetic sometimes. They were dressed in white from the very first day they set foot in England. Fuegia, as the only girl aboard, delighted everyone with her clothes. York Minster's and Jemmy Button's suits were no less elegant. Despite the fact they weren't very tall, the white material set off the mahogany-brown of their skins. Unfortunately, York Minster was extremely jealous. He wanted to marry Fuegia. She was certainly a lovely little thing, strutting about the deck. There was also a young missionary aboard. His name was Richard Matthews. He was to live in the Land of Fire together with the three natives. He was strongly motivated. His dearest wish was to spread the Christian gospel. The natives were nomadic. At Río de Janeiro Fuegia Basket learnt how to serve tea.

The journey to the Land of Fire took a year. By the time they saw their native coast again, three years had passed since they'd left it. Matthews had never set foot outside England. The London Missionary Society had provided them with wine glasses, soup tureens, teapots, white table linen, cutlery, candelabra, plates for each meal, good footwear and beaver hats against the cold of that region. No other people live so far south. Civilization ends six hundred miles further north at El Carmen near the Río Negro. Even though the Beagle arrived in the middle of summer, they had to struggle to round the Horn. They anchored in Beagle Channel. The place had been christened after the first Beagle expedition. From the deck they could see glaciers sweeping down into the indigo-tinted water. The passengers and almost all the crew were on deck, the passengers in their finest clothes. They gazed up at the lofty, snow-decked mountains. Imagine, Roberto, the suspense as a woman paddled out towards them. She had shells in her hair. Her face was painted and the upper half of her body was covered in a llama skin. The skin slipped off and exposed her breasts. She took no notice. She looked at the men and the lone woman at the ship's rail. She paddled back. The crew and passengers rowed ashore. They were well received. They were served bird, dolphin and penguin meat. The natives wanted to compare their height with that of their guests. One took one's place in the queue. Back to back. They grimaced at one another. They laughed when some of the crew began to play musical instruments. Terrified, Fuegia Basket ran back to the boat. Jemmy Button trotted. York

Minster was already back aboard. Matthews was looking worried. He said:

"It's no worse than I expected."

The captain ordered four boats to be launched. They rowed through Beagle Channel with all the provisions. They would visit Jemmy Button's home. Nearly a hundred people met them. Three tents were erected. One for the missionary, one for Jemmy Button and one for the other two. Jemmy met his family again. His mother, two sisters and four brothers. When they saw him they began to beat their faces.

"Do you not recognize me?" he asked in English. He tried Spanish.

"Yammaschooner," they answered.

FitzRoy presented one old man with a silk scarf. He smiled and made noises that sounded like he was calling chickens. His face was painted, all except for a band round his eyes. He gave the captain three friendly slaps on the breast before doing the same to himself. He recoiled when the captain wanted him to try his gun. He wouldn't lay hands on it. Knives were obviously familiar to him. Up to this point not one word had been exchanged that everyone could understand. The old man pointed to the knife Don Carlos carried in his belt and said cuchilla, the Spanish word for knife. When the captain asked him if he knew more Spanish words, the old man looked blank. FitzRoy loaded the gun and fired two shots over the water. The old man shook his head and looked inquiringly at his guests as if to ask whether it was a noise, or just a gust of wind he'd heard.

The four were set ashore. The crew returned to the Beagle. They spent ten days sailing along the coast before returning to see how things were progressing. Matthews came running towards them. They were in fear of their lives and their possessions had been ransacked. He was clutching a seven-branched candelabra to defend himself with. Fuegia was sitting in her tent. She didn't want to meet the white men.

"Believe me, captain, I have tried. Genesis and the simplest English words. But all they say is: 'Yammaschooner. Yammaschooner.'"

The missionary returned to the ship. The natives remained. The Beagle sailed north.

Don Carlos shook his head. He had to press on.

"Good day to you," he said and disappeared.

I walked across the plaza. It felt as if there was nothing between my wound and the cobblestones.

When <u>God created man</u>, he must have overrated his powers.

I was standing a short distance below the fort. One of the milk boys almost ran me over with an empty churn. He leapt up on to a great, black horse and rode off in the direction of San Lorenzo. The boy couldn't have been more than ten years old.

"Be off!" I shouted trying to give the impression that he'd cost me the deeply ruminated thought being neatly turned in my mind when he'd tried to knock me down. Riff-raff!

Until then, and as discreetly as possible, I'd been watching the women washing and bathing below the fort. They often bathe in bevies. They run out into the waves, splash one another, giggle, scream, run back out of the sea, dry their hair and comb each other's long tresses . . .

My assignations with the English lady are all too rare, alas.

While the women were taking their morning dip, a wild horse had come galloping. One of its legs went into a crab hole and broke instantly. The scantily dressed women rushed up to it. Horses can suffer pain too. Three of the women ran up to the fort. They were confronted by a sentry. They talked to him. One of them boxed his ears, while the others tore his musket from him. They shot the horse. They threw the musket in the water. They continued bathing. The plundered soldier was laughed to scorn by his comrades. It was almost time for church.

I walked rapidly up to Calle Bolívar, and stood beneath the poplar trees watching the women's small, energetic steps. Most women aren't as young as their make up would have you believe. Their frocks are of European cut. Over them, the ladies wear a mantilla and their maids a rebozo of thicker material. The churchgoers amongst them are dressed in black silk. The women go arm in arm. Unmarried girls are accompanied by their mothers. They often put a red flower in their hair, a plumerito.

The spring, the flowers, the trees, the avenues, the globes of the gas lamps, the carriages that sped past, the Sundays, the women, the women. The siesta stilled the city's buzz. It was very hot for October. Torrential rain had fallen the day before.

It was quiet, I walked towards the Plaza de la Victoria. The thought of going home was unbearable. I had argued with Signóre Alborello all morning about the rent. He tried to cheat me. The man's a swindler. His vegetable stall is doing badly. Why should I suffer for that!

I stood on the edge of the plaza. The sun was oppressive. The water sparkled behind the fort. I sat down. The lilac-blue flowers of the jacaranda tree had burst into bloom. The sun stupefied the city, which had collapsed, sated with joy. Those who dozed must have felt delight in their own decay. The square was deserted. I awoke. From the cathedral emerged a tall woman. She came down the steps. She came towards me beneath the infinite azure-blue sky. Her face was sad and haggard, perfectly matched to the stately weeds she wore. She formed a shining black speck against the light. She came alone. Her tight-fitting dress accentuated her slim figure. Her parasol permitted me to see her face clearly. Tears had made her rouge bleed.

Her huge head of curly black hair gave her a lazy and triumphal air. The sea breeze lifted a corner of her billowing skirts and exposed her magnificent calves. I wouldn't have shifted my gaze if someone had begun shooting at me.

Denis Diderot, a Frenchman, whose work *Encyclopédie* I discovered in the library, tells of a Spaniard who wanted his inamorata painted by the finest artists. Mindful of his own jealousy, he did not wish the artists to meet her. Instead, he described her proportions minutely, her nose, mouth, neck, eyes etc. He sent a hundred copies to the hundred best portraitists. He received in return a hundred paintings which were all faithful to his description, but not her likeness. Roberto, I am unable to describe her. There is always that something else which I can't communicate.

In spite of the reserve in her face, in spite of her obvious need to be alone with her grief, I felt an unbridled desire.

I followed her to the intersection of Alsina and Bolívar by St. Ignatius' Church. She seemed to be going in the direction of the university. Today I was glad I didn't meet Don Carlos. He seems embarrassed by my interest in women. I looked at the spot between her nose and forehead, her arm movements, her hands, the way she walked. The glimpse I got of her face as she crossed Calle Alsina, caused images to spread out like a fan in my memory. She's probably never hated a man so much that she returned his trinkets.

I looked at her. I wanted to get close enough to her to smell the fragrance of her perfume. I called out to her. She turned and increased her pace. I was walking ten yards behind her. She stopped. I stopped. She turned. I kept still. She came towards me. She stood in front of me. I kept still.

"Kindly stop following me. I don't know who you are, neither have I the slightest desire to be introduced."

I looked at her.

"Go way!" she shouted.

I knew her. I am her lover.

Dear brother. The candle is burning on my bedside table. The wound in my foot has got larger. Yesterday I thought I'd gotten a fever. But I haven't. Again, early this morning I felt I must be feverish. In the afternoon I was certain I wasn't. I've lost yet another casual job at the shipyard. I took my wages and went to the apothecary. I stood in front of the counter. Awaiting my turn. I studied the assorted earthenware and glass bottles on the shelves along the wall, to each of which was pasted a white paper label in gothic script. I looked at the scales and the clock in the corner. I was tense and nervous. Because of what I'd come for. It was my turn. I pulled a scrap of paper from my pocket. An Irishman at the shipyard told me it was possible to buy opium at this shop. He'd done it himself! The piece of paper had the name of one of the assistants written on it. The Irishman told me that opium is dried juice from the unripe seed pods of the opium poppy. An annual from the Orient. Smoking opium is said to be a heavenly experience.

"Can I help you?" asked the man behind the counter. He was wearing a pince-nez. Could this be the apothecary himself? Just as my tongue was about to form the words and my right hand, with the note, was moving towards the counter, I saw Don Carlos come through the door. He saw me. If only I could have evaporated into thin air. What bliss it would have been to know that I'd vanished. Out of all reach.

"Nice to see a familiar face," he said.

"Is it?" I said.

"Pardon me for butting in," said the man with the pince-nez. "But in a moment, perhaps, you might be good enough to say what you require?"

"A bandage."

"Very well. I hope we have one of the right size." He went into the back room.

A large selection was placed in front of me. I took a roll that looked as if it might do. I paid and told Don Carlos I was in a hurry.

"See you later," I said and went out into the street. After a few minutes the episode began to irritate me. In the first place, I blamed Don Carlos for being there. Was I frightened of him? If he found out about my real condition I would no longer be eligible as a traveling companion. My prospects of escape would be ruined. I must keep that possibility open.

Roberto! He's forcing me to lie and do *everything* to hide my agonies! What if the rumor were to spread to the shipyard? I'd never get a job again.

When next I met him I had to get him talking. I asked if he'd made any interesting finds on the journey so far. That gullible scholar began to speak of his most important finds to date. Not a word was said about the episode in the apothecary's.

Don Carlos talked unceasingly: HMS Beagle sailed southwards. They crossed the equator. The water became bluer. The navigational charts less detailed. Not far from Nueva Bahía Blanca near Puerto Belgrano, they dropped anchor. The seabed was shallow and muddy. Legions of crabs crawled about in confusion.

Don Carlos set off with his assistant, Sims Covington, a cabin boy and fiddle player to whom he had taught the arts of filing gathered material and stuffing animals. The coastal landscape was flat and dry. Far off in the distance they could make out the three magnificent peaks of the Sierra Ventana. Captain Robert FitzRoy stood on deck and waved. They rowed ashore.

They hauled the boat up the beach. Argentine

soldiers surrounded them. It was the 12th of September, 1832.

"El Naturalista?" the soldiers queried suspiciously. They examined the belted pistols and every single geological hammer. The soldiers wanted to be certain that these strangers were not in league with the Indians who were to be driven off the pampas. The sky was wide and clear. The soldiers let them go. They followed the shoreline northwards. Mile after mile. They shot at a jaguar. They saw orchids and the tucu-tuco bird. It was black with some white and red on its breast. But what a powerful bill! Long, yellow and curved at the tip. Its eyes were blue and yellow with black pupils. They walked down to the edge of the water. Evening fell. Darkness grew. The trees, which the fine weather had brought out in a blush of red blossom, tossed gently in the breeze. The landscape of Punta Tejada dipped its blueness in the stiff grass. The waves crested, flattened and streamed up the beach. Their foam left behind. Dear brother, I can imagine how the wind must have written in that foam and erased characters no one can read. The sand was reddish. The water fell back. A new wave swelled. Don Carlos was already hacking away at the bottom of the slope. On the other side were small, scattered sand dunes and shrubs.

"Over here," shouted Don Carlos.

Covington ran towards him. Don Carlos had found the skull of something that looked like a hippopotamus, an enormous hippopotamus. They began to dig with hammers, small spades, hands. They found bones and joints. From their size, some must have belonged to an animal so huge it would have had to bend down to graze the trees. They found the bones of a creature that appeared to be an enormous armadillo, and a prehistoric version of a wild llama. The bones had been protected by sand and shells. Time was short. Night fell. They dug. The Beagle was to sail next evening. The skeletal remains of a horse came to light. Don Carlos thought: wasn't the horse unknown in South America when the conquistadors arrived? Did certain species develop to a particular stage and then die out? An armadillo scampered behind a sand dune topped by a bush. Is present-day man different from the man God first created? Is it a constant process? How could there have been room for some of the largest of these monsters in Noah's ark? The sweat poured off them. They hammered away. They shoveled. They dug. They ran their fingers over the bones of the past. The sun rose, a red, shimmering ball on the horizon. Covington stood up. He straightened his back.

His right arm was numb. He saw a sea-turtle swimming towards land, navigating by the waves. They caught it. They carried it ashore. They studied its awkward movements. They turned the turtle upside down and shot it. The waves got whiter with each hour that passed, and bluer. Day dawned. Covington was holding the bones of the prehistoric armadillo. They looked at the bones and skeletons around them. They had no words to describe what they saw.

"Perhaps the Bard, no, perhaps Shelly in *Prometheus Unbound* could have described it," Don Carlos said.

Roberto! There is something about Don Carlos I find almost moving. While total chaos reigns in the world about him, he collects, sorts and classifies his finds. He must believe that knowledge can organize and guide our lives. There is something in this naive optimism that I find superficially attractive. But on deeper reflection, it makes me pensive and melancholy. Do you remember when we each found a fossil in the cliff face at home? Mother told us that fossils were relics of the Flood.

How I envy you your belief! Was the creation anything like that? When God began making man, all went well with the eyes, the arms and the legs.

They, at least, were practical. But why make a skeleton capable of walking upright? Had he but spared us that! And why endow us with the ability to think? Lungs have their use, but conscience? Those critical questions?

This city has a superb library. Reading makes me question more and more. I can assure you that having an ever-inquiring mind doesn't bring happiness. My conversations with Don Carlos have prompted me to dip further into the works of three scientists, one English, and two French. Their books lie before me. Whilst I read, I kept the small fossil finds of our childhood in mind, Roberto. Charles Lyell is English and, no doubt, an acquaintance of Don Carlos. Lyell believes that we can decipher events way back in geological time from what we can see today. For example, erosion can tell us a great deal about what mountain ranges looked like in the past. Dear brother, permit me to lay two heretical French notions before you. Georges Buffon considered there was a connection between the faunas of Africa and South America. I'm leafing through. The African lion shares so many points of similarity with the South American puma that it can't be coincidental. Or what about the African rhinoceros and the tapir? Buffon believed these animals must have lived

57

on the same continent at one time. Today they represent separate evolutionary branches of a common root and tree.

Jean Baptiste de Lamarck, who died two or three years ago, believed that when an organism had developed to a certain stage, it became more and more dependent on its surroundings. Quite an observation, Roberto! As I understand Lamarck, there were extremely few bird species in the dawn of time. Some of these species ended up in areas with plenty of water. They had to be able to swim to eat. The ability to swim became crucial to survival. They had to spread and extend their claws in order to swim. Gradually the skin got stretched. These developed characteristics were then inherited by the next generation. The generation after that would have yet more webbing and so on, until we arrive at the stage we're familiar with today.

I'm not referring to these discoveries in order to shake you in your belief. I mention them to show you that even great and respected men harbor sinful thoughts. If nothing else, it may perhaps be a comfort to know you aren't the only one with a brother who's a heretic.

Brother. When I mentioned to Don Carlos that I

was the lover of an Englishwoman here in the city, I said it principally to shock him. I had the feeling that his reaction would be to stop and question me. He didn't ask me about Mrs Black, and I dropped the subject, since I had achieved my main aim — to get him to continue the conversation from that occasion outside the cathedral.

One day we were walking by the sea below the fort. The women were washing clothes. Don Carlos stared straight ahead. I looked to the side and, after a while, stopped. I watched the women fill the big baskets they carried on their backs with heavy, wet clothes. I saw the way their bodies swayed under the weight. Their legs quivered and the arteries in their necks swelled. I noticed a pretty young woman. Barely twenty. Her look was full of concentration, her lips parted. She followed the line of other women climbing the steep path to the street in a swaying column. In their unladen arms they bore baskets of bread, meat and wine. I watched these mute, beautiful pack animals. I gazed once again at the young woman. Her hair was blonde. Sensational enough in these parts. Should I run after her and offer to carry her load? Don Carlos tugged at my shirt sleeve.

"I thought you had a mistress already?"

"So you registered that?" I said.

"Yes," said Don Carlos.

"You can't object to my stopping awhile to look."

She disappeared over the brow of the ridge. I glimpsed a sharp look about her mouth and a vertical furrow between her eyes. She was looking at me. I drew my own conclusions. It is one of the best things about living in a city like this. Women pop up everywhere. When I see a beautiful woman, life suddenly quickens, gets racier, more daring, the blood flows faster and the eye becomes keener. At such moments I repress the thought that my relationship with Mrs Black is hopeless. I don't dwell on the fact that her excuses for not meeting me over the past few weeks, mean that she, too, is coming to the same conclusion. There was something in Don Carlos' whole demeanor that made me unwilling to discuss the matter with him. Because we are so different? Possibly. But first and foremost because he is an innocent young man, and I a lustful libertine.

My wound has been weeping more today. I've found it hard to use my foot.

Dear brother. Are my days spent sponging off a rich, young Englishman? Don't tell me the thought hasn't crossed your mind! Don Carlos went off. A black slave stood right in front of me. The city is crawling with them. He stared at me. I picked up a newspaper from the ground. "General Rosas To March In Next Week." "England Occupies Falkland Islands." "Export Of Wool Increases." I threw the paper away. A beggar took it. Illiterates sleep wrapped in newspapers.

There was a smell of tobacco, sweat and dust. I picked up another newspaper: "385,000 Animals Slaughtered Already This Year." "We Ask For Peace." The black man asked for money. I went behind a wall. I squatted on my haunches. He squatted down beside me. I lay down on the ground. He lay down. He looked me in the eyes. I jumped up quickly and kicked him in the face. He bled. I ran round the block. I leant up against the wall and caught my breath. I opened my eyes. He was standing right in front of me with his bloody face. He asked for money. I gave him a counterfeit coin of a far greater value than he could have imagined. He asked for money. I struck him. He asked for money. Slaves have no fear of death. I shall end here. This tale has gone on long enough as it is.

Before, when I saw a dead man, I would ask myself: "What was the point in his being born?" Now I ask that same question every time I see a human being.

I saw a man outside the cathedral. He was blind. Invalidity can excite compassion. He was selling lottery tickets. So, he was not a total destitute. I felt aversion. Particularly on account of the endless destitutes who are neither brave nor aggressive enough to become lottery ticket sellers. The ones who suffer in silence and absolute dignity. *That* is what should be required of the genuinely doomed. I gave nothing. I went home.

The pain was excruciating. I shall try to relate Don Carlos' experiences on the pampas, Roberto. If nothing else, it will make me think of something other than my foot. As you can see, the writing paper I now use is better quality. I stole a small wad from a shop in San Telmo when my stock gave out.

Dear brother. Don Carlos is good at describing landscape, no doubt about that, but it's strange how much he puts up with from General Rosas. He's practically been dependent on him. Is it surprising he's able to reconcile religion and science? No one could accuse him of being unable to make compromises!

The clouds had gone leaving the men alone. The pampas stretched before them. Don Carlos was making his way to Buenos Ayres. There were seven riders in all, Don Carlos and six gauchos. The gauchos had been procured in El Carmen by Harris, a friend of FitzRoy's. On the 11th of August this year they'd set out from Nueva Bahía Blanca. On their journey overland to the capital, they would have to pass General Rosas and his army. Harris told them that the general's camp was in the vicinity of Río Colorado. From there his supply lines reached all the way to the outskirts of Buenos Ayres. In several places they saw the remains of Indian massacres. The Indians were no longer able to organize their resistance. They were scattered across the pampas. They were trying to hide. They had never seen a gun. When an Indian contemplates the stars, he believes he is looking at his ancestors. The Milky Way is the place where his forebears hunted ostrich. The night-time clouds are the feathers of the hunted birds. Don Carlos learnt how to use a bola, a rope with a stone tied at the end. The gauchos learnt to use them by chasing dogs at full gallop. The bola wound itself round the neck of their prey. Don Carlos is mad about hunting. As a boy he loved standing in front of the mirror and snapping his gun to his shoulder. Ostriches were the easiest to catch. At full pelt they would ride after flocks of twenty to thirty animals. These ostriches were slightly smaller than their African counterparts. Once the sling had twined itself round the victim's neck, he would bring his horse to a sudden halt and the sling tightened until a small snap was heard. They arrived at Río Santa Cruz. In front of them several small heads were floating across the river. He rode closer. They were fleeing ostriches. He hadn't realized they were such good swimmers. On his way back to the others he shot a llama and an armadillo. They built a fire and roasted the armadillo in its shell.

"It's almost a shame to kill them. They're so quiet."

A skunk strayed in amongst them. The smell spread. Don Carlos looked at Enrique. Enrique clenched his teeth. He tensed his jaw muscles. The corners of his mouth moved out and down. His eyebrows rose. Finally, the raised eyebrows were pulled towards each other. He was annoyed.

"Get it out of here," Enrique shouted.

They smoked and played the guitar. The maté went round. Ricardo sat with his poncho tight about him. His black, broad-brimmed hat fell down over his eyes. They finished the meat and kept the bones for the next meal. The bones served as fuel.

Enrique was the eldest. A thickset man in his mid-forties. He asked Don Carlos to ride with him while the others had a siesta.

"You ride in that direction. I'll go the opposite

way. In an hour's time we'll meet here and see how many animals we've managed to round up. Then we'll kill them."

The way Don Carlos related this, one might almost imagine he wanted to be a gaucho in the next life. That evening they arrived at an estancia owned by an Englishman. The tenant, the estanciero, a native Argentine, gave them reasonably detailed instructions about how to reach Rosas. They stayed the night and rode on. The landscape was dry and barren. Ahead were small clumps of umbu or eucalyptus trees. The hills about them carried the sky on their stony necks.

After forty miles on horseback they made camp. He remained by the fire. The others had turned in. He stared straight ahead. I imagine him getting up to fetch John Milton's *Paradise Lost*. The book was in his saddle-bag. He read. He closed the book and gazed up at the clear sky. He tried to find Orion. He thought it over. The constellation must be almost upside down compared with what he'd been used to in Shrewsbury. Sirius was almost directly overhead here. He pulled out his notebook. Why had that huge armadillo died out? He made a sketch of what it might have looked like. A huge, heavy shell and a tail that looked a bit like a mace. When attacked, it could brandish its tail and pull its head into its shell. But the weight of lugging that fortress about! Possibly the heaviness of its shell had contributed to its extinction. The deposits of calcium in its skin might have been the decisive factor.

He dozed off with the second volume of Lamarck's *Geology* in his hand.

The stages got longer and longer. For several days they rode well into the evening. The moon, night's luminous gemstone, was all they had to navigate by.

General Rosas' camp was where they'd been told it would be. His army was composed of Spanish immigrants, creoles and Indians who had surrendered. Don Carlos saw a number of Indian women standing round a large cart. They had been spared. Two of the women stood out. It seemed they were Spaniards who had been kidnapped five years previously. From that time on they had been dressed as Indians. The general went about in uniformed undress. He shouted out commands. He made snap decisions, engaged in banter, fed the horses, spoke bluntly and was concerned with just two things: massacring Indians and regaining power in Buenos Ayres. He was the gauchos' man. When he was not being a general, he was an estanciero. He owned several slaughterhouses. But he had begun his career as a gaucho. Everyone knew that. The soldiers worshipped him. He lived as they did. He was not scared of work. He might have been brutal and brusque, but he was theirs. A bull-butcher. Courageous, virile, stoical. General Rosas regarded the Englishman. Don Carlos felt that troubled beast, a thumping heart, within him.

"To get to Buenos Ayres? No problemas." It could be arranged. But just now it was unsafe.

Next day the army surrounded two or three hundred Indians. The majority were massacred. The strongest of the young male Indians were offered the chance to surrender. Those who spat at the commanding officer were shot. One of the younger women, whom Rosas had thought to spare provisionally, approached, fixed him with a look, and said in broken Spanish:

"What are you good for, pigs!"

He made as if to shoot her between the eyes.

To die is to join the majority.

"Aim here, you devil."

She pointed at her heart. He aimed.

"All you are fit for is to murder us without mercy, butcher trees and build houses. The white man spreads across the pampas like death. Only two things exist: death and conscience."

Don Carlos felt the pulse at his throat. The general laughed.

"He is at his most dangerous when he laughs," one of the drunken soldiers whispered in Don Carlos' ear.

One can't live forever even if one isn't worried about the price of coffins.

An Indian on the edge of the group grabbed his small son and sprinted towards a horse without saddle or reins. They hurled themselves on to its back. The father kept one arm round his son as he bent forward and urged the horse on. A gaucho with long, dark, curly hair threw his bola round the two fugitives. They ended up lifeless on the ground. Rosas ignored the episode. He was still aiming at the Indian woman. She wanted to get it over.

"Maybe first we should tie your arms and legs to four stakes, the way we dry animal skins, and let you fry a little in the sun?"

Close by a soldier drank the blood of a slaughtered llama and vomited. Rosas leant against a small tree. The tree was about a yard in diameter and had a thorny trunk. It was thick with branches. The waleechu tree is the Indians' altar. Animals, trinkets, cigarettes, everything is offered to this tree to keep their horses from tiring. Rosas looked at her as he slowly began snapping the branches.

She looked toward the mountains of the Sierra Ventana, the home of the gods, before she threw herself at him. They closed their eyes. A shot rang out.

Dear brother!

Goethe died last year.

Don Carlos hadn't mentioned his offer during our last few meetings. He left me to worry alone.

There is a host of small, spartan restaurants in Buenos Ayres. At times, when I have the money and want a little peace and quiet, I go to one of them. It was just after five o'clock. I stood outside the "Tollini," one of my favorites. I felt in my pockets. Why I did this I have no idea. I knew what I'd find. Not one single peso. Even though the lining was intact. I wondered if I should go in. I seated myself right at the back of the restaurant. I picked up the discarded newspaper from a neighboring table. The waiter stood before me. I looked down at the table.

"What can I get for you?"

I looked at him. He did not seem in the least unfriendly.

"May I see the menu?"

He was benevolence personified. He placed it before me.

"Anything there that takes your fancy?"

"Yes, I think I can safely say that all the dishes whet my appetite."

"Thank you. That was most kind."

"You think so?"

"Something to drink first, perhaps?"

"Certainly, but I must think about it a bit."

I looked down at the menu and found myself somewhere between bife de lomo and bife de chorizo.

"Of course," said the waiter.

I looked up. He had gone. I glanced at the newspaper. I saw an advertisement for soap. Another diner sat right in the corner. Whenever I'm in an eating house there is always someone whose appearance arouses my interest, even if that person doesn't intrigue me initially. This man had a pale, rather inconsequential face. The anguished expression he wore did nothing to heighten my interest. But, the pain expressed in his eyes was hard to define. It looked as if he might have known several varieties of suffering. He seemed disposed to seek them out. At the same time there was a nonchalance about him that indicated he had been through much. He ate quickly and ravenously. When he had finished he examined the other guests thoroughly. Me and three others. It looked as if he wanted to etch our faces on his memory. The waiter returned.

"What would you like?"

"I haven't made up my mind."

I quickly spurned the idea of ordering, eating and then leaving without paying. That would be very short-sighted. I patronize the place now and again. On the other hand my belly was screaming out for food. Ragged, black clouds encircled the city. Beyond the harbor entrance the clouds pressed closer together. Above the northern reaches of the city they had gathered into a single, dark cloud with grey arms and claws. The sky was clearer to the west. The heat was making the air oppressive. The sun had lost all its power. A fine, light rain began to fall. The man with the intense eyes got up and left. I followed him. The waiter stopped me.

"Don't you want anything today?"

"I'm too full at the moment. I'll come back another day."

The prospect at once filled me with elation. I could simply come again another time. With head held high, no remorse, no explanations nor fear of reprisal. I heard my own laughter, which more than anything sounded like an exhalation of relief. What a marvelous day this promised to be. I followed the man down the street. He had a perfectly normal back. It was not the least hunched. A little stooped perhaps. He walked quickly. His clothes were respectable. Was it a woolen suit he had on? The suit was a uniform dark grey. He had nothing on his head to protect him from the rain. The rain increased. He carried a paper bag under his right arm. Pretty soon the rain would tear holes in the bag and expose the contents. The way he carried the bag indicated that it contained something that would be damaged by rain. I felt a sort of affection for this man and his trivial, sorrow-tinged life. Perhaps he was a kindly family man walking homeward. Let no one say I am ungenerous. I can even feel tenderness for the felon on his pallet. I regard him as a sleeping child. There is no difference between killing a child and a sleeping man. The back before me disappeared. The rain slanted away in another direction. A light and welcome freshness coated every shining surface. In reality it takes so little to make me feel content. It was enough that the rain had stopped. The sun came out in the southwest. Round about me I could see flowers and trees. Azaleas blossomed not far off, and over there, a really shining example of the paraiso tree with even more florets than the jacaranda.

I walked down the street my eyes wide open, but still no one recognized me. It began raining again. A little of my disquiet is in each drop that falls. It's important not to let this feeling carry me away too far, or my throat will tighten and choke out the breath of life. It eased. The happiness of people who never realize they're unhappy irritates me. They really have every reason to feel sorrow and helplessness. Yes, the right word might even be wretchedness. Their existence has as much sensitivity as a stone's, and events that should have been like knives piercing their souls, are just so much dust blowing past! A blissful breeze caressed my brow. I stood still. Four young women were walking towards me. I didn't know them. They were singing. They seemed carefree and happy! I had a feeling of bitterness. Was that really what I felt? Yes, indeed. It was bitterness. Not against them, but myself, perhaps? I refused to let myself daydream. Dreaming is a cowardly attempt to retreat into oneself. But this waking life, with this miserable soul, is that any better? Especially when one has the sort of soul that only manifests itself in other people's dreams as they lie snoring, shaking the mask of death, while the stars pale to nothing in the morning sky.

I felt the exhaustion in my body. My eyes smarted. I stood watching everything about me with the great, open eyes of insomnia. The tower clock was silent because all about it was silent. I was a silent sea in a landscape which didn't exist. I felt my head perched on top of my body. I breathed with my lungs. The melancholy rain increased in strength before it eased off once more. I looked up at the sky. Far away there was the rumble of thunder. I lowered my eyes. The bulk of dirty, grey rows of houses framed the street along which I walked. Clothes hung out to dry in the rain. What was it Don Carlos had said? "Is there anything I can help you with?" I am nearly old enough to be his father. Is there anything in my appearance to make him think he can ask me such a thing? When he began to pull out his money, I waved him away. It must be his youth that makes him so inept. I was shaven. He had been tactless in the extreme. Did he think I would prostrate myself for a few miserable pesos from a young Englishman? Might he actually be stupid, after all? If I'd gone down on my knees like some miserable wretch, held out my arms, cupped my hands and begged for some stinking money, would he have been content?

I got home and went to bed. It had stopped raining. I wouldn't be able to succumb fully to sleep that night either. The moon's molten mock-silver spread over the neighboring houses until it congealed and turned black. My eyes tried to press sleep beneath their lids. I must have slept for a few minutes. Suddenly I felt an almost inexplicable tenseness. If it wasn't a moment of sleep that had calmed my body, perhaps it was the beautiful slanting light of morning? I am the distance between what I am, and what I'm not. To put it more plainly: I am somewhere between what I dream myself to be, and that which life has made me. No, this world is not for those who possess both mind and heart. I was born into a world of unceasing metaphysical and moral dread. The childish, commonsensical beliefs of Don Carlos are razing religious faith. Clearly this young man understands nothing! He turns the Bible into a litany of vague myths. And not only that: religious questions of a fundamentally metaphysical nature are also brushed aside. Doesn't he know what he's doing? I could find no words to express my growing irritation with Don Carlos. Feelings cannot be explained logically. Let me take an example. Just then I wanted to go down to the park behind the Cabildo. Why? To analyze one's desire is to destroy it. To gain insight is often to suffer dejection and melancholy. Insight destroys illusion. Reason does not increase happiness. When the heart is banished from the body, one is as good as dead. This is not something I consult a pathologist about.

Not far away I could hear someone practicing the piano. It occurred to me that it must be some rich man's daughter doing her scales. I can still hear those scales. The repeats. The mistakes. I didn't see the pupil, but I was certain it was a girl with long, black hair and a bald, bespectacled teacher. She had pink bows in her curly hair. He was feeling nervously for the handkerchief in his pocket.

I sat down on a bench beneath a huge umbu tree. A bed of marguerites was the last thing I saw before I fell into a slumber. I felt that for centuries I'd known, deep within me, all the trees in the park, all the flowers and myself, before an overwhelming tiredness, a black fire, consumed me in its verdure. As a bird emptied the contents of its bowels on my head I heard it twitter: "You are mine. Just mine." I woke up. I felt fever's mild intoxication spread a numbing cold throughout my tortured body. The sleep had not been enough to rid me of my enduring tiredness. Let me forget my irritation over that young English puppy! Let me preserve my broken, quavering passivity with its occasional, diffuse visions skimming the edges of ideas before being totally bewildered by the startling feelings barring their way.

I rose from the bench. I put my hand in my pocket. It was empty. I felt in the other. Empty. It was evening. I have no idea how many people have contemplated a desolate, thronged street in the way it merits. The pedestrians walked on the cobblestones as if the street was deserted. They walked, as if enclosed in a thin bubble of glass, without touching the cobbles. They walked as if oblivious to everything.

There is a weariness associated with the burden of thought. This kind of weariness is the worst of all. It doesn't weigh down in the same way as physical tiredness. It is a weariness to do with one's consciousness of the world. Don Carlos increases, extends and deepens this weariness. This young man's saving grace is his naïveté. One can't be angry with him. I daresay.

Should I, perhaps, try to understand my melancholia? Folly. That would be to credit reason with an exaggerated importance. Reason can't assuage melancholy. Melancholy is a humor of the body, black bile. And why should I embark on such efforts and the physical ordeals they would demand? I wiped away some saliva from the corner of my mouth. I couldn't think how my mind could have even posed the question. The muscles of my body were exhausted by labors I had no intention of performing. The scent of eucalyptus reached my nose. The Indians believe eucalyptus can soothe fever. The blue evening sky was peaceful and clear with a few, frolicsome clouds in harmless confusion.

Then a woman appeared leading a child, perhaps it was her daughter. The child was clutching a doll. The doll was treated as if it were a living thing. The doll fell on to the cobbles and smashed. Her sorrow was as great as if her mother had dropped dead. That little girl would have considered glass more precious than gold. And tell me, why is gold more valuable? Who is it that has set the values we adhere to, or more accurately, are addicted to? What wouldn't we adults do for gold?

I looked down the street. Isn't it odd how we organize our whole existence? I saw the signs, gas lamps, cobblestones, the planted trees, all arranged as the result of intensely organized intellectual effort. All built on neat patterns. People walked down the street as if they had as little understanding of this as dogs. At the end of the road I saw a bald man with glasses and a girl with long hair and pink bows. I decamped.

Roberto, I sit here alone with my skeleton. Nothing wears down the spirit more than its refusal to formulate vague thoughts. My writing shows you whether the pen point is moving quickly or slowly. When the letters almost fill with ink, do you draw your own conclusions? Perhaps you think I feel sorry for myself. Dear brother! Feeling sorry for oneself doesn't necessarily mean it isn't justified!

★ ★

Roberto! Don Carlos gave me a substantial advance yesterday. I accepted it. I placed myself under no obligation whatsoever. I haven't signed a single document. With the money I can buy ten tailor-made suits of the finest cloth. I can have fresh flowers delivered to my mistress for months. I can stand fifty dinners with wine. I can pay the Alborellos a year's rent.

I've bought some kegs of rum. He gave me the money in San Telmo. When I left, I made sure he wasn't following me. I've thumbed through and counted, counted and thumbed through the money. The notes and coins are lying on my bed. I've tossed them in the air. I've balanced small piles on the top of my head. I've tried to see how many notes I can squeeze between my ear and the side of my head.

Send all the world's beggars to me!

Roberto! I gave Don Carlos a useful bit of advice. He was obsessed with the idea of finding a dentist. He'd suffered toothache for several weeks. I knew of a dentist. Lefebré, a Frenchman, is an experienced practitioner. He is looking for patients. He had said Don Carlos' jaw and teeth were perfectly normal, everything was whole, nothing broken. Then he'd asked:

"Have you been in severe pain recently?"

"No, not particularly," Don Carlos replied.

One must hide behind a mask when one meets the gods.

"Sit down," said the dentist.

"Yes," said Don Carlos.

Even though the brain makes up only a fraction of our body weight, it uses something like a quarter of the oxygen we breathe.

"Sit calmly, don't break it."

"Ah," said Don Carlos.

A thousand years ago a German dentist died. He was buried with his equipment: knife, awl, scalpel, a spoon and an iron bar.

"There!" said the dentist.

"Ah," said Don Carlos.

The dentist filled the bad nerve with arsenic and told him to come back in a fortnight. The nerve would then be mummified. The dentist pulled out a keg of brandy and placed it on the table under the mirror. He poured some into a glass.

"Here you are, sir. This is for the pain."

"No, thank you," said Don Carlos.

"Very well," said the dentist and knocked the whole lot back in one gulp.

This puppy, Roberto, who can't accept a nip of brandy, is the man I put on airs for!

Just now, nothing pleases me so much as sitting on a bollard down by the harbor and watching the waves.

I can't remember when I first realized how important sea air was to me. It must have been some time after father took me to the Ligurian Sea. We stood side by side on the beach. There was an off-shore wind. The waves rolled away from us. He pointed to the left and then to the right: "Over in that direction is Genoa, and there you can almost see Corsica."

"Corsica," I repeated and imagined castles, fairies, men in armor, snow-capped mountains and tall towers. When, some years later, in '27, I signed on aboard the Spanish schooner, Bolara, I experienced a similar association. We berthed at St Petersburg. A few days later we were to sail on to Stockholm. I'd never heard of St Petersburg. I'd never seen anything like it. A huge city built to humor one man's desire for sea air. Peter the Great was sick of the inland air of Moscow. In 1704, after weeks of traveling on horseback and in carriages, he spied the sea. The ground they stood on was a broad, level swamp. The Gulf of Finland looked inviting. As the Tsar filled his lungs with the marvelous air he made his decision. He pointed: "The city is to be built here!" His retinue looked about them. Not a hillock, not a hut could be seen for miles. The soil was clayey. No one spoke. The Tsar broke the silence. He pointed towards the estuary of the Neva. "Inform the provincial governors that they must supply forty thousand workers each year. The city is to be built on piles like Amsterdam. Use the forests round here." He lifted his long stick, his dubina, flung it into the swamp and roared: "This is to be our future capital!" In his mind's eye he must already have seen the world's widest avenues, and palaces decorated for banquets to celebrate victories over the Swedes and Turks. Peter the Great was the Tsar.

I saw the sails out in the Río de la Plata. I let my nose breathe in quantities of air so that my brain would have plenty of the stuff to appreciate. Was this some of the same air I inhaled as a child while standing at my father's side imagining Corsica? Father pointed and said: "You'll go there one day, my lad."

Peter the Great was standing at Vitus Bering's side in 1724. They were looking at the map. Siberia and Alaska was just a blank space. "You'll go there, my fine Dane," said the Tsar.

I was with Vincenzo Camorotti and Don Carlos on the seashore a short distance from the city center. It was evening. We were going to walk in the direction of Lezama and Plaza de la Residencia. We had been watching some horse racing. No whips were allowed and absolutely no saddles. They raced in pairs. A lot of money was at stake. Bets were laid all evening. The man who wins the jackpot is wise to carry a knife in his boot. Men from every walk of life take part. Last year I lost a month's wages. Camorotti wanted me at his side to make sure he didn't lose all his money. His wife had only allowed him to go on that condition. She is sweet. Vincenzo lost out early in the wager.

We walked to Lezama and looked at the residence of the Scotsman, Daniel McKinlay. The Royal Philippines Company had a warehouse where they kept African slaves in the old days. The buying and selling of slaves is now carried on in the harbor of Retiro. Don Carlos asked us why it was called "the Englishman's house" when the proprietor was a Scotsman. I suggested a walk to my work place, the Admiralty Shipyard. The war against Banda Oriental (Brazil) had turned the shipyard into the biggest in Argentina. Somewhat unwillingly, he accompanied us. Once down the hill of San Pedero, we were to follow Reconquista to the harbor. The rain of the past few days had made the roads almost impassable. A water wagon pulled by two oxen had overturned. One of the oxen had drowned in the mud. The huge wheels were just about to disappear. The water seller was hauling for dear life at the horns of the second ox. We tried to help. Several others came running. The water seller wept with rage and despair. When there was no hope left we made our way to the Matador Slaughterhouse to borrow a horse and cart from a man I know. The slaughterhouse yard contained several small enclosures belonging to various slaughtermen. Though it was evening and the weather was wet, work was in progress. The beasts were driven through the city streets into the enclosure. The matador rode toward the steer. His lasso of metal wire tightened about its neck. The muscle between its thigh and knee was severed. One knife thrust into the jugular. The blood spurted straight up into the air, before splashing over the entrails of the previous animal, which had emitted the same gurgling noises. The steer was butchered with an axe, its head severed, its carcass cut into three pieces lengthways. The long, dismembered pieces were loaded into the wagon which would take them to market. A couple of pigs wandered the enclosure eating the left-overs. A carrion-crow, a bird not unlike a seagull, snatched a piece of gut. Don Carlos left. He still had a toothache. A rat ran towards the head on the ground. I kicked the rat away. I didn't see where it went. Rats always live in the vicinity of man. Who will survive longer? Them or us?

I was drinking wine in the bar at 119 Carlos Calvo. I was eating bread. Four of us sat round the table, Fredrico, Marco, Miguel and me. I was reading in El Telegrafo about the uprisings in Paraguay. Suddenly, Miguel sprained his wrist. At first he yelled. Then he went almost completely quiet.

I called out: "It's my round!"

Someone said: "Giovanni, you've never bought a round before. Have you . . ."

The sun shone. Inside it was dark. Someone lurched into the stack of crates. One landed on Fredrico's head. He took it philosophically. He was speaking:

"Rivadavia is the best president we've ever had."

The rain arrived. We looked at one another. We ordered another round.

"No, the best was General Belgrano who decreed in 1812 that the flag should be white and blue," said Marco.

Fredrico: "Mariano Escobar was a fisherman."

Marco: "His father scolded him."

Fredrico: "His grandfather, old Escobar, died in his sleep."

Marco: "'I'm so frightened of dying in my sleep,' Mariano used to say. D'you remember?"

And with that there was a lull in the excitement. I drank again. Dreams are rent by irreconcilable acids.

Fredrico: "Do you remember Christina?"

Marco: "What about Iris Estaban's calves?"

Fredrico: "She could wiggle her ears."

Someone was singing.

Was it the creole in the corner?

I: "In a world without sorrow the anaconda would burst into song."

Marco: "Come here, damn you, I want more!"

We got more. I drank. We drank.

Fredrico: "Iris's sister was toothless."

The wind moaned outside. The sun set.

Marco: "They say General Juan Manuel des Rosas is not in Buenos Ayres."

Fredrico: "Did she take everything off?"

Marco: "We kissed each other till we sank."

Fredrico: "We're all fond of horses."

I: "Who?"

Marco: "He hit the mark at long range. Old Escobar was quite a shot! Bragging? Not a bit of it."

It got darker. We drank.

I: "One more!"

Fredrico: "Iris's sister was toothless."

I: "Really."

Marco: "Rich man Edson's little zoo is mostly full of flies."

Fredrico: "The empty cages are kept locked to stop people getting into them voluntarily."

I ordered soup.

I: "Is this soup?"

Marco: "Did anyone hear gunfire?"

I: "A new house goes up in Boca every day."

Fredrico: "Iris's sister was toothless!"

Marco: "Yes, we heard!"

Fredrico: "One of Almirante Brown's illegitimate children, right?"

No one had heard a thing.

I: "I'm not paying for the soup."

Late evening. We drank more. The moon's face looked very swollen. A knife was thrown at the wall.

Fredrico: "Shall we go?"

It was *then* I blurted out: "Fredrico, d'you still remember Cecilie?"

I rose. Fredrico lashed out. I regained my senses.

Fredrico: "Come outside!"

I: "All right."

We went outside.

Fredrico: "You monster! And you call yourself a human being!"

A hen walked past.

I: "That's mine!"

Fredrico: "Now, by God, he's even grabbing that defenseless chicken."

He turned to the others who had crowded around us.

I: "What?!"

Fredrico: "Don't let him get hold of it."

I: "Now I've got you!"

Fredrico: "Watch him! Push him away!"

I: "I'll wring . . ."

Fredrico: "He's in the right mood to do it."

I: "I'll stick my knife in you and you won't even struggle!"

There was a rabbit in a hutch under the table outside the bar.

Fredrico: "Listen, now! Don't let him nab the rabbit as well. Get rid of him!"

Nobody moved.

I: "Coward."

Fredrico: "Kick him away."

Some of them obeyed the command.

I: "My leg!"

Fredrico: "Hard!"

I: "The deuce!"

Fredrico: "Don't just stand there!"

I: "Me?"

Fredrico: "Get that rabbit off Giovanni!"

I: "Lay off!"

Fredrico: "Hard!"

I: "I'll give you some of your rabbit!"

Fredrico: "All of it, damn you!"

I: "Not on your life!"

Fredrico: "My God, how that rabbit's screaming."

I: "Piss off!"

Fredrico: "Sit on Giovanni!"

I: "You son of a whore!"

Fredrico: "Don't let him wolf it all in one mouthful."

I: "My hunger's not that easily satisfied."

Fredrico: "There! A decent blow from a stick."

I: "Murderer!"

Fredrico: "Harder?"

I: "Go on!"

Fredrico: "Calm down!"

I: "I wish I was a cannibal, not so much because I would be able to devour you, as for the pleasure of spewing you up again."

Dear brother, I haven't been able to write for several days. My wound is worse. It's suppurating just as much as before. I've lost the feeling in certain parts of my foot. This has afforded me greater freedom of movement. At the beginning of last week Don Carlos and I went on a major excursion. It was the first — and perhaps the last? — time I saw Don

Carlos on horseback. We were between San Lorenzo and Boca. We rode down by the shoreline of the Río de la Plata. It was then that we, or rather he, saw it.

"Isn't that a Cephalopoda?" said Don Carlos reining in his horse and looking down into the water. He was a skilful rider. No doubt about it. He had borrowed the horses from Mr Lumb.

On my suggestion we were going to look round the area where the new shipyard is to be built. The navy wants to increase the strength of its fleet for the war with Banda Oriental. Perhaps I might get a permanent job?

"Have you ever gone into a church just to be completely on your own?" I asked. I drew up by the side of Don Carlos.

"No," he said peering at something smooth and slimy on the water-line.

"But you did study theology?" I said.

"One may enter a church without studying theology," said Don Carlos.

I wanted to move on. He rode into the water.

"Well, there's no doubt about it. It's an octopus."

"Isn't the wonderful thing about going into a church that one may discover more about who one is? But you, I suppose, were able to find that out aboard the Beagle?"

"On the occasions I am alone in the cabin, I hear nothing but the endless sound of the captain's *twenty-two* chronometers, while my thoughts mainly revolve around the nausea of my ever-present seasickness."

He dismounted, picked up a handy stick and began to prod the repulsive creature. He didn't look at me as he spoke. I remained on my horse.

"What do you want with it? Can't you leave it in peace?"

"It appears to be a prize specimen. When I find anything of interest, I send it to London."

A fly settled on my nose. I swiped at it.

"A common or garden fly," said Don Carlos. He was trying to lift one of the octopus' arms. I got off my horse. I saw we wouldn't be moving on immediately. I stood close by my horse to indicate that I expected to ride on soon. The horse was defecating in an easy, untroubled way. Excrement is a kind of rejection, something to be rid of. Cats cover their turds by scratching with their feet. With a little imagination, horse muck smells of hay and grass. The manner in which my horse rid itself of its excrement bordered on the elegant. The fact that the smell wasn't worse, contributed to my reasonably positive attitude. The excrement of men or swine could never have put me in that frame of mind. Pigs and humans are omnivores. The sweetish smell made me think of something rotting. An incredibly fat man rode up, a vulture's dream of a man. He looked at Don Carlos, then at me, and shook his head. I looked at my horse which hadn't finished. Don Carlos looked at me.

"It's not like the guanaco."

"What?" I said.

"The guanaco on the pampas always defecates in special places. Eventually the piles get so large that they can be up to eight foot in diameter. The horse is quite different. Messy and unsystematic."

One of the creature's arms had got hold of Don Carlos' right knee. The octopus had strayed into the shallows. Don Carlos stood in the water. He was wet to the middle of his thighs.

"I do believe it's caught a crab," he said as he beat another arm, which threatened to bring him down, with the stick. I found a knife in Don Carlos' saddle-bag and was about to go to his aid.

"Keep calm! A couple more whacks and it'll let go of my knee and concentrate on the crab!"

He dealt it two, sharp blows. Its grip slowly loosened.

"See how it changes color," said Don Carlos enthusiastically. He looked at me as if anticipating an outburst of elation, or at least an interested glance.

"At first sight octopuses can look harmless. They seem to have too many arms and tentacles to coordinate an attack. Think how many insects have been tricked by flowers. There's nothing so peaceful as a flower. Take the carnivorous plants, the cunning sundew or the lady's slipper. First they lure insects to them, then kill them, slowly. Can you see the octopus' beautiful eyes?"

I was trying to find the gun in the saddle-bag.

"Put it away! Get the notebook out of my shoulder-bag over there! I must find out if it has eight or ten arms. I'll try to lift it up. You count the arms! Count the tentacles as well." He lifted it by its head. Two of its arms still clung to the crab.

"You're being strangled!" I shouted.

I tensed.

"Come on, count!" he commanded.

"Eight! Two tentacles!"

"Thanks! Now you can help me get it out. I've got to study its suckers."

"Shall I fetch the gun?" I asked.

"I'll catch it alive, don't worry! The octopus belongs to the highest order of molluscs. Its ancestors frequently had a shell covering all their internal organs, like snails do. Look at those eyes! They're emerald green, wouldn't you say?"

A rider halted a short distance away. He paid us no attention. I was relieved. He was clearly making for the peninsula opposite. He dismounted. He took off his upper garments, re-mounted and rode out into the water. As his horse began to swim, he slid off its back and grabbed its tail. When the horse turned its head to see where he was, he splashed water in its face. This was repeated several times before it swam straight ahead.

When I looked at Don Carlos again, he had managed to get the creature ashore. The octopus had taken hold round his chest and hips. He said not a word. He had the stick in his right hand. He was using it to raise one of the arms so that he could examine it from beneath. I stood still, the Englishman's notebook in my hand. He freed himself after dealing the animal a few further blows.

"I know of an estancia not far from Palermo. One of Lumb's friends owns the place. We'll take the octopus there," said Don Carlos.

"Aren't we going to look at the shipyard site?"

"Later, later. You see, this man can help me send the octopus to Professor Henslow. *He* has connections!"

He put the eight-armed beast to death. Together we hoisted it on to his horse, which shied and whinnied as we laid it on her back. Before he tied it on properly, he asked me to hold his horse and the octopus while he made some notes. Never before had I held a warm, snorting horse with one hand whilst propping up a cold, slimy octopus with the other.

"Watch out for its salivary glands. There may still be poison in them."

I jumped and let go. The octopus fell on top of me. The horse bolted. It stopped a short distance away. Don Carlos rushed forward. He took hold of the octopus' head and dragged it off me.

"What came over you?" he inquired in alarm.

He looked at me stretched out on the ground.

"A cold and heavy blanket," I replied jovially.

When we arrived at the estancia, we called out:

"Ave Maria! (Be greeted!)"

The owner appeared in the doorway and returned our greeting:

"Sin pecado concebida! (Conceived without sin!)"

We were warmly received. Soon after, the owner, Señor Hernandez, sent three of his men out to fetch food for dinner. The steers were rounded up in front of the houses. Bolas twined around three well-grown animals. They were slaughtered in the yard. Some of the meat was roasted. The rest boiled. Water was served with the food. After the meal we smoked. A woman sang some songs from Salta, a place further north in Argentina. The other women sat in an adjoining room and talked amongst themselves. The owner and Don Carlos did the talking. Don Carlos wanted to know if his host had some formalin, by any chance? The animal could not be allowed to rot. Hernandez had never heard of the stuff. The conversation turned to Don Carlos' experiences in the Sierra Ventana.

"You realize the Sierra Ventana is the highest range of mountains on this continent east of the Andes? They're over 3,500 feet high. They resemble an altar. It's rumored that the mountains contain coal, gold and silver. I've climbed several of the peaks. Essentially they are composed of hard, white quartz. When the mountains lay under the sea, the water must have eroded the looser, upper layers. Earth and gravel must have been aggregated and removed from the mountains one sees today. Have either of you read the geologist, Lyell? On my last night I slept on a rock ledge. It was cold, but I remember the great satisfaction I felt at having managed to climb the Indians' holy mountains. Before I fell asleep I thought that there must be Indians several hundred yards further down. I slept like a log."

Hernandez shot me a questioning glance. He turned his gaze to Don Carlos:

"Has any sort of mining operation been started to win the minerals from these mountains?"

"Not that I could see," answered Don Carlos.

"Forgive me," said our host smiling, "but since I cannot help you with this . . ."

"Formalin," put in Don Carlos.

"Could we not roast the creature?" our host inquired.

"I'm full, thank you," I replied.

"It's most definitely not for consumption! We'll take it back with us to Buenos Ayres," put in Don Carlos.

Our host noticed that Don Carlos hadn't seen the funny side of it. His voice had a conciliatory ring when he asked:

"But how do you manage to transport all you find?"

"The first skunk I found, I tied up in a silk scarf. I have to use whatever comes to hand. Now, months later, and after innumerable washings, the scarf still smells of it. Skunks aren't frightened of gunshot. They're so used to being hunted on horseback with the bola. I bagged most of mine on foot with a gun.

"The tucu-tuco bird is perhaps the easiest prey. The Indians gave the bird its name. It can barely hop or fly. If it senses danger, it makes helpless tucu-tuco noises. I once put my hand over the eyes of one specimen. It wasn't frightened. Not the slightest bit! I laid my fingers over its big, yellow bill. Without showing any fear it waddled, dumpily and clumsily, forward. It was so tame I put it in spirit on the spot.

"The agonti hare is more of a problem. It's twice as big as its English counterpart. Its movement is more reminiscent of a rabbit than a hare. It's good at running in zigzags. It's not easy to catch, unless there are several of you."

Hernandez offered round some expensive cigars.

"It seems you're making good use of your time down here. Mr Lumb tells me you've found bones of animals that don't exist any more. How do you know they're extinct? I've heard rumors, especially from along the River Paraná, that people have met with these mammoths quite recently."

"That's impossible. These animals must have died out a long time ago," answered Don Carlos.

"But what did they eat? Did the pampas have a more luxuriant vegetation at that time?" I asked.

"I'm not at all sure, but I don't think that's the

explanation. From the pictures I've seen from Africa, relatively large animals, like elephants, live in areas of sparse vegetation."

Is there anything he doesn't know?

Before darkness fell we left the estancia, Don Carlos, the horses, the octopus and I. On the outskirts of Buenos Ayres dusk descended. The olive, peach and jacaranda trees looked as if they were cut out of black cardboard as we rode by. Don Carlos told me that from the first he had been struck by the dimensions of Buenos Ayres. Its population of nearly eighty thousand, its wide streets and huge plazas of which Plaza de la Victoria formed the natural focal point of the city. The size of the buildings around the plaza, the cathedral, the public offices, the Cabildo, what had been the Spanish viceroy's palace prior to the revolution and the fort facing the Río de la Plata had all created an impression.

In the twilight we met a caravan on its way to Mendoza. The wagons were nearly seven yards long and were hauled by six oxen. It would be fifty days in the mud. They looked as if they were going to war. Weapons poked out beneath the roofs of the wagons. We rode by the water. Suddenly Don Carlos pulled up his horse. The octopus was about to fall off. He dismounted and began tightening the ropes.

I jumped down realizing we wouldn't get to see the shipyard site. I was just about to skim a flat stone on the calm water, to see how many times I could make it bounce.

"Stop!"

Don Carlos held my arm back.

"Isn't that feldspar?"

"It's a stone," I said pushing him away.

Kindly but firmly he took the stone out of my hand and put it in his own pocket. He spoke of the countryside. The landscape here and at Punte Alta was almost equally flat. The night sky lowered its lid on the land.

"Fascinating," I said and smacked what was now a rather dark octopus with the flat of my hand, without Don Carlos noticing.

The moon was full. My head was empty. The moon has not moved for several years.

The next day found me journeying to Francisco Javier Muniz. I needed some scientific arguments I could use against the conceited Englishman! At least something that might make him pause for breath and think twice. I passed General Rosas' sumptuous home on the outskirts of the city. The district it stands in is known as Palermo. Large numbers of soldiers were on guard round the house. It was rumored in the city that he had a huge telescope he peered through in the evenings. As I rode past I mused over what a telescope might look like. I knew it was an instrument used to observe the stars. But I had no notion of its shape! The ability to see the stars close up must imbue him with a special power! An advantage. The houses behind the Cabildo and Santiago de Linier's house at Venezuela 459 were the finest private houses I had seen up to then. I had never been in this part of town before. The houses fringing Recoleta cemetery were not to be sneezed at either. Outside the house Rosas' soldiers were shouting:

"Rosas is assuming the mantle of Argentina's savior, San Martín!"

In the city the rage against Balcarce is increasing. Many believe the governor and his ministers will flee. Everyone is in turmoil. I don't give a fig. The decisive battle is imminent.

Muniz lives way out in San Isidro. A day's ride on horseback from the capital. It's a lovely place on the banks of the Río de la Plata, several miles north of the city. A number of rich families live in the area. I had no precise address. I only knew he lived in San Isidro. He was actively opposed to Rosas. He had

supported Governor Rivadavia from 1822-27 and was made Principal Doctor in 1826, five years after he had finished his medical training. A year later he became Professor of pediatrics and pathology. He has a considerable interest in life and death. At the age of twelve he became a cadet in the Andalusian Regiment under the command of Colonel José Merlos. He took part in the defeat of the English in the streets of Buenos Ayres in July 1807. He fired at the Englishmen from the roofs of the small houses in San Telmo. He was wounded, but got to safety. He was decorated, at twelve years of age. Later, he took part in several battles, including that of Ituzaingó against the Brazilians in 1827. In the field, he was a surgeon of commissioned rank. When Rosas came to power in 1829, he lost all his posts and positions. Muniz shared Rivadavia's ideas, which are also the ones prevalent in France and England. He is in favor of free trade and increased contact with the great European powers which supported the emergent mercantile bourgeoisie in Buenos Ayres. England lent Buenos Ayres one million pounds sterling from 1822-27. Muniz believed his country was dependent on this contact. Rosas, the landowner and gaucho, champion of populism and national chauvinism, is hated by Muniz.

Muniz felt insecure and kept his whereabouts more or less a secret. The house stood at the end of an avenue of eucalyptus trees. I had first seen eucalyptus outside the post office on the corner of Carlos Calvo and Balcarce. Out on the Río de la Plata lay a Norwegian ship, probably laden with timber. I could smell roast meat. It was Saturday. A black servant was roasting assado at the back of the house. I was hungry. I tied my horse to a tree. A garden, painstakingly made and lovely, surrounded the house. The servant went in.

"Is Francisco Javier Muniz here?" I called out. The doors at the front and back of the house were open. The building was white. Two floors and a roof garden. No one answered.

Was it jealousy that had led me to run one of Argentina's great experts to earth? Yes! In addition to his other accomplishments, he had been to Patagonia and traveled around the pampas and had uncovered prehistoric animals. I'd asked Don Carlos if he knew Muniz. He'd never heard of him. It was time to make contact. I'd heard about Muniz shortly after I settled here. Suddenly, he was standing in the doorway. A man in his late thirties.

"Are you Francisco Javier Muniz?"

"Yes."

What was I to say?

"I am a great personal admirer of yours. Did you not send prehistoric animal skeletons to the King of Spain?"

"I don't know you," answered Muniz.

"You have also been a good doctor to the family of Marco Silvani of Boca. It was he who told me about you."

"Oh?"

"Do you know of Charles Robert Darwin, an English naturalist?"

"Get out, you police spy!"

All the doors were shut. He took out a rifle from behind the door.

"I'll shoot!"

"You've made several prehistoric finds by the River Paraná, haven't you?"

"Be off!"

I leapt on my horse and rode away as fast as I could. The smell of the assado became fainter and fainter. I galloped in disorderly retreat, having failed in my wicked designs. I dug my spurs harder into the horse. I didn't look round.

Marco Silvani told me this sad tale about Muniz and Signóre Bagli:

Salvatore Bagli got a fishbone stuck in his throat. Boce are fickle fish. The doctor was summoned. Doctor Muniz examined the patient. He knew that Bagli had suffered from an irregularity of the heart for some years.

"He's dead," Muniz pronounced.

His widow wept. The others in the room embraced her. They wept. Next day he was buried. Wreaths and flowers were heaped in great profusion. Everyone wore black. The mourners went home. Bagli banged on the lid. The grave-diggers had also gone home. On the third day, a grave-digger heard him.

"Stop that row, Old Nick!"

He banged on the fourth day too. One of the grave-diggers got him out. Bagli contemplated the withered flowers and dusted himself down. He went home. Signóra Bagli screamed:

"Go away, you apparition! My family and I have suffered enough without this as well!"

He went to his children and grandchildren. They would have nothing to do with him. Sharing their sorrow, he clutched at his heart and died.

I had just lain down. I had dreaded it long before exhaustion forced me into bed. Lately, a figure had appeared as soon as I'd closed my eyes. He was there before me. This time I took courage. On previous occasions he had driven me from one side of my bed to the other. I asked:

"Are you the Devil?"

"Yes, of course I am. Don't tell me you can't see that?"

"No . . . ," I said.

His tail was covered in what looked like wolfskin. He had two horns on his head. He pointed to his head and his tail.

"Well?" asked the Devil.

"You haven't asked me how much of Don Carlos' advance I've got left?"

"It isn't my job to ask *that* question. But what did you imagine I'd look like?"

"Like this," I said and turned inside out like a glove. It was very dark inside myself. I felt a bit embarrassed. I didn't know what he could see. I'd like to have seen it too.

When I turned right side out again, he was running away with his tail between his legs and both hands pressed to his ears. His mouth was open wide. He screamed and screamed until he woke me. At last we were even.

Roberto, is it the Devil or the fever that fills me with such dreams? There is not the slightest thing to indicate that life will get easier. Nothing. Let me think about that. No. I would prefer to say: absolutely nothing. Despite this, before sunrise tomorrow, I shall put on my threadbare breeches and shirt. I'll make sure they're on neatly and will stay up all day. Not only that. If anyone were to set out a little food, I wouldn't say no. Certainly not. A keg of wine? That, too. A more substantial repast of several courses? Most decidedly.

I pulled the blanket over my head and tried to sleep. I believe I can remember feeling that birth was a disappointment. I arrived to find others there before me. I'd had no prior warning at all. It wasn't just the odd one or two I'd have to live with, but people in such quantities that, strictly speaking, being one of them seemed even less than not existing at all. I lay beneath the blanket. Outside the trees bowed down.

I stood looking up at the vast vault of the sky. It has in me a patient and devoted student. Don Carlos was talking about Francia the Paraguayan dictator. The newspapers that support Balcarce are rejoicing.

"Now the dictator has fallen, noble and upright

men will come to power."

"Have you been to Paraguay?" I asked.

"No."

"Are there any names you'd care to put forward?"

Either he didn't understand my question or he ignored the irony in it.

"They're obviously barbarians," answered Don Carlos.

"Assuredly."

"South America would have been quite a different place had Englishmen, and not Juan Díaz de Solís and his Spaniards, been the first to sail up the Río de la Plata."

"Quite so. But you were the first to reach China, weren't you? But that apart, it seems European states are quite willing to cooperate on matters of substance."

"What do you mean?"

"Potosí."

"What?"

"A town in the Bolivian Andes which was the largest in the world in the 17th century. I first heard of it last year."

"I've never heard of it," he said.

"In 1545 the Spanish began mining there. Renaissance Europe was short of metals. Silver for one.

They eventually sank five thousand mines. Six thousand Negro slaves began work. The rarefied air at 14,500 feet was too much for them. They died. The Spaniards enslaved the local Indians. They lived on coca leaves and didn't succumb so quickly. Up to now almost seven million Indians have perished for the sake of silver!"

"You said Europeans had cooperated?"

"The monarchs of Europe have used silver to mint coins for centuries."

"I've had a letter from Professor Henslow in which he tells me that England has just outlawed slavery. It was a great comfort to receive that news. I shall never forget an experience I had in Brazil. An Irishman, who owned a cotton plantation, had captured an elderly Negress. He took his eye off her for one moment. She threw herself over a precipice and faced death without a scruple rather than be taken into slavery."

We stood talking at the end of Calle de Empedrado. The city's first cobbled street. Lights were burning in the house of the old patriot Mariquita Sanchez. We walked towards Plaza de la Paz.

Don Carlos suddenly fell silent. I heard our footsteps on the cobbles. He broke the silence:

"I sometimes experience a loathing that turns into a nausea I can't shake off. As a matter of fact, there are few things that irritate me so much as the man with easy solutions. I still remember how my father, the doctor, suggested I eat raisins as a cure for seasickness. After I'd spent two nauseous years at sea! Raisins! But one tries anything, doesn't one? I got a handful from the ship's cook and vomited in the galley. I hate every wave in the sea. But still I persevere with this mad voyage. According to the terms of my articles I can return home whenever I wish. I just don't do it. I won't ever do it. After a couple of days at sea I feel a vague revulsion which gradually increases. This revulsion is replaced by an overweening nausea which eventually fills my entire body and head. I go up on deck, stand there, bend and stretch before returning, exhausted, to lie in the cabin. This nausea is like an enveloping swell. And then at some point my head reminds me that some years ago, in this same cabin, the crew found Captain Pringle Stokes with his throat cut. He was my age. I hear the twenty-two chronometers around me."

"But what made you compare . . ."

"I hate feeling nauseous, but I expose myself to it daily. The smell of assado makes me feel sick, but I eat it. It passes. A meal passes. When I began to think about the Negress who jumped, I felt a nausea that reminded me of the extreme biliousness I experience on board. It lasts a long time, and the worst thing about it is I never know how long. That nausea holds me totally to ransom. And, as if that wasn't enough: it's a condition I've subjected myself to voluntarily."

He looked at me. His eyes were listless. His expression was more one of searching, inquiry than anything else. I said:

"We are so used to waiting, so used to accepting every condition whilst adapting to the future, or to an illusion of the future, that we have invented the term mortality merely because we understand the necessity of waiting an eternity for death to claim us."

He clearly didn't realize my words had any connection with the dilemma he'd placed me in.

He said nothing. We stood on the outskirts of the city. Four fishermen were down by the water. Between an ox and cart and a horse thirty yards off they had strung a huge fishing net.

Don Carlos and I went to a restaurant in the Plaza de la Paz and had a meal of bife de chorizo. A huge, succulent steak. As Don Carlos cut into his meat, he recalled an incident from the pampas. He poured some water from the carafe. Yes, Roberto. He was paying!

"I was sitting by the camp fire with the gaucho who was my guide on the last leg to Buenos Ayres. Earlier in the day we'd caught an ostrich. My God, how hungry we were. Just as I was about to cut the meat from its haunch, I noticed it!"

"What?" I asked.

"I asked the gaucho to stop eating and took the bone he was gnawing out of his mouth. I put the bone and the remains of the flesh together, trying to reconstruct the bird. No doubt about it! The Argentine ostrich was obviously smaller than the African, with which I am well acquainted from the collections at Cambridge and the British Museum."

"What's the meat like?"

"I haven't started yet."

"I mean ostrich."

"Good, very good."

"Marvelous steaks in this country."

"Yes, but this is tough. I've been struck by the fact that certain animals have such strong wills that they transcend even death itself. In the jungle round Río de Janeiro, a Portuguese priest and I took a shot at two wanderoos sitting side by side in a tree. We bagged them. We waited for them to fall. Nothing happened. We ran up to the tree and saw the two animals hanging by their tails. We had to cut down the tree in order to get them off."

The meat was rare inside. The juice on my plate was faintly blood-colored. He looked at me.

"There's something beautiful about that, don't you think? It wasn't just their will that was impressive. The suspended apes struck some noble chord in the priest and me.

"Would you like a little water? It's been a long day. Let me treat you to this meal. You've been quite a help in finding the right shops. And at the Post Office: what would I have done without you?"

I had to let him ramble on. I hadn't a single peso on me. I studied the face in front of me.

"Thank you," I said and ate all I could.

"Have I told you about the penguins and dolphins of the Río de la Plata? No? On the first occasion we sailed southward, I remember some of the officers standing by the ship's rail. They were silent until one shouted: 'Aren't those dolphins, and there, aren't they . . . yes, penguins.' They weren't far from the ship's side, ten or twelve yards perhaps. One of the officers called out: 'Look at the dolphins, they're swimming side by side. They're stopping, lifting their heads above water, are those noises coming from them? Are they talking? They're talking to the herds ashore, to the cattle.'

"That was tasty at all events. Can I pour you some more water? We don't want any wine, do we? Take some bread!

"At first I thought the officer had gone raving mad. But the dolphins really were making noises. He wasn't imagining it. I wouldn't go so far as to say they were communicating with the animals ashore. But that's what it seemed like. How I'd love to get to the bottom of that mystery! We lack the knowledge, the instruments and the imagination to understand the animal world. Did I mention the cattle? The Spaniards introduced them. The first animal arrived in Mexico in 1521. In 1619, the governor-general wrote that eighty thousand cattle could be rounded up each year for their hides alone. By 1700 it was estimated that there were 48 million head of cattle on the pampas. In 1535 the Spanish arrived with 72 horses. The Indians no longer needed to cultivate the land. Or to be more accurate: it was no longer possible to have fields under cultivation. It's like the importation of artichokes from Europe. The artichokes colonized rapidly to the detriment of the indigenous plant species. Am I talking too much?"

With a strange intensity, Don Carlos told me about the Jivaro Indians of Ecuador. I told him to calm down. He spoke faster and louder. We drank heavily, more heavily. What I find surprising is that, to this day, I can remember what he said in detail. When a Jivaro Indian has killed an enemy, he cuts off the man's head with a bamboo knife. He then makes a clean incision from the neck upwards and carefully flays the head. He tosses the flesh to the anacondas. The scalp is boiled for less than half an hour. It must not boil too long. Otherwise the hair will fall out. Once boiled, it will have shrunk to a third of its original size. The headhunter scrapes off any remaining flesh from under the skin. After that he sews up the mouth and the incision in the neck with strong thread. Five or six plum-sized stones are warmed in the fire and then carefully placed inside the scalp. They are put in one by one in such a way that the face takes on its original appearance. The heat from the stones makes the head shrink. Hot sand is added when there is no more room for stones. It takes a couple of hours' work a day for six days to produce a shrunken head.

Everything went black. I drove my elbow at Don Carlos' forehead. I shoved him backwards and left him.

Not far off, a small animal lay injured in the gutter. It turned out to be a stinking, grey cat. I gave it some nuts I had in my pocket. All at once I took on an importance for that poor creature, more enigmatic, more mighty than anything philosophy could bestow on one's own existence. We were two outcasts who clung together in the depths of our loneliness.

I stood up. There was Don Carlos again. I lashed out at him. He continued to stand in front of me. It's not my wish to make myself complex. An anger, an aggression I can't explain boiled up within me. I raised my fist and knew that it couldn't be lowered again until it had found its mark. I saw red. It was anger that had raised my fist. The same anger that makes the crab wave one of its claws. Makes the stallion kick at its adversary's gonads. Makes the cat arch its back. Makes the tortoise rise on its flippers and hiss. Makes the turkey's head turn blue. Makes the chimpanzee puff itself up. Makes the rabbit stamp. Makes the hippopotamus yawn. Makes the mouse rear up on its hind legs before hurling itself at the cat. Makes the dog lower its tail and ears while baring its teeth and snarling.

Every definition of madness I've tried to come up with has incorporated a large chunk of reason. I can't remember the last time I was angry. My memory is as poor as ever. There must be a reason for it. My fist was traveling with some force towards Don Carlos' face. He leapt out of the way. I punched the thin air. I pounded and pounded as if he were part of a war I was fighting out. Everything went black. I fell to the ground.

"How goes it?" asked Don Carlos, unscathed.

Roberto. I can crush him, but in spite of this I feel so weak. A pessimist is a person who is forced to live with an optimist. He's given me the opportunity of leaving this demented city. I haven't even given him an answer, and he treats me with the greatest kindness! I'm jealous of this carefree sycophant! He's the sort of man who would profit greatly from dying. He's the sort of man who doesn't understand that the danger of a long life is that one forgets what one has lived for.

On my way home, I stumbled. My right foot was swollen. I raised myself on all fours. Pulled myself up with the aid of my left leg and my arms. I lowered my right foot gingerly. I cried out and fell forwards. I got up again. Jellyfish have no backbone. I have. I got almost all the way home. There was a light in my neighbor's window. Someone tweaked my ear.

I turned. I raised my right hand. I clenched my fist. Don Carlos was observing me benignly.

"What marvelous ears you have!"

"My mother said that as well," I replied.

He didn't let go. His thumb and forefinger were rubbing the upper rim of my ear.

"This small thickening here corresponds to the tip of an animal's ear. Yes," he said thoughtfully, "it must be so. I've seen some excellent examples in the fetus and neonate, but in an adult? Never!"

I shook myself loose and felt my ears.

"Can you feel them? Aren't they superb?" said Don Carlos.

* * *

Several miles outside Buenos Ayres, in the vicinity of Quilmes, I saw some of Rosas' men leading a prisoner from the government forces.

"President Balcarce will punish you," yelled the helpless prisoner. The soldiers shrugged their shoulders. I caught myself doing the same. What straw doesn't one cling to when one faces irrevocable doom? The words were as impotent as the twitchings of a hen after her neck has been wrung. The prisoner shouted his entreaties to the soldiers who were holding him. They did nothing to silence him. No blows, no words. The officer in command rode some ten yards behind the prisoner and the half dozen soldiers on foot. They moved on a few hundred yards. The officer shouted "Halt!" The prisoner jumped. It went quiet. The officer got off his horse. He stared at the prisoner for some seconds before asking: "Have you made your peace with God?"

"Yes," replied the prisoner without any surprise.

"Good," said the officer. "Lower your head!"

The prisoner obeyed. The sabre found its mark. The officer calmly picked up the head which had rolled round a couple of times on the ground. He held it up by the hair, turned to his soldiers and suddenly transformed himself into a professor of anatomy. His voice became measured and factual. He explained that the cut was made vertically on the neck, and proceeded to reel off the names of all the organs visible in the cross-section: carotid artery, windpipe, spinal column, nerves, muscles. He gave the head a chivalrous kiss on the cheek and dropped it on the ground. The head landed in a small pool of blood that had not yet congealed. One of the soldiers ran forward, pushed the head on to a stake and slung the body in the ditch by the side of the road. The officer had long since mounted his horse and ridden on. The corpse was of no interest to him. There is room for everyone lying side by side in heaven.

I was headed for Quilmes. My right foot has improved recently. I was recommended some herbal ointment for it. My horse was tired. Buenos Ayres was surrounded by Rosas' forces. Riding in the area was hazardous. An hour after crossing the city boundary, I found myself encircled. I explained that I was journeying to my cousin Lugi Camboresi. He had some temporary work in Quilmes. He had borrowed money from me. Now I needed it back. I was penniless again. Totally penniless. The soldiers stared at me. A few began laughing raucously. Some thirty rifle muzzles were pointing in my direction. Should I try asking them to see if they had their boots on properly? "Hurry up and shoot him!" shouted a gaucho with a bandage round his head. He was pushed aside.

"Let's do the thing properly!" another called out.

Fear is, perhaps, the greatest asset in the fight for survival. The thought of death forces us on.

Three of the soldiers had set about organizing a grandiose execution. They were about to fasten a dirty, white rag over my eyes.

"Hurry up and shoot this Balcarce devil!"

It was the same ruffian who'd just wanted me killed on the spot. I began talking. Fast and incoherently. As soon as I'd been captured I'd realized instinctively that it was my only chance. As I talked, my eyes wandered to and fro over the band of soldiers, before alighting on one I took to be an officer. He was totally indifferent to the impending execution. He was studying what looked like a map. I had no idea what I was babbling, but at the sight of the officer I shouted:

"But it's General Roco, isn't it? Long live General Rosas! Down with Balcarce!"

He looked up from the map. His eyes were grey. He was unshaven. His hair was greasy and grey.

"How do you know my name?"

I could see from the expressions around me that they had begun to feel uneasy.

"But of course I recognize such a patriot as yourself. My brother fell at your side in the south, near the Río Negro."

For a moment it looked as if he were deliberating before he screamed:

"Pigs! What do you think you're doing!"

He ran up to the three soldiers who were holding me. He wrenched away the dirty kerchief. It was meant to be the last thing I saw. He stuffed the kerchief in one of the soldiers' mouths.

"Do you want me to court martial the lot of you for murder?"

He was aiming his gun at the soldiers. I breathed more easily. My anxious speech was over. It seemed I'd managed to stay the execution. I'd read in the newspapers that Roco operated in these parts and that he had formerly taken part in the southern campaigns. I'd taken a chance.

I turned to the soldiers, letting my gaze fall on the most blood-thirsty of the lot. Roco had his arm around me. I raised my right fist and shouted "Long Live Argentina!" After some hesitation, everyone joined in three choruses of "Long Live Argentina!," before we all rode on together towards Quilmes. Roco kept his horse next to mine. We began to speak of "my brother." His courage, his marksmanship, and his way with women. I let him talk. He was more than willing to talk. He rode forward to the three who had formed the execution squad. He cuffed and abused them before returning to my side. I realized that sooner or later I might be forced to be more precise about "my brother" and my own background. I fed my protector with humbug and chatter that might appeal to his vanity. A characteristic that proved to be boundless. I was liberal with remarks that extolled gaucho life, Rosas' stratagem and his heroic military deeds. Some of these were unknown to Roco, but all the more interesting for that. Military heroism clearly appeals to these soldiers, was my spontaneous notion. If one wants others to leave one in peace, there is only one course of action. Allow them to blossom. Allow them to wallow in their own vaunting. There is no such thing as intelligent vanity. It is crude and instinctive. There is no man on earth who is not first and foremost vain. My task at this moment was to play the admirer. My relief changed to muted joy as I realized that, perhaps, I wouldn't need to say very much. My countenance had only to display admiration. When he had finished an anecdote, the punch line frequently accompanied with a loud, raucous laugh, or a somewhat longer story, I would interject:

"That could have come straight out of the pages of a history book."

If he didn't carry on immediately, I would fill the vacuum with comments like: "Not only are you a great soldier, but an outstanding raconteur into the bargain."

After a couple of hours he pronounced me to be simpatico. An hour later, highly intelligent. And the soldier who, earlier in the day, had wanted to shoot me without even asking my errand, was now able to find innumerable pleasant sides to my character. I sent a shower of praise back. I saw how the blood flowed easier in the soldier's veins after that. His look brightened. His blood-shot eyes were suffering the effects of some inferior liquor. My warm words practically made them swim. Somewhere in those eyes doubt of a sort must have lurked. He hid it well.

My conversation with Roco gradually became less military. He talked about women. By and by he rambled so much that he wasn't able to pick up his own thread. He started to become drowsy. I had to think up some way of escape. He fell asleep in the saddle. A rider came over a nearby knoll at full gallop. They recognized him. Clearly some scout or orderly. He spotted us. He rode up to Roco's horse and cleared his throat. Roco woke up.

"What the hell is it, Marco?"

The young rider looked terrified. His clothes were muddy. His face clearly bore the signs of a man who has seen something he didn't like. Roco's reaction was like that of several other officers I've seen. Fear is the worst thing that can grip a military unit. If you're unlucky enough to have a soldier in the clutches of this demon, it must be exorcised promptly. Half-asleep, and after only one glance at the young, tortured face, Roco could diagnose the condition.

"Well, out with it!"

His chin quivered so much that he could only force out small, petrified barks, like a young puppy yapping in its sleep. It was hard to tell if he were speaking or sobbing. Roco found the performance painful. He gave me an apologetic look. His face was flushed with rage. For the third time, he asked for an explanation. At last the man managed to stammer:

"Rafael has been shot."

"Well, what of it!?"

"He was shot as he was going for water."

"Well, what of it!?"

"He was unarmed."

"Well, what of it!?"

"He died on the spot."

"Is that all?"

"Yes, general, sir."

"What about the water?"

I had escaped military life up to then. Now, suddenly, I was part of one of Rosas' companies. We and our horses were thirsty. At last we found a river. We heard shooting from the direction of the city bounds. The horses are lucky. Even though they're forced to see the war to its conclusion, no one makes them choose between one and the other. No one obliges them to look as if they believe it. Enthusiasm, panegyric, folly, that's our accursed fate.

There was talking behind me. I was sitting on my haunches drinking water. I heard two voices:

"Death in battle would save us a lot of grief."

"Shut up, he can hear you!"

"My God, how lucky the old men are to be out of this."

"Shut up, he's over there."

"I bet our women are as randy as cats and the old men have got their mouths full and their hands up skirts and in pockets. Just imagine a tender, loving woman who'd give you her all. Let your hands wander over her body."

"Shut up!"

"Arsehole!"

I never cease to marvel at man's lack of dignity. Perhaps it's my own form of vanity. I have just one wish. Not to be burnt. To rot in a churchyard or on a battlefield, yes. But burnt, no! A skeleton still resembles a human being. It's a framework, a specifi-

127

cation, a start. It is easier to re-awaken to new life, than a mere pile of ashes. As ash one's demise has been more elemental. Something to be strewn about, something that cannot be reconstructed. If one finds a skeleton, one can imagine how the bones and joints fitted together. One can imagine how that person looked and how they lived. A pile of ashes might be a burnt pig, a newspaper or a human being.

My vanity assumes that I will decompose with dignity. On maturer reflection, I can't see why.

The pair behind me were beginning to raise their voices. Out of pure consideration I said:

"Keep it down, lads, or Roco will hear you."

The look in their eyes showed anything but gratitude. They began to glower. They came towards me. My little comment had united the two quarrelers against a common foe. I was saved, yet again, by the general. He wanted to drink with me. He pulled off his boots and waded out with a bottle of strong apple brandy. My two enemies stripped off and began splashing water at one another. They were hairy from top to toe, more or less. As they were about to go ashore they were beset by a vast swarm of mosquitos. Roco roared with laughter. He slapped his knees in an attempt to express his mischievous joy. Now in retrospect, I'm glad that, in a fit of arrogance, I didn't give the smallest vent to the feelings within me, which were perhaps most reminiscent of a flood that has finally breached a dam. What a satisfying sight to watch the mosquitos suck the blood out of them and pump their veins full of poison. I thought:

May syphilis shred their veins! May alcohol perforate what little liver they have left! May the sun scorch their eyeballs! Perhaps they would meet their deaths in the nearby Paraná delta? They leapt about hysterically, as the other soldiers laughed uncontrollably. I rejoiced in each stone they trod on. We made camp. Night fell. The campfire was lit. I kept close to Roco the whole time. He did a number of chores in the meantime, popping in and out of the light round the fire. His face came and went. If you lift a death mask after three thousand years, the face beneath is whole for an instant, before it crumbles to dust.

I drank. Everyone drank. I had to try not to get too drunk. I had good grounds to feel uneasy. I got drunk. My last clear thought was that I had to get them to relate their wartime escapades. That might save me. It didn't fail.

I woke up. It was morning. I remembered where I was. I looked about. Was this my opportunity to get away? Some others were already awake a little further up the slope. I put the thought out of my head. The general was up already. Had his mood turned? Was I being watched? He nodded, but without smiling. It might mean that everything that had passed the day before was merely the prelude to a slow and painful execution. My mind conjured forth quick, competent executions by marksmen whose one shot might find its mark between the third and fourth ribs on the left side. I had no guarantee that Roco hadn't found my story about my brother a little too plausible. Perhaps he wished to punish me with silence until my trivial, physical execution took place. One after another they rose. The majority had hangovers. I was expecting something in the nature of breakfast to be prepared. Five of the soldiers began to clear away ammunition, rifles and provisions. An area about fifteen square yards was cleared. To say that I felt increasing apprehension was to put it mildly. A false description in an attempt to distance the event. I stood as stiff as a candle. My fear was the burning wick. My nausea was the wax that held the wick up. Two leather belts were tossed on the ground. The soldiers crowded round the improvised square. No one paid any attention to me.

"Fifteen lashes!" I heard Roco shout.

I closed my eyes. My neck was so tense I could barely turn in the direction of Roco's voice. I waited for the rough hands that would hurl me down into the dust. Before me lay sprawling the young messenger of the previous day. He was given fifteen lashes for spreading despondency amongst the troops. He lay there like a young donkey that has never yet felt the stick. He put up no resistance. The experience was obviously new to him. He didn't know how to protect his body. The soldiers said nothing. The victim tried to close his eyes. Perhaps with the vague hope of losing consciousness? He said nothing. He began to bleed from the mouth and nose. He rolled backwards and forwards in the dust. After the fifteenth stroke the general shouted:

"Ten more!"

The youth clearly hadn't heard this new sentence. He attempted to crawl to his feet. He was on his knees. The sixteenth lash hit him across his back with great force. His white shirt was soaked with blood. Roco ran forward and tore it off him. The boy lost control. He writhed on the ground. The dust swirled about his stomach. It was mixed with blood and spittle. After the twenty-fifth stroke, two soldiers were ordered to carry him off. He would be needed in the ranks over the next few weeks. The general lit a cigarette and came ambling over to me. He smiled:

"My good friend, when we get to Quilmes I'll take you to a wonderful brothel. They have a splendid Negress there. What magnificent breasts! She's been nicely brought up by the nuns in the town. She can do everything, pick lice, lance boils and entertain without being too tiring, or thoroughly exhaust you in a most enjoyable manner. The choice is yours."

He began describing one of the other women at the brothel. The one with the fat, white thighs. He spoke with enthusiasm. After the women, the country's brothels and my experiences in Genoa were exhausted as conversational topics, he gesticulated expansively.

"When the war is won, we shall visit the best places together."

He really believed it.

"Let's exterminate this pack first. We must get this war won!"

"Have you ever met Balcarce?" I asked to shift him on to a new subject. He painted a picture of the country's president with a broad brush dipped in a bucket of excrement. I let him fill canvas after canvas with Balcarce. It was quickly done. Balcarce was, after all, the arch-enemy. The dagger at the heart personified. "At the country's heart," he added. To get the general's tongue really wagging I asked:

"General, sir, after your forces have captured Buenos Ayres, what punishment would you deem fitting for the president?"

Some people labor under the foolish misconception that soldiers, and in particular officers, lack imagination. What a misjudgment! Balcarce was executed nine times. If I include the time he was brought back to life to suffer the torture yet again.

When I pointed out the difficulties of killing a man twice, he asked me how I could be so certain. I declared that I'd posed the question in total ignorance. We ate mutton. The soldiers slept again. The general explained this by saying they were building up their strength for the battles to come.

It's sad watching people lying down to sleep. One realizes they don't give a fig about what happens. They simply don't understand what they've been put on earth for. They can sleep anywhere, whether bloated, full, hungry, filthy, drunk or sober. They've always got clear consciences. How could I manage to get away? I was in the process of being assimilated into the company. I felt like a terrified pig in a market place, surrounded by a throng of laughing, shouting people. I tried to hide my snout in a small bundle of straw that had been thrown down in front of me. But when I attempted to push my snout into it, the straw parted in all directions. The people were still standing around me. Grunting and kicking was no good either. Pissing would be even more futile. At the far end of the market the butcher appeared with his big knife.

I was not the least bit sleepy. I was surrounded by snoring. Only the four sentries and I were awake. A couple of hours later the reveille sounded for the second time that morning. We rode to Quilmes. The houses looked deserted. I attempted to explain to the general that I wished to visit my cousin Lugi straight away. I wanted to find out if he and his family were well. He laughed. It sounded like the bark of a dog.

"But you haven't forgotten about my showing you the brothel?"

"No."

I had forgotten.

The brothel was in full swing. The general took two of his officers and ordered the rest to stand guard outside. The envious glances of the soldiers almost made it worth while.

The madam welcomed the general cordially. Eyed

him from top to toe and kissed him.

"Wonderful to see you alive. What can I do for you today, general?"

It sounded as if she were selling vegetables in the market. Roco turned to me.

"This gentleman would like the Negress."

"She's run off!"

The general was speechless. A consuming fury shook his face and frame. He blackguarded her roundly. He demanded to know what steps had been taken to recapture the Negress and bring her back. The madam said she'd soon turn up. It just needed a little patience. Roco would not allow himself be pacified. She put her arm round him and whispered in his ear loud enough for us all to hear:

"But I have a surprise, general. A revelation! A flower."

"Tell me!" cried Roco.

"No, see for yourself! Melissa!"

A lovely, dark-haired woman suddenly stood in the doorway. The madam had spoken the truth. A showpiece. Her eyes looked a little lusterless perhaps, but that might change.

I remember thinking to myself: just imagine if Roberto and Don Carlos were here now.

"She's yours, my dear friend," said the general

pointing at me. The Indian woman took me upstairs to the first floor. She knew a few words of Spanish. I walked behind her, my appetite was boundless. What youth, elasticity and suppleness! I moved on, muscle by muscle. One limb after the other. Her skin color, which I'd normally viewed with condescension, was beautiful to me. Stimulating in every respect. She was a goddess under my hands, which sometimes stroked, sometimes groped her eager body.

I heard shots outside. The soldiers were being encircled by government troops. The door burst open. Roco screamed:

"They're trying to surround us. Get out!"

That was the last I saw of the general. Together with his men he took to his heels with the government troops in hot pursuit. A few minutes later all was quiet. I was alone in the brothel without a peso to my name. I was getting dressed when the madam entered.

"Don't worry. The general has paid."

She took the Indian woman by the arm and escorted her out of the room. The madam soon returned. She wanted to know if I had lodgings for the night.

"I'm visiting my cousin. He owes me money."

"What's his name?"

"Lugi Camboresi."

She laughed.

"You'll be waiting a long time for that money!"

"Why?"

"Because he fled, or is lying murdered somewhere."

"I think I'll investigate that for myself."

"Fine by me."

Just outside the house one of Roco's men sat slumped against the wall. It was difficult to hear what he was saying. He was rambling. Two bullets had pierced his torso. He was only wearing a thin tunic which he'd managed to unbutton. I felt his stomach. It was tense. Unfortunately for the soldier, the bullets had probably not caused much internal bleeding. If they had, his stomach would have filled with blood and the whole thing would have been over in a few minutes. The stomach lining fills and death ensues. In his case it would take time. His wounds were in more time-consuming places. Poor devil. His stomach was swelling slowly. He was fretting. He sweated and babbled. It's in situations like these that I have to keep a certain distance in order to bear up. The last thing the fellow managed to say was: "I have no money or rings." As though that were not plain enough.

Lugi was impossible to trace. I had to try to ride back that same night so as not to be killed or taken prisoner. Late next morning I arrived home, worn out, hungry and thirsty. Not far from home, I saw a butcher slit the throat of a goose. The blood gushed. I almost screamed, but his happy smile constricted my gullet. I can still feel that scream in my throat. I'll do anything to be rid of it.

Late last night a letter was pushed under my door. Its sentences were long and detailed. I did not recognize the handwriting. The letter pointed up my inadequacy. It embroidered and magnified faults I barely knew I had. What an incisive portrait! What precision! No sender's name. Who could it be from? What was the point of it? Was there ever a more malicious, more direct, more unveiled chronicle of a man's worthlessness? Where had this friend of truth, who had not dared sign his name, come from? I mulled over one or two names. I read on: "And you, who have renounced your faith, spend your time writing a letter that is nothing more than a vulgar plea for forgiveness and indulgence." The writer was familiar with all my secrets and was more than willing to reveal them, but not his own identity! There was no mention of any extenuating circumstance. The long sentences were stifling me. An anonymous letter deserves no attention. The missing signature compromises its probity. I awoke. Who is it that makes me dream such dreams? I jumped out of bed. I paced the floor. It must be the Alborellos. Surely, it can't be Don Carlos? Was my irritation over the letter caused by conceit? Of course it was a dream, but who is it that's plaguing my head with such thoughts when I so badly need sleep? Who was this intruder? It must be Don Carlos. A cockroach lay on its back in the flour. What if I were to pull one of its legs off and send it by messenger to Mr and Mrs Lumb? On the envelope I could write: "To Don Carlos. Urgent." Nothing more. I must get the letter sent. Imagine the collector's reaction! He receives the letter. He weighs it in his hand. He holds it up to the light. He sees nothing. He makes some comment about the lightness of the envelope. Perhaps the thought that there is nothing inside it crosses his mind. Nothing at all. But the "Urgent" on the outside would make him open it all the same. He's quite clearly not the sort of man who'd hesitate to open anonymous letters. He'd stick two fingers into the envelope and, after a few seconds' fumbling, feel the serrated leg of the cockroach with the tip of his middle finger. At that moment he wouldn't even be thinking about the sender. He would glance round the room. Where are the tweezers! Carefully, he extracts the leg. Examines it carefully. "But isn't this a perfectly ordinary cockroach's leg? But were it perfectly ordinary, would it have been sent to me?" He would ponder the question the entire morning. After a while he would begin to turn to the identity of the sender, but only after an hour's hectic searching through reference works, repeated measurements of the leg etc. What if I sent the letter? I stretched.

It looked as if it was going to be a fine day.

It was the afternoon. Signóra Alborello was outside. At first I didn't notice what she was carrying in her arms. At a distance the city is no bigger than a half-shut eye. As I got closer I saw what it was. My God! She was clasping that filthy dog of theirs! The creature's eyes were closed. Stone dead.

"Giovanni, hurry up and help me, won't you!"

"What's the matter?"

"Get hold of the spade! Dig under the tree!"

I rejoiced in the knowledge that the animal which had meant so much to Signóra Alborello, had ceased to bark. I took hold of the spade, lifted it, and screamed as I felt the infernal pain in my right foot.

When using a spade, the entire body weight must be on one foot. The other guides the spade into the ground. Both feet are required. My damaged foot was too inflamed to dig with and too weak to support me.

"I have an injury," I remarked doltishly to that enterprising woman.

"Hand me the spade, then!"

She thrust the dog at me and I held out my arms and cradled the stiff beast as if it were my firstborn. It began to rain. The drops fell in an uneven tempo. First, a slow fall of light drops, almost bereft of force. Not far away, above the tin roof to the right, the drops became smaller, about the size of barleycorns. The next moment the rain was like a thin pall. The dusty pelt was soaked, and dirty water trickled down my shirt and breeches. Signóra Alborello dug energetically beneath the tree. Why are dogs always buried beneath trees? I did not ask. The thing was heavy and cold, but it hadn't begun to stink. It smelt bad enough, God knows, but the smell was mainly of old dog. Perhaps it had dug its holes here where we were standing? The rain was falling, heavy and straight, without tact or finesse. She told me to lay the animal in the grave. I explained that my foot would prevent me from doing that. I could have dropped my burden into the hole. I'd quite likely have enjoyed doing that. Except that the rain water would have spurted up and caused me to fall because of my impaired balance. Before I had time to think another new thought, she tore the creature out of my arms, knelt down and laid it tenderly in the hole. What had been my contribution to the funeral? I hadn't dug, I hadn't laid the deceased in the grave, but I had held it. I had held the dog above the ground. The same ground it would lie in until decomposition had done its work. I was presumably the only living being who hated that animal. And now I stood there. The heavy bundle had been lifted from my arms and buried. I was wet.

I shall always evolve in loneliness. I shall always be lonely. I talk to people and am lonely. Never for one instant would Don Carlos admit that he was affected by the same consuming disease. I write letters and am lonely. I try to make myself understood and am lonely. I have moved to a larger city and am lonely. My room, or more accurately, the room I rent from the Alborellos, is more like a cell than anything. The walls are cold. Melancholy is a very lovely state. I slide into it easily and often. I generally get up in the morning. Why? I try to swallow one meal a day. Why? I go to bed almost every night. Why? I dress now and again. Dear brother! Perhaps it would be better if I abandoned this story about myself and turned to something else. Perhaps it would be easier for me to accept a world untarnished by my presence. Some are born syphilitic, I was born serious.

I looked out. The clouds chased onwards, worn and worried by the wind. Had I been patient enough, I should have seen the moon. I shut my eyes. I heard the wind mingling with my breath. Words and images spun round in my head, welled up, and were dissolved, consumed. What was it Alborello had said? That the old horse outside had been bought whilst on its way to the knacker's. Alborello had heard that it would drop dead as soon as it was put to work. Alborello is a horse-fancier. "The eyes are what's most important. Nothing else matters much," he always says. He looked it straight in the eyes outside the knacker's yard, and it repaid his glance! It'd traveled sixty miles to get to the knacker's.

"I'd have been happy if the horse had lasted ten months after I bought it. It's been two years now."

Whilst he spoke, he kept a watchful eye on his son, Vincenzo. The boy began to wail because of some trifle or other, as if he wanted to protest at his father's smug recital. The horse's front legs gave way. Some rabbits die before they have been butchered. When lifted out of its hutch by the ears and laid ready on its back, the knife is often plunged into a corpse. Alborello beat the horse across the back with a stick. It forced itself up, but then the old sluggard went down on its knees again. The boy's father gave him a slap on the bottom for frightening the horse, and then beat it to its feet. He tied the worn-out creature to the tree and then turned to me:

"It'll be all right."

I went up to my room to be solitary. I looked out of the window. Father and son had gone inside. The four-legged creature, which could hardly be graced with the name horse, was still under the tree. It was looking down at its own cool shadow.

Was it my imagination or did I feel a mounting irritation over Don Carlos' boundless interest in animals? Rather slyly I inquired:

"Wouldn't you like to be able to understand animal language? Wouldn't that solve a lot of riddles?"

"No," was his emphatic answer.

"Why not?"

"Because we mustn't be frightened," he said smiling.

"Would we be frightened?" I asked flabbergasted. "Now I understand," I said. "You mean that we have reason to be frightened because they are of a lower order. Certain species are thoroughly repulsive. I remember once in Entre Ríos," (I was talking fast and gesticulating) "I saw a shoal of piranha and a beautiful white horse in a river swollen by the spring floods. The horse was going to mount the bank, its front legs were on firm ground. Just as it was about to lift its forequarters out of the water, the attack came. It stood stock still. I didn't understand why at first, until the horse fell over on its side. Its entire body up to its neck had been devoured."

He interrupted me equably:

"I'm not certain, but I believe that some sort of selection and development is taking place in animals. The species can't be static and unalterable, can they?"

"Selection?"

"Take the elephant. You've seen drawings of them?"

I nodded.

"They breed very slowly. But despite that, in a couple of hundred years they would have colonized the entire earth if selection were not a controlling element. It's a kind of regulation that prevents that from happening."

"But you can't deny that animals are of an inferior order and more brutal than men. We're bad enough, but aren't they worse?"

My irritation was growing.

"In Roman times, hunting was brought into the cities," Don Carlos answered calmly.

"No fewer than seventy arenas were built within the Roman Empire. During one spectacle at the Colosseum five thousand animals were killed. Once there were elephants in North Africa, hippopotamuses in Nubia and lions in Mesopotamia. They were eradicated for the sake of entertainment. Nothing more."

"No massacre precludes the next."

"Just so!"

He had become voluble:

"What is extraordinary is the thoroughness with which the extermination took place. I won't be drawn into any bombastic opinions about who are the lower orders."

I asked him to talk about something else. He said nothing. We sat silently side by side for a moment. I began to speak of the time I had seen General Rosas surround a village. On the outskirts of the village, the soldiers were doing weapon training and practicing hand-to-hand fighting. When they got hungry, a few of them went on a wild career through the village square and stole the meat they needed from the butcher. They could have got the meat almost anywhere, but these soldiers enjoyed the hint of danger in riding into the square, as there were still snipers in the village. The next day the butcher decided to take his steer to market instead of cutting it up in his own shop. Just as he led it into the square, four soldiers rode towards him at full gallop. They stopped, cut up the beast, and disappeared.

He listened. Was he put out? He might just get up and go, and never come back. I hadn't thought through the consequences. I looked at some beautiful blue violets and the lovely garabato tree with its clusters of yellow flowers. He looked in the same direction. The sight must have had a conciliatory effect. He stayed put. We were sitting side by side on a bench in Retiro Park. I had the feeling this might turn out to be one of our last meetings. Again he began speaking quickly and fervently. I was almost relieved. He clasped the shoulder-bag he had on his lap.

"I mentioned the sloths I came across in Brazil, didn't I?"

"Yes," I said out loud.

"Good, but I didn't tell you they have three fingers, eat leaves and weigh nine pounds. The stomach alone weighs three pounds. It's usually full of undigested leaves. They're aptly named: in the course of twenty-four hours they move forty yards at most, and it takes them a month to digest their food. The prehistoric sloth must have been enormous by comparison. I'd hazard some six yards in length and four tons in weight."

"Wasn't it hard for them to hang in trees?"

"Certainly," said Don Carlos.

"But how are *you*?" I asked.

"I've at last managed to do most of what I planned here in the city. And that's no mean feat considering the insane chaos that reigns here in Buenos Ayres."

Hadn't he heard what I was asking?

"Well, there is a civil war raging!" I said.

"When I returned to the dentist, it was shut. I haven't got all the time in the world, either."

"Why was it shut?" I asked.

"There were bullet holes in the walls. The door was gone."

"Had he disappeared?"

"I discovered where he lived and got him to extract the atrophied nerve. I couldn't go about much longer with arsenic in my bad tooth. Just imagine if my tongue had come in contact with it. He was skilled for a Frenchman. Highly skilled."

Don Carlos opened his bag. He placed two trays of beetles on the bench. Some had been fixed with small pins. Others were loose on the trays. By each one was written the date and place it was found and its Latin name, if he knew it. He put both trays side by side. With the aid of a pair of tweezers pulled from his inner pocket, he adjusted the beetles and their labels.

"Well, what do you think?" he said.

He gazed proudly across his army of beetles.

"Impressive!" I said.

"I shall be sending them off soon."

"Where to?"

"I've got to send them to Professor Henslow in London. I send all my finds to London. Each day while I'm here I try to find small boats bound for Montevideo, now that the harbor here in Buenos Ayres is blockaded. Goodness knows how many pounds of bones and skulls I've sent home. When I get back to Shrewsbury I shall try to put my collection in order."

I couldn't contain myself. I asked:

"But are you enjoying it? I mean, it can get lonely

after a while when you're collecting, classifying and traveling all at once. And you're only a young man, aren't you?"

"The finds Covington and I made just north of Nueva Bahía Blanca near Punte Alta are my most important so far."

He picked up one beetle tray and pointed at a black beetle with a lateral green stripe. Suddenly, Don Carlos was caught by a bola which twined itself around his neck.

"I'm no wild llama!" shouted the collector. He fell forwards with the tray he was holding and knocked the other one with his knee. The beetles were scattered in front of the bench. The "hunter" was a terror-stricken young boy behind some nearby bushes. He fled once he realized what he'd done. Don Carlos tried to tear off the coiled rope, which only made it tighter and tighter. Red in the face, he got down on his hands and knees and arranged his beetles. Quickly and methodically he replaced them in orderly ranks without removing the rope. Half an hour later everything was back in place. In the meantime I'd unwound the rope from his neck. I hadn't said a word. He pointed at the black beetle with the green stripe and sighed. I asked:

"How are you?"

He looked me straight in the eye, slapped me lightly on the knee and said:

"I'm a collector. Yes, that's what I am. Flowers, beetles, bones, skulls, leaves, feathers, yes, I even collect stones and types of rock. I catalogue my finds as best I can. We need too much material rather than too little! First and foremost we'll make a survey of the fauna and flora here in the south. It's not for me to verify or refute any particular theory. I'm too young. Henslow's the one with intimate knowledge of the various evolutionary theories, not I. But I'm inquisitive by nature, yes, extremely inquisitive."

Just as a rising feeling of irritation began to take hold of me, a pacifying thought gave me temporary comfort: Don Carlos hadn't mentioned my limp. Was it out of tact or egotism, or self-absorption and lack of interest in other people that my painful foot had not been mentioned? He had given up his medical studies because he'd not been able to stomach being present at postmortems. He couldn't bear the sight of blood. He was scared I'd show him my foot! What a miserable creature!

He rose quickly from the bench:

"It's been pleasant talking to you."

Always these courteous phrases.

"Unfortunately, I must be on my way. I have to

speak to a skipper who's promised to smuggle more than four hundred pounds of bones to Montevideo tonight!"

He waved and broke into a run. I sat on the bench.

"What a nincompoop," I said.

A couple of yards away I spied a sheet of paper he'd left behind. I didn't call out.

Don Carlos returned. He'd realized he'd left the sheet behind. I asked:

"I can't understand why you gave up your medical studies. There's money to be made in that line. And anyway, one isn't a proper doctor before one's killed a couple of patients. Couldn't you have steeled yourself to endure the postmortems? Perhaps you weren't good enough?"

Don Carlos stared into space. Englishmen don't strike you in the face. They just don't invite you to dinner. He said nothing! He turned to me:

"I was certainly no scholar at school, but is that to my credit or discredit?"

I was spared the necessity of replying. An irate father approached dragging a boy of about ten. It was the scamp who had almost asphyxiated Don Carlos.

"Beg the gentleman's pardon!"

The father tweaked the boy's ear, and the lad went

down on his knees.

"It wasn't that bad," stammered Don Carlos. He was reddening beneath his beard. Don Carlos didn't even box the boy's ears. The father was profusely apologetic. After repeated cuffs from his father, the boy made a muted apology. They departed.

"Why do you drink?" Don Carlos asked.

I looked at him. He stared down at the ground, as if searching for the dust from his own face.

"I'm sorry . . . ," he began.

I interrupted:

"To make the people I meet more interesting."

"There's a lovely smell of flowers in this park. Is it the marguerites that have such a strong scent?" said Don Carlos looking at me. He was still blushing.

I walked home. I was cold. The fever was making me shiver. I felt as if it was my skeleton that was walking. With the flesh cut away. I passed crowds of people. I drew their gaze, even though it was not intended for me. What do they believe in? That God is on their side? Those with money and power know that he is. I walked on. Even though I am not rich, I endeavored to look useful. One of the church clocks began to strike. I walked past Admiral Brown's house. I caught sight of a huge four-poster bed on the ground floor. Perhaps it was the admiral's revenge for his narrow berth aboard. Perhaps the four-poster was a tribute to the sea?

Almost every city is beautiful at sunset. Its reliefs are more subtle, its spires more pointed, its recesses deeper, its rooftops sharper, its statues more expressive. I went into a church that was open. I listened to a mass in a Latin I didn't understand. The fact that the language was foreign, increased my concentration. I smelt the melting wax from the altar. I vowed that if I met Don Carlos again I would be polite and sympathetic. Had he eliminated me as a traveling companion? As I stared into the burning candles, I felt sure I'd be able to keep my resolution.

Dear brother! Reason is my greatest sore. Is the loneliness of being thrown upon reason God's chastisement? Is this how God overtakes me? The fact that life is an accident, that I am worth no more than the dust I shall become, causes God to rub his hands.

Roberto!

The problem with being a non-believer is that one has a limited number of prayers at one's disposal.

Formerly, I used to wish that God would intercede. Now I've come to the realization that this will not happen. As I don't believe in miracles, I'm even denied the means of wishing for the impossible. For several months I've tried to fold my hands together. They wither and lose all strength. Roberto, I'm not one of those who must have proof of God's existence to believe. Certainly not. Reason cannot obliterate God. Belief demands a total surrender of the self that I am unable to make. I have begged several times for this self-effacing gift so that, at least at certain moments, the consciousness might leave my body. The body is my prison. The distance to God is insurmountable.

There could be no mistake. It was Francesco Como from Brindisi. I recognized his voice. He was holding forth about his best fighting cock at the end of Calle de la Ribera. Francesco's training program had recently secured the cock a series of victories. There was a little money in it, too. He was voluble. His genius had made him phenomenally big-headed from dawn to dusk. Even at night he got no rest. He clamped himself tightly to the bed so as not to be deflected from his steady stream of ideas. He never kept his genius in check. Should one come home late at night, one would be sure to hear Francesco Como cackling in the dark.

A crowd was gathered around him. A group from San Telmo arrived. They'd brought along a fighting cock in a cage. I positioned myself on the edge of the crowd. I'd been to see Dora. She sewed some buttons on for me. We made love. "Lift me up, my rhinoceros," were her last words before we reached that most exquisite of all insanities.

A ring was prepared for the two fighting cocks. By now several hundred people had turned up. The owners goaded their black cocks with orange-brown collars. Newly sharpened metal spurs were fastened to their feet. Their red combs shook nervously. Francesco stuffed chili pepper up his cock's vent and beak.

"This is the big moment, Themistocles!" he shouted. He looked the cock in the eye. I tapped the shoulder of the man in front of me and asked:

"Who's Themistocles?"

"When the Athenian general, Themistocles of ancient Greece, was about to engage the Persian King Xerxes, he halted en route so that his soldiers could watch a cockfight before the battle. Cocks fight neither for gods, the security of their progeny nor vague notions of freedom," replied the man.

"Why do they fight, then?"

"Because they don't want to lose."

The fight had started. They struck with their wings. They pecked. They kicked with their spurred feet. The San Telmo cock fell beak first and bloody into the sand. Francesco lifted his arms in the air.

"*Themistocles es mi gallo.* Themistocles is the cock for me," he exulted with uninhibited joy. His neighbors embraced him. The referee held out his arms and shouted that the fight wasn't over. Wild shouts of protest. The owner of the San Telmo cock was allowed into the ring. He sucked his tattered cocks's throat and nostrils clear of blood. It didn't help a lot. The cock was placed on the ground. Again it fell over.

Francesco whooped for joy. We, his neighbors and fellow Boca-dwellers shouted: "Themistocles! Themistocles!" Just as Francesco was about to lift up his cock in triumph, its near-vanquished rival leapt up and delivered the coup de grâce to Themistocles who fell down dead. Francesco ran to his lifeless friend. He lifted it up, kissed it, gave a heart-rending cry and made a dash for his house.

It was I who discovered him, later that evening, down by the water. His head was just a pulpy mass. It had been blown to pieces. He was still clutching the blunderbuss. Themistocles lay at his feet. The gun was in his mouth and poked right through his skull like an crowbar. Mincemeat, hair, mucus, clotted blood, his eyes had been forced out of their sockets. I shouted for help to lift him up on to the bank. I had to pull out the gun. I was frightened his head might disintegrate. Themistocles, you ass.

One day Don Carlos mentioned some of the dishes he was served at the Lumbs'. Just then I noticed I had a headache. It's unlikely it started just at that moment. Presumably, the pain had been seeking shelter at the back of my head for several months. I noticed that when Don Carlos mentioned Yorkshire pudding, my brain associated the headache with the fact I was short of something. The brain is a demanding and, at times, odd master. Above all I prize the brain's ability to repress. What a brilliant attribute! With mild affability it maneuvers unpleasant thoughts behind the scrub and thicket of the untended parts of the mind. When I suddenly realized I lacked money, a new thought sprang from the less accessible areas of my brain. I would visit the Military Hospital. I had been feverish earlier that morning. After making my way through the main entrance, I told them I was Doctor Escobar's cousin and had some money for him. Eventually I found the Pathology Department. It was cheek by jowl with the crematorium. I had come to the Pathology Department to sell parts of my body. I wanted a small advance so that I might pay for a few basic necessities.

"What's your business here?"

A man in a gory apron stood before me. It struck me that pathologists must love the development of disease.

"Do you purchase organs? I am wondering if you wish to buy mine?"

"Which ones do you want to sell first?"

"My bowels," I replied without hesitation, "my bowels have given me so little satisfaction recently."

"Do you want to hand them over now, or wait a few days?"

Didn't he understand what I meant? Without waiting for a reply he said:

"Get out! We've enough on our hands at the moment, without worrying about live bodies as well."

"I don't think you understand! You'll get my body after I'm dead. All I need now is a tiny advance."

"Get out!"

He turned on his heel and went into a whitewashed room with a marble floor. A dissected body lay on a wooden table. He didn't bother to check if

I'd complied with his order. His back was broad. He was bald. The cadaver on the table had red hair. I left the hospital with rapid steps. I felt I'd been held in low esteem. Did he think me a fool? What would he have said if I'd lopped off one of my arms right in front of his eyes? I did not pursue the thought. He might have asked why I didn't cut off the other one as well. What would I have done if he'd lifted me by the ears to check my weight?

A bit later that day I went into one of the more superior outfitter's shops. A male customer caught my attention. His spectacles were what interested me. He was obviously short-sighted. He placed them on the counter. He held a pair of trousers up to his eyes. I stole the spectacles and ran off in the direction of San Lorenzo. I hid in one of the narrow alleys there. Later on I pawned the spectacles.

I had a magnificent meal with the money. Numerous courses. Wine, white and red. No expense spared! I indulged myself in a bottle of brandy after the final course. I ate as if it were my last meal. The red meat was like fire in my veins as soon as I swallowed it. Alcohol eased the pain. I folded my napkin and wiped the sweat from my brow. I was certain my fever had evaporated. I was just about to leave when I spied the man whose spectacles I had stolen earlier in the day. He was wearing a new pair. He tripped on a cobblestone, right outside the restaurant window. His spectacles flew off. I could see the pained expression on his face when he thought they'd been smashed. He crouched down. After some groping about he found his spectacles. He felt them. He raised them to the sunlight. He squinted at them and smiled, patently relieved. He put the spectacles on. He disappeared towards the optician's. I left a generous tip. I rose. There he was back again! I sat down. His spectacles were now secured with a cord round his neck. I noticed that the cord was red. Had it been black it would have blended in with the man's hair. Perhaps the color had been chosen to facilitate finding the spectacles in the morning. He came past the window. He tripped over the same cobblestone. His spectacles flew towards the ground. He fell on top of them. When he got up, he was holding the cord in one hand and the shattered spectacles in the other. I retrieved the tip and put it back in my pocket. Roberto! I won't let Don Carlos treat me any more. I walked out. I looked around to see if the man had disappeared. I went slowly home. Limping takes time.

I fell forwards. Manzoni and Pellico tried to hoist

me up. I was unwilling. I sat up with my right elbow resting on a cobblestone. I had plenty of time. Some of my teeth were loose. I reached for the wine keg that had slipped from my grasp. A wonderful landscape stretched all about me: well-formed stones washed by the rain. I sat up. My friends tried to hurry me along. I took a few pulls from the keg. I stumbled on. I drank a bit more.

We were stopped by a constable. He was the spitting image of the constable who'd warned me as I'd entered the bar up the street. Manzoni and Pellico gripped me tightly. They tried to relieve me of the keg. I managed to get a little more inside me before it was rudely snatched out of my life. Some of the wine ran down my face. I felt a smarting. I raised my hand to my cheek and forehead. Cuts and scratches. They were bleeding. The constable was speaking to me. No doubt about it. It was me he was talking to. My mouth was full of wine, which explained my disinclination to converse at that precise moment. The constable pointed out that I'd been lying right across the street causing a general obstruction to the public. The highway belongs to everyone, he said. As if I didn't belong in that category. A horse and carriage halted nearby. I saw the horse's lean and steaming flank in the gleam of the lights and the coachman's hand on the door handle.

It would be good to die without too much agony. Shut one's eyes beneath the blind, black sky. Let one's eyes sink into the cranium and then *quickly* turn to carrion. That's the advantage of drowning. The crabs can't arrive too soon. I'd rather not have crows peck at me when I'm half-dead. Am I asking too much?

I heard the sound of the horseshoes clopping nearer and the jingle of the harness. Then all went quiet. The horse stopped. It looked at me. Whinnied. Would it attack? Where were Manzoni and Pellico? Drinking cronies, have ye forsaken me? The horse stood still. I looked away. I tried to think of the thighs of a woman I'd never had. How there really was flesh and life in them. How they could feel. She had such a lovely laugh when she and I were alone together. Perhaps she'd liked me? Elvira was her name. I looked the horse in the eyes. The constable was talking to me even more loudly. My friends hadn't forsaken me. They still held my arm firmly. They promised to take me home and make sure I'd never end up in the same state again. They explained that I had sixteen children under four years of age at home and my wife was waiting for me. I belched. My friends carried on speaking. An Indian from Tucumán had once taught me never to stare an eagle straight in the eye. Eagles are the only living creatures that can look directly at the sun. Is there some connection between horses and eagles? I'm not sure. I looked away from the horse's eyes. Do horses never sleep? The coachman might have tied it up.

He mounted the horse. Man, who looks rather helpless on an elephant, is more in his element on that restless wind-bolter, the horse. The horse inebriates itself on air: swallows it, breathes it, goes mad on it.

My friends managed to win over the authorities. They dragged me home. Above us, at the top of the night's quivering stalk, shone the moon. The moon drew the waters to her. I could do nothing about it. They laid me down in front of the house, beneath a bush. I awoke at dawn. I saw a dew-drop on a leaf. It didn't want to fall. I saw how tightly it clung on. Its belly swelling. It became a large, almost majestic, drop. It fell, splash, a wet patch on the stone.

I lay on my back. My heels, calves, thighs, buttocks, back, shoulder-blades, arms, elbows, hands and the back of my head took the weight of my body between them and spread it on the ground. My thanks to the ground for giving me that brief respite. It was raining. A hard sheet of smothering rain. It was raining so heavily my flesh felt like something wet and fluid around my own perception of it. I heard time fall. Drop by drop. I was, I realized, an individual, but of absolutely no importance. The privilege of being nothing affords me the opportunity of imagining myself as anything I want. The Tsar of Russia, for instance. The King of England certainly has no such opportunity. The realities of his situation bar all escape. Don Carlos has taught me that much. It rained. The drops grew, dilated, quivered and fell between the small branches and leaves on to my head and body. At that moment I had no sense of my clothes being between me and the drops. Quick and hard, and not without precision, they landed in sensitive spots like the corner of my eye, my temple or deep in my ears. I had no sack to pull across my face. I tried to think if there was any comfort to be drawn from the way the drops struck my face. They would smooth out the wrinkles on my forehead!

The day was about to rain itself dry. After the final shower I got to my feet. That was quite enough! The rain moved southwards. All that remained was the wind that had blown it away.

I couldn't find my key. The thought of rousing

the Alborellos wasn't tempting. I walked towards the city center. I was soaking wet. The weather was comparatively mild. I walked down Calle Bolívar. People hurried to and fro. It was the morning rush. I wanted to walk. Walk, amongst that living forest of people, where each face is created in the very instant I look at it, as my arms, hips and nails solicitously brush the masses gliding past.

Some of the people I jostle, will live through great changes, dissolution, chaos. This leads me to believe that my life too, in some mysterious way, will be altered. Rather like the old man who watches his friends pass away. I didn't say it would worsen, but alter. I catch snippets of intimate conversations, about "the other woman," "the family," "the brothel." The true expressions of the passersby I cannot see. They dissimulate. Are they mocking me? I find that only natural. I'm glad I didn't meet Don Carlos, or you, dear brother. I wouldn't have wanted you to look into my eyes. The sun had begun to gather strength. At that moment I hated this city. Outwardly, perhaps, it is beautiful. There are carnivals and religious processions. But beneath its catholic innocence and exemplary European architecture, lurks the stench of pestilences the conquistadors brought with them. On every street corner sits a beggar stinking of disease.

I became sober and my clothes dry. I took courage and went into the barber's shop of two acquaintances at the bottom of Calle Bolívar. Alfredo looked at me:

"Well, take a seat."

I hadn't said a word. He placed two warm towels round my neck. The act of sitting made my body realize how tired and exhausted it was. But at the same time, the warm towels gave me a feeling of well-being and luxury I sorely needed. I leant back in the chair and breathed deeply. I made the most of it. I shut my eyes. Alfredo took out his long cut-throat razor.

"Where's Ricardo today?" I asked when I realized that his partner was not in the salon.

"He died yesterday."

I said nothing. Alfredo finished what he was doing. I asked if I could pay him next day. He made no reply. I left.

I grieve for the faces that vanish from the street scene. Not necessarily because they meant anything special, but more perhaps because they were symbols of life as a whole. The lame beggar who always cajoled with that infernal voice, Señor Zenga the waiter. What has become of them? They who were a part of my life, because I saw them over and over again. One day I shall cease to walk these streets. People will remember me vaguely with a "what's happened to the man who, what was his . . ." And everything I do and everything I feel and everything I experience will end up as just one pedestrian less in Buenos Ayres. A city anywhere. My body's volume in air.

Future couples strolled past. Seamstresses sauntered arm in arm. In doors here and there lounged listless shopkeepers. Some soldiers went by. All this was played out under my gaze. I walked on, savoring without bitterness my insignificance. No Christ had died for me. The sun was about to set. Yet more people thronged the streets for an evening stroll. Young men and women whiffed romance. Perhaps the hours spent before the mirror would be crowned with success. I heard a snatch of conversation: "Her husband died in front of her very eyes while he was fully conscious. He turned white from the roots of his hair down. That last sip of tea had ruptured his main artery." I walked home. I felt happy. I didn't drink tea.

The following night I awoke in my own bed. Three pigeons had managed to get in through the half-open window. Great, fat pigeons that had settled on the bedspread. I loathe pigeons. They were covered in dust and filth. They gave off a sweetish odor. When they flapped up in front of me, their wings looked like hostile pennants. They made me want to retch. Fear spurred me into action, a panic-stricken decisiveness. I got the book from beneath my bed and hurled it at the hateful creatures. Of course it missed. They flapped against the window. They couldn't get out. I dived towards the bottom of the bed. I got hold of one of them, squeezed it and threw it out of the window. The other two followed, after a ten-minute battle. Outside, the moon peered down through the cloudy night sky on to the sleepy city. I turned the pages of the book. I didn't read. My heart was still pounding. I saw the shadows on the walls. I dropped off to sleep.

The moon fell like a gilded lid in front of the house. It began to burn, spitting sparks before it turned into a black lump of coal. Where the moon had previously been there was a hole. Falling stars are one thing, there are lots of them after all. But there is only one moon. I awoke.

After the early morning rain the sky had regained the blueness that had hidden up in its grey void. Puddles slept in the streets. Three men in dark clothes entered the Dominican church. They looked as if they were going in to pray. As soon as they were inside, each took his candle. They disappeared into the gloom. Does one pray for mercy? What did I have to pray for? The day promised me nothing but itself. I only know that it runs its course and comes to an end. The morning light invigorated me, but didn't better my situation. My consciousness of the city was, deep down, merely a consciousness of myself. Perhaps the city had once been seen as an ordered universe. The city walls the bastions against the chaos outside. The walls have been torn down, and the same thing has happened inside me, too. I walked the street. I saw nothing. That is, I looked about and saw what everyone else saw. I was lost in my own reverie. From a bakery I recognized a smell so delightful that it caught at my throat. For a moment my thoughts had dulled my sense of smell. Now, suddenly, I caught the scent of fruit from an overturned cart. I stopped by a puddle. In the water, the clouds which had sprung up in an interval between nothing and nothing looked like a body of soldiers marching everywhere or nowhere. On the fringes of the Plaza de la Victoria I heard a horse neighing frantically. Its owner had to slip its tether. The people, who were keeping their distance, had to retreat even further. The air about the horse was charged with fear. Most fearful of all was the horse itself. Around the agitated animal, several other horses lay dozing in the shade. Perhaps it'd had a nightmare. After a while, its owner managed to calm the animal using persuasion and his whip. The scraggy horses were similar, but each had its special features. They looked like elderly beer-drinkers round a table. The market in the plaza was in full swing. It occurred to me that I should use the opportunity to look for a bag. The stalls were packed closely together. The one touching the other. A young man crouched on his haunches surrounded by his wares. He hardly needed to stretch to reach all his bags. The man in the next stall was selling the same kind of goods. And so it went on all round the plaza. Every kind of leather bag in Argentina was on sale in the Plaza de la Victoria. It would have been no surprise if the bags had got up and started dancing. I could feel the goods, test them, talk, tell my life story. The stall-holder sat unperturbed. I was wise enough not to mention prices. "Just having a little look," I repeated all the way round. If I'd mentioned a price, I'd have had to go all through the haggling ceremony. Spare me that.

Nearby, a blind beggar began to call out. It was

impossible to tell what he was saying. Imagine waking up and not being able to speak any of the world's languages. How he bellowed! He repeated the same sound. He was in that call. The fast, regular repetition turned him into an entire group. He put me in mind of beggars generally. How often have I been told that God will bless me if I give all beggars a shilling. I looked at him. Suddenly, he made a rush towards me, like a menacing animal. His face certainly didn't arouse my pity. I was frightened he would crush me bodily. His clumsy movements, added to his speed and weight, made me fearful. He humped towards me on his crutches. He had one leg. I managed to run to safety on the other side of the square. Here there was a long line of bread-sellers, women with round loaves. Mature women. Well rounded loaves. Amongst them was a young woman. She was too young for the bread. The women tossed the loaves into the air, patted and turned them, patted them once more, audibly. After these caresses the loaves were replaced on the pile.

—Next to a stack of vegetables stood one of the most wretched donkeys I'd ever seen. Its hide was mangy. Its bones protruded. The donkey couldn't possibly be fit for carrying anything. It was a mystery how it even managed to stand up. Its master tried to make it budge. He addressed it:

"You can go a bit further."

The donkey made no reply.

From somewhere or other arose the sound of a fiddle. What a mournful noise! The donkey turned its head, trying to discover where the sound was coming from. But taking another step was out of the question. Its master began to beat it with a stick. Hard, harder. Then, from between its hindquarters an enormous member appeared, pointing diagonally forwards, stouter than the stick the animal was being beaten with. The bread-sellers began to giggle and point. The blows rained down more heavily on its tormented back. I have no idea what thoughts had found their way into the donkey's head. Nor do I know if it was the music or the savage blows that, using its last ounce of vital force, had made its member stand up for duty. The whole of its decrepit frame seemed to form a cowl over its desire. The donkey dropped down dead.

The blind beggar went quiet for a moment. He'd put a coin in his mouth to feel the denomination with his tongue. Only then did I realize he had no hands. He began to shout again. Unintelligible sounds.

When Christopher Columbus landed in America, the first words he said to the natives were: "As-salam alaykum!" He'd learnt the greeting from the Arabian seafarers in Genoa. The natives had looked at each other doubtfully.

The beggar continued to bellow. I went to the river to bathe and cleanse my foot. Later in the evening I got in the back way to see Mrs Black, my passion. Her husband had gone to Mendoza the evening before. She pressed her bosom to me. I smelt her arm, an evaporating acacia scent. Between her lips I saw the small teeth I knew so well. She touched my arm. I could smell her finely mottled scent of skin, her small, almost invisible freckles. She raised herself up on her elbow. Her back hollowed. She turned her rump towards me. I undressed. She didn't see my foot. I got ready and she arranged herself so lusciously in the dark. What a scent she had. We lay on a clean sheet! Afterwards she served up the choicest dishes.

"Why aren't you eating? You don't see that kind of food everyday, do you?" she said.

I jumped. I was sitting imagining her teeth in my flesh. I felt her tongue lifting me to the roof of her mouth, swathing me in spittle, pushing me under her sharp eye-teeth. I was sitting there before her, but at the same time it was as if a part of me, or all of me, was in her mouth being crushed and torn apart fibre by fibre. I wasn't completely passive, for as I was being chewed I affected her, too. I occasioned the slight tremors that shook her body by penetrating her further than I'd ever done before. A couple of hours later I had to leave stealthily by the back door so that the servants wouldn't see me. She would give me a signal the next time I was to come. I was about to protest. The door behind me closed. I walked home. I threw myself on my bed. I lit the candle. Two cockroaches were trapped in the open flour bag. The light had scared them. They couldn't get out. I looked at the flat, brown bodies covered in flour. I looked at the long, powerful, notched legs. I lifted them out of the bag by their legs and threw them out of the window. The rest of the night I spent drinking rum to dull the pain in my foot.

★ ★ ★ ★

I heard that Don Carlos was out of town. His letters of introduction and passport for Santa Fe had been arranged. At the Lumbs' I learnt that he was expected in a few days time. HMS Beagle was to sail from Montevideo at the end of October.

"But it's the 13th of October already," I said.

"I can't say any more. Some of his things are here," one of their servants told me.

He could have got malaria, or been killed by Rosas' soldiers. A week later I assumed I'd never see him again. In the city spontaneous protest marches in support of Rosas became ever more frequent. "Viva Rosas," "Viva Rosas." The bullets whined in the streets. The attack might come at any moment. On the 23rd of October I saw him. Thinner than ever. He was busy. He had to reach the Beagle in time! He'd been ill in Santa Fe. When he'd realized time was short, he'd made his way down the River Paraná on a small, single-masted balandra. It was too slow. He left it at Las Couchas on the outskirts of Buenos Ayres. He was surrounded by soldiers from General Rosas' army. Don Carlos gathered that the general's brother had command of the troops in the area. He was taken to the brother. He spoke of the cordial relationship he and the general enjoyed. The general's brother was magnanimous. Don Carlos would have to leave his horse and belongings behind.

"And Covington, your assistant? Where is he?" I asked.

"He was to remain outside. But, by a stroke of

unbelievable luck, we got him in yesterday."

"A little money oiled the wheels, perhaps?"

"Don't ask. Think what you like. We've made some fantastic finds."

"But how will you get to Montevideo?"

"We'll see, but then, Rosas can't have known about the rising in Buenos Ayres."

"They say his wife is behind it," I said.

He looked astonished. The next day they'd left. I don't know how, presumably by boat. Ciào. Farewell. Would I see him again, or was he a chance acquaintance who vanishes into a sack that is tied up tight, never to re-emerge?

The pain in my foot was unendurable. I knew this was to be my last wandering in the streets of Buenos Ayres. I'd never get another chance to leave the city. I'd never be able to repay my debt to Don Carlos. He wouldn't even reproach me. I began to think of the cactus that feeds on itself like a flame. Burnt out and dry, it blooms. I am no cactus. I am a man who doubts he'll live to see 1834. God says: "Is it I that have created you, or have you been impudent enough to invent me?" "None of us can live alone," God says. Just as I thought I had been spared any more: "I have ceased to love mankind, they dabble at inventing gods for their own petty needs . . ." "ita med Dens adjuvet et sancta Evangelia."

Roberto! It isn't true. I invent no one. I am doomed to live with my body in the absence of God. My body is *here* regardless of what I think. We die of it. The body is moving towards itself, its essence, its disappearance. I recall a piece of scripture Father Razio often quoted, Ezekiel 37, 6: "And I will lay sinews upon you, and will bring up flesh upon you, and cover you with skin, and put breath into you, and ye shall live." Roberto, how we fear the thought of our own fleeting nature!

Don Carlos is dependent upon some higher, organizing power: God or reason. Don Carlos doesn't quite trust either of them. That is why he makes confession to both God and reason. He is riding two ostriches that run in opposite directions.

Not far from my window the Río de la Plata flows like a distended artery. Man is a trusting creature, dear brother. How often one hears people ask the fruit-seller what his oranges are like. They ask in order to hear the reply: "They're beautiful today!" It's like searching for love in a whorehouse. We wish to be deceived and seek out the lie where we can.

I'm in bed, and I should be lying to you were I not to add that the walls surrounding me, the ceiling and the floor, will be my coffin. My happiest moments are when I am not thinking of anything, not dreaming, but sunk in torpor like a withering plant. I can't pace restlessly up and down the streets any more. I sit up in bed writing from the land we thought was El Dorado, that land of wealth in the continent that was named after our countryman, Amerigo Vespucci.

I'm often struck by dismal thoughts about the things we put up with. At the shipyard there is only one privy. There are four hundred of us to that one hole into which we empty the contents of our bowels and bladders. The Admiralty dock at Riachuelo has plenty of work at present, due largely to the war with Banda Oriental, but our masters will not give us more than one privy. Chaos reigns in front of its door all day long. It's amazing how quickly one adapts to a daily occurrence. It only takes three or four days and one's reconciled to it. One has no choice. One accepts it, one does as others do and makes no fuss. Like pigs trying to get to the trough, we elbow the weakest away from the door. Each day, the same people get there first, after punching and kicking the more sensitive parts of their fellows.

Mortal dread keeps the whole thing going. The Emperor Nero was proclaimed winner of the race even though he fell off his chariot before the finish. No one complained.

I've heard people say that we're angels, imprisoned in bodies, just waiting to be free of them to return to heaven. Was it Thomas Aquinas who said it? The rowdies in the privy queue have convinced me it's not angels we have within us.

I'll shortly be laying down my pen. I look at my right leg. I have wrapped the foot and calf in rags. I've got gangrene. It stinks.

When I watch the gauchos rounding up cattle, I find myself smiling each time I see one of the beasts attempting to escape. What am I smiling at? The defiance of death? I don't see how it can be anything else. My smile is a self-delusory postponement. Maybe you're wondering how this fits in with my English mistress. It was an infatuation. I see infatuation as made up of three elements: hate, love and knowledge. It gives me a special satisfaction to name the third. Perhaps that feeling of control is a comfort? Let me set out my reasons. I don't necessarily regard love and hate as opposites. Knowledge has a strangely sympathetic role. When one becomes infatuated, one alternates between a feverish love and the hatred of being in someone else's power. Knowledge is a loyal servant to both feelings and seems either to strengthen one, or smooth the path to the apparent emotional opposite. I don't want to see her again! Did she notice my foot in the dark after all? Did she make the connection? What of Don Carlos? The animal skull over there in the dark will survive me.

To me Don Carlos appeared reasonably gifted, so far as I can judge such matters. What impressed me was his vitality, his fervent belief in what he was doing. Whether a man collects rags or bones, or both, is all one to me. He is first and foremost a pious bloodhound who, in some obscure way, knows that his various finds will lead him to a great and liberating thought. Isn't that beautiful? Haven't you heard it before? I've actually reconciled myself to his enthusiasm, youthfulness and drive. I try to muster sufficient trust in the notion that there is still something noble and tender in mankind, at least as long as man attempts to understand the world he lives in. Another voice within me says that great theories are the immediate cause of yet more schism and suffering than exist already. Haven't we sufficient ideologies to jade us? Take the newly born child. Its parents first brush aside every genuine and original feeling it may possess. Then the church takes over and crushes the remnants of its soul according to the dictates of the state. There are quite enough as it is! I wish I hadn't been shot in the foot. I don't know if the bullet was for or against Rosas. I don't know which cause I'm dying for. I survey my foot, the congealed blood and pus. It looks hideous. I won't attempt to describe the smell. No writing or other thoughts can shut it out.

Am I afraid? I'm like the scared rabbit's eyes in the magician's hat. Once in a while I contemplate the boundaries of understanding. It's here my greatest privation lies. If only I had a retreat in heaven and in God! What nonsense! That's as mad a notion as believing I could achieve a state of grace now if I took up my faith again. Not with this helpless, stinking carcass, Roberto! No! Roberto, be patient with my broodings one last time. I'm taking a swig from the rum bottle under the bed. You noticed a long time ago that they weren't just ink-blots covering the last pages of this letter.

Roberto! Why must I mention my need of God yet again? And especially to you!

Don Carlos is a liar. To attempt to reconcile belief and science is to remain uncommitted to either. Had he relinquished his faith, he would have had to trust in himself and his science. He has chosen science, without realizing the consequences. Is it fear of loneliness, cowardice, or sheer immaturity that enables him to accept this unholy alliance? I have only one explanation. His instinct always warns him to leave an escape route open to his native faith, like a fox with its various boltholes. He's too craven to put his trust in man and reason alone. Don Carlos dreads reason as I have dreaded death. What twin founts! I see now that though I renounced the religion of my childhood and tried to rely on reason and knowledge, I've permitted this young man to burden my mind with a question that has given me illusions and jumbled notions about escaping from this city, just as I forsook Genoa. I've lied about my condition in the insane belief that I could cheat reason and death just as Sisyphus tried to cheat Hades before receiving his well-deserved punishment. I'm now able to write and tell you that I *won't* take Extreme Unction. Reason has re-established its sovereignty over my mind. I shall die alone. I shall manage it. This is my own kind of dignity.

I write. The nib is scratching. It makes more noise than the revolving earth. The candle is still alight.

Is my breath as determined now as at the moment of my birth? When I've placed the pen and these sheets on the table, I shall sing as I look at the skull over there in the corner.

Farewell, dear brother.
Giovanni

P.S. Dear brother. I haven't told all. So I've had to re-open this letter. I didn't tell you of my intent after I signed it. I managed to drag myself unobserved down the stairs. I crawled to the street corner. I waited for the right moment. A covered wagon hauled by a pair of fast, black horses approached at speed, up the Calle de la Ribera. What I did next was fully premeditated on my part. Just as the horses and wagon were drawing level, I threw myself in front of its wheels. The plan was that my head should be crushed instantaneously. My burning desire to get the whole thing over made my left leg over-compensate. My right leg and foot were extra amenable. Mind and body were one at last. My will was so strong that my body passed too far under the wagon. My head suffered nothing more than severe concussion. My left leg was uninjured. Apart from a few insignificant bruises. My right foot was crushed by the right front wheel, before the rear right-hand side wheel repeated the action a second later. I passed out. I closed my eyes in the belief that I should never open them again, and that without telling you I'd taken my own life. I regained consciousness. I was lying across two seats in the wagon I'd just thrown myself beneath. Over me stood a man with a knife. I've never liked the sight of knives. The man who loomed above me had wielded them before.

"Give me another field knife, Pogo, before he comes round."

His assistant was on the spot immediately. I was unable to shout that I was conscious. Perhaps I wasn't completely awake? I felt nothing as he cut me. Had I lost all feeling in my right leg and foot? It seemed like it. I noticed that my sense of smell was the first thing to return. The kennel in the middle of the street didn't just contain washing water. The sand between the cobbles was churned up. The dust found its way to my nostrils. Even so, it was the smell of blood that predominated. The man with the knife had amputated my right leg beneath the knee. As he held it up in front of my eyes, I noticed that he had rolled up his shirt sleeves. His shirt was white and the material clearly expensive. His hands were bloody.

Pogo, an elderly Indian, took the leg and disappeared behind the wagon. I raised my head slightly from the seat and looked down my body. I don't know whether it was the pain or the fact that I'd lost a piece of me that made me cry. I'm not talking about hysterical weeping, or the sort that can be confused with demented laughter. I'm talking about ordinary, everyday weeping. The kind that makes the whole face crumple. Followed by a fitful sound superseded by tears from the eyes petering out as snot. The weeping was over the moment I blew my nose on my coat which was lying on the seat beside me. I sat up. For a moment I was alone in the wagon. The man who had amputated my leg climbed back in.

"Lie still!" he ordered.

I lay back and stared at this energetic man. The man before me was Francisco Javier Muniz, the army surgeon and naturalist. He didn't recognize me. He was on his way to the front to tend Balcarce's wounded and dying. Pogo carried me up to my room and my bed. Muniz gave me a crutch from the back of his wagon.

The bleeding has stopped. I haven't quite got used to my new condition. Outside my window there is nothing more important than a couple of roses.

Your brother, Giovanni
15th November, 1833

Giovanni

Buenos Ayres, 15th February 1837

Dear Roberto!

There is just one thing I regret. I have tried to kill a man, without succeeding.

Do not build up your hopes. I have no moral scruples about what I have done.

When I wrote to you last I was certain I would die. One believes one is dying long before one does. Most people have no idea what their last moments will be like.

You have not replied. Was my letter offensive? Were you affronted because of your Christian faith? Perhaps you simply did not want a letter from me? Presumably you had already got used to the idea that we should never again walk in the park at Varazze, or visit father's grave, or go on excursions together to Genoa.

I am tormented. I must write. I hate myself because I have not managed to obliterate the face that haunts everyone in Buenos Ayres like an incubus.

Roberto, I suspect you have received my letter and burnt it. Even if I had got gangrene and had tried to kill myself, you would not have answered! Admit it: you have wished me dead from the day you realized what happened seven years ago on the quayside at Genoa. That time, behind the warehouse, when I lied to you and said you could not sail across the Atlantic in the Santa Maria because there were not enough berths.

As if that were not enough: now you know you have a brother who is capable of murder.

You do not want to hear from me. That is the truth. The fact that you will never open this letter imparts a certain lightness to the pen-nib.

I lean forward slightly so that the people around me cannot see what I am writing. There may be spies in the reading room as well.

On the occasions I have surfaced in your consciousness, you have brushed me away like some plaguesome insect. I am like one of those black beetles we played with on the beach. We dropped big stones on them. Each time we thought we had got rid of them, they turned up again. I remember what father said: the albatross is the incarnation of the souls of dead seamen. Prolonged retreat across vast ocean expanses. Portent of bad weather.

My meeting with Rico Trappatoni has had fatal consequences. I screen the paper with my left hand. I look up before bending over the paper again.

We could not kill him with a knife or firearm. That would have caused the most insane reprisals. It had to look like a natural death.

I bend even further over the sheet. No one has raised his head to look at me.

In Varazze Catholicism and sunlight are constant factors. The park, the houses, the river change with the seasons. The seasons are the same. You and your friends are the same. It is a miracle the blood does not coagulate in your veins.

Roberto. You hate me. You are too cowardly to admit it.

What Rico and I have done . . . I turn cold, my face blanches. The thought of the consequences fills me with dread. The blood rushes from my skin and into my body's inner organs. My circulation is affected. My brain receives too little oxygen. There is a pricking behind my eyes. The contractions of my heart pump the blood round my arteries. I breathe deeply. My left hand is clamped tightly around my right arm above the elbow. I loosen my grasp. I tighten it again.

I am afraid of dying.

I can feel the pressure of the blood in my upper arm. There is no pulse below the elbow. I loosen my grip. I rise. I look at the people concentrating around me. They are reading. I stand before a plain wooden chair. I sit down. I am in the National Library. It seems the secret police have not discovered this place yet. At least there is no visible presence.

It is a cruel notion that you wish me dead. My eyes search for something that can bring temporary respite to my mind. At one of the tables a pedantic apothecary sits with head deeply bowed. He is poring over a volume of botanical plates. Next to me is a priest, elbows on the table and hands over his ears supporting his head. He is reading about the pious Francis of Assisi. He yawns. Before me lies an open volume on European architecture. The reading room overseer and the others must think I am making notes.

Strangling him would have been too risky.

Dear brother, peace of mind is short-lived. This will be my last letter. No complications have arisen after the successful amputation of my right leg below the knee by the army surgeon and naturalist, Francisco Javier Muñiz, three years ago. I could have got gangrene again in one leg or the other. The wood leg and crutch I walk with have given me enough exercise to keep my circulation going. A painful blood-letting with leeches and cupping glasses was also beneficial. The Spanish conquerors have long believed that gangrene can be prevented by boiling the fat of dead Indians and rubbing it into the wound. I have not tried it.

The only letter I have received in the past three years was given to me last week by a freed black slave. He now works as a servant to the Lumbs, an English family. The letter was from Don Carlos. In England he is called Charles Robert Darwin. When I last wrote to you, he had just left the city. I have not seen him since. He is convinced he will become famous.

What could Rico and I have done differently to escape detection? Should we have been even more daring and determined? Did we hesitate? One second might have been enough.

Don Carlos' letter was posted on the 20th December, 1836. It is a long letter. He thanks me for what I did for him on the three occasions he was in Buenos Ayres in 1832 and '33. Don Carlos mentions our conversations. He writes that they have enriched him. Hypocrite! He praises me because he knows I cannot take advantage of it. Not once in his long letter does he mention the money I owe him. Enclosed with his correspondence was enough money for a suit of clothes, some liquor and a couple of excellent dinners. When I saw the name of the sender I decided to open the letter. It stank of money. He wants the return of the prehistoric armadillo skull he gave me.

Don Carlos believes the skull may be important for him. I accepted it because I was fascinated by the young man. That was then. His professor, Thomas Henslow, believes that the skull may have belonged to a glyptodont, a gigantic antediluvian armadillo.

I got rid of the thing long ago. I used up the money yesterday. Were I to be arrested with money on me, the police would take it immediately. So I have at least made sure I spent it all. Every last damned patacón!

They want to take me alive.

This letter, Roberto, is my last chance to speak of what has happened. I want to confess everything to you. You are my brother, after all. No, I am not noble. I am thinking mainly of my own well-being. The secret police, la Sociedad Popular Restaurador, are known as the mazorca. The pronunciation is exactly like mas horca: more hanging. They are the dictator Juan Manuel de Rosas' most effective tool. Rosas' wife, Encarnación de Ezcurra, is in change of the secret police and the Ministry of Propaganda. If they allow me one last wish, before they cut my throat — which is their signature of death — I shall ask them to send my letter to you.

I can feel the strength palpably draining out of my hand. I am numb.

A few years ago I would have called my acquaintance with Rico Trappatoni an unreserved pleasure. I would have characterized his skill with a gun as something I could have greatly profited by.

Not a single message or effect of his remains.

Did I make the blunder that will be so decisive for us both? Did I leave one or more damning clues in Rosas' home?

What an hysterical abundance of detail there is in Don Carlos' letter! What self-absorption! What energy he displays in describing his own homecoming.

On the 6th October, 1836, he arrived back in Shrewsbury. He had been away from home five years. Eighteen months at sea, and three years, three months on dry land. Never had such a seasick man walked ashore more firmly resolved to avoid going to sea again, he writes. It took him two days in a post chaise from Plymouth to Shrewsbury. He managed to gain entry to the elegant, ivy-covered, three-story brick building. It was nighttime. He crept unnoticed into the house. Next morning his four sisters and his father, Robert, sat unsuspecting round the table. Don Carlos surprised them just as a child might have done. His brother, Erasmus, was living in London. Don Carlos was thinner and his hair had grown. Despite the five intervening years his face and appearance had hardly altered. His father, the country doctor, was just as florid, talkative and stout as before. According to Don Carlos he weighs twenty-five stone. Parked outside the window was the yellow gig he used on his rounds.

The idea was to kill quietly and unobserved!

Roberto! This baby of twenty-seven is in the process of writing a book about his journey round the world. Without the slightest compunction he has entitled it: "Journal of Researches into the Geology and Natural History of the Various Countries Visited by HMS Beagle under the command of Captain FitzRoy from 1832 to 1836."

What a conceited nincompoop!

When he was staying here in the city he was an unknown young whippersnapper. The letters he sent Professor Henslow were read to the Cambridge Philosophical Society. In London, Henslow had spoken about him in glowing terms to William Clift of The Royal College of Surgeons and shown him a Megatherium skull. All the experts wished to meet this braggadocio. The very same fellow who stood beside me in the Calle Bolívar. Together we ogled the women from behind. And what was his comment? "The Buenos Ayres women glide through the streets, while in England they saunter like lazy sows." I recall him offering me a cigar as he made these academic observations. Don Carlos maintains he can remember just how Shrewsbury looked during the fireworks' display of 18th June, 1815, after Napoleon had been defeated at Waterloo. Shrewsbury was quite unchanged when he returned from his voyage round the world. Just as Varazze will remain the same sleepy, God-fearing town until doomsday.

In the library here I have discovered that Shrewsbury is situated south of Liverpool. The map shows the town far inland at a bend in the River Severn. Shrewsbury is said to be full of steep, narrow streets. The remains of the city wall encompass it still. A red sandstone castle rises proudly from the middle of the town. The inhabitants live from the pottery industry, cattle and tanning.

Roberto, I still remember your birthday: the 12th February, 1809. At the moment you were born in Varazze, Don Carlos was born in Shrewsbury. Two provincial European towns. My thoughts fly back and forth between Buenos Ayres, Shrewsbury and Varazze. After Galileo, after the Earth was turned into a marble, any fool can roll it back and forth on his palm!

Rico's full name is Ricardo Claudio Trappatoni. Rico is not merely a convenient abbreviation. The sound of the name conjures up generosity and warmth.

One of the first things he said to me was: "If you start mulling endlessly over right and wrong, nothing will change. You must stop thinking, you must act if you want to stop injustice."

I started. I remember what he said next. He was looking into my eyes.

"As I stand face to face with death I shall have the chance to be a decent human being. That's when life begins. Death gives life meaning."

Rico has always been a man of action. He is one of those rare and old-fashioned bodies who harbor concepts of what is just and unjust. Rico often says: "Everyone believes God is on their side. But those who have money and power know that he is. The others must content themselves with relics. A relic means a remnant of something, a remainder. Splinters from Jesus' cross are the most coveted. Today his cross weighs five hundred tons." I support the revolutionaries while their ambition is as yet unfulfilled.

Roberto, what would you have said if I had knocked at your door? Would you have let me in? No, I do not reproach you. Why should you? Since I wrote to you last I have repudiated the existence of God. Necessity is what drives me. I write to you, Roberto, rather than turning to God.

You are both equally silent.

★

Roberto!

It is probable the police will get hold of this letter. I shall wait with my confession until I no longer have any choice. A couple of months ago I threw away the key to the room I rented on the first floor of the Alborellos' house. After my amputation the landlord, Signóre Alborello, displayed a mounting interest in me. Increasingly he would ask me how my work at the shipyard was going. He wanted to know if there was much to do, if I enjoyed it and, not satisfied with that, would ask detailed questions about the tools in my carpenter's bag. For a long time I assumed these were expressions of consideration and kindness. He got me to expound on the advantages of the various gouges, of the many awls in my bag, of my splicing tools and not least the seaming palm: the padding I must wear on my hand to force the needle through sail. The best timber plane in my white canvas bag I had stolen once when on a job in Genoa. I had a well-appointed bag. A craftsman might also have noticed that it contained small, home-made tools for doing all kinds of tackle-work. Because of his former trade as a cabinet maker, Alborello could see it was the tool bag of a skilled artificer. The bag's treasures said it all. Take something like the marline spike that doubles as a handle for the boot hook on the other end. As soon as one looks at this tool one knows one is dealing with a real craftsman. The wear on the hook betrays if he has the necessary skill.

Alborello displayed a professional interest in my carpenter's bag. He got me to talk with enthusiasm and delight. He got me to divulge that the casual jobs I got from the shipyard were becoming fewer. I had no misgivings because I paid my rent punctually. He never asked me where I got the money from. I did not regard this as a bad omen. After a while I realized that his consideration and interest were anything but sincere. I had opened my heart as one might to a doctor. Alborello took several months to make his diagnosis: Giovanni Graciani pays promptly now, but will not in a few months' time. His attentions were about as cordial as those of a condor circling over a carcass.

Roberto. You are lucky. Thanks to your religion you can invoke the Devil.

When the Alborellos' game became clear to me, I threw away the key, took my carpenter's bag and a blanket and left without paying the rent. I pawned all my tools during the first week. The only thing I kept was an awl. For some reason, I felt sure I would need it quite soon.

Some acquaintances let me live in a secret tunnel that runs beneath the network of streets of Buenos Ayres. I shall not divulge its precise location. Its importance to the smuggling trade is well known. Especially after the Spanish king commanded Buenos Ayres to trade with no one except Spain.

Until a few days ago I lived there with Rico Trappatoni. We were in the process of cementing a friendship. How many years is it since I had a friend? He missed his four-year-old son who is living with an aunt in Rosario. He was a widower. The considerate way in which he spoke of his son was suffused with a tenderness I appreciate. Was it this quality that made him constantly ask if I needed help as I was handicapped?

I miss my trips to the Catedral Metropolitana. The police are stationed at strategic points in and around the cathedral. I must content myself with looking at the beautiful building from afar. Above the twelve Corinthian columns in front of the door there is an embellishment within the triangular tympanum. It shows the meeting between Joseph and his family in exile. Some of my acquaintance say this wonderful piece was created by a convict who was set free after the cathedral was finished. The credit has been taken by others. The convict's name was Daniel Massaro. He was executed a fortnight ago.

Lately, I have only been able to view the cathedral from the opposite side of the Plaza de la Victoria after dark. I have had to content myself with my memories of all the beauty within the cathedral's main doors. I shall never again see the pieces of Venetian mosaic. Nor the High Altar with its baroque lines, nor Francisco Parisi's Italian renaissance paintings nor the altars dedicated to Saint Peter and Our Lady of Sorrows, Nuestra Senora de Dolores. I have seen for the last time that most hallowed spot for all Argentines, the mausoleum in the cathedral. This mausoleum is raised over the grave of the hero of independence, General Don José de San Martín. San Martín liberated Peru, Bolivia, Chile and Argentina from the Spanish crown.

When evening falls I leave the library. In the dusk I can make out the Grenadier regiment and the governor's bodyguards. From my vantage point it is impossible to make out the colors of the uniforms at this time of day. Red and blue were chosen by General San Martín in 1810. I can only just see the pyramid with its classical lines in the middle of the plaza. All honor to Francisco Cauete, creator of this work of art that can be seen by one who cannot approach the cathedral more closely. In the half-light the cathedral looks like coagulated civilization. One of the city's best brothels is directly opposite it on the other side of the Plaza de la Victoria. At present, the tunnel, the brothel and the library are my only fixed points.

I once stood on the edge of the Plaza de la Victoria and watched Mrs Black glide across the square. What made that beautiful and wealthy woman choose me for a lover? At that time I had a gangrenous foot and an insecure job at the shipyard. That my looks, or for that matter my so-called innate qualities, could have appealed so strongly to this Englishwoman, I find laughable. Was I a random choice? Did she want her husband to discover us? And what of me? Was I flattered? Did I wish to observe more closely how the rich lived and thought? All of a sudden I am alarmed that I cannot picture her face. How could I have allowed this, of all faces, to slip my memory?

There! I just caught it again! A mental picture. What a sweet pang.

Is love not the most carnal of all illusions? To love is to possess, but what does one possess — the body?

I raise my head. I look out.

After countless rainy days the sky has regained the blue that has been hidden high above the wide, grey expanses.

The last money I earned honestly was as a letter-writer to the illiterates about the Calle de la Ribera. I got the idea from Rico. The level of literacy in and around the Genoese community in Boca is distinctly low. I used to meet my customers outside the National Library or by Nuestra Senora de los Nieves, the church of Our Lady of the Snows.

The National Library is the pride of the young state. It was built before Rosas' time. Reason, and the French notions of enlightenment and freedom have set their stamp on the collection of books. A considerable number come from Real Colegio, the Jesuit college, and some are private gifts from, amongst others, Bernadino Rivadavia's wealthy friends who supported the French ideals of education.

Letter-writing was a welcome addition to my income from sporadic jobs at the shipyard. There are no limits to what people want letters written about. An Indian with roots in Peru asked me to write a letter to his prospective father-in-law. As he described the job I could not help noticing that his teeth were still green from coca leaves. The Indian wanted to marry a Spanish woman. Her family was originally from Grenada. The letter was to be addressed to her father who lived near San Telmo. The young woman had several times attempted to explain to her father what sort of faith the Inca Indian of her heart adhered to. The Inca asked me to formulate a convincing letter. I undertook the commission well knowing the task to be impossible. Rico had advised me to have nothing to do with the fellow. After checking that his coins and notes were genuine, I was ready for the dictation. He began with a lecture on the history of the Incas!

"The Sun is our ancestor. Our history has been written by the Inca, Garcilaso de la Vega."

"I'm waiting for the gist," I put in.

"Our people lived in a desert. They were helpless until the Sun saw their pitiful plight. The Sun decided to send his two children to enlighten mankind and give him laws and rules. They descended by Lake Titicaca."

"I've heard it all before!"

"They began their wanderings in the area around that vast lake. When they halted to eat or sleep they would thrust a golden staff into the ground. If the staff sank right in, cities were to be built. They were to act as enlightened noblemen by virtue of their wisdom and goodness. They were to rule over everyone. The Sun's son was called Inca. His sister, Mama Ocllo. Of course you know that the realm of the Incas came into existence without a written language."

"Get to the point!"

"In 1530, when your people came to my country with Pizarro at their head, the Incas were thirty million strong. Forty-two years later there were one and a half million Incas left. The last Inca to lead a rebellion against the Catholic faith was beheaded at Cuzco. The head of Tupac Amaru, as he was called, was mounted on a stake. But his head would not decompose. Quite the reverse, my heathen brothers believed his head shone with a celestial radiance for weeks. Thousands of Indians studied the head until your people decided they had to remove it."

"I'm off!" I shouted. "Sentimental ramblings! Think of your 'father-in-law,' you dolt!"

Only then did he stop. Why did it never occur to me that this innocent fool might be one of Rosas' agents?

Roberto, I can assure you that the man with the green teeth possessed not the least jot of irony. I do not know whether his petition was born of a boundless devotion to that Spanish woman, whom I should dearly love to have seen, or an enormous self-assurance unaccompanied by any insight into himself. He got no answer to his letter. When he came to me the second time I tried to look serious. I expressed great surprise that he had not had a generous offer of the hand of the old Spaniard's only child. I said that the whole thing must be due to a misunderstanding. I offered to write another letter. As soon as he had scraped enough money together and I had followed my usual procedure for checking the quality of his coin and paper money, I was ready for dictation number two. My client showed an infinite admiration for forms of address, imaginative ways of acknowledging banalities and precociousness in wishing his beauty's father good health, sleep, digestion and Christmas. The fact that the Christmas greetings were sent in February did nothing to shake the Inca's faith in my qualities as a letter-writer, quite the reverse, they were, rather, an expression of even greater care and consideration. The Inca wanted me to sign his letters "Pepe." He thought it the most Spanish name he could imagine. And, in addition, best calculated to appease his future "father-in-law." The fellow was an out-and-out, servile groveler. Nevertheless, there was one thing about this Indian that aroused my curiosity: his attitude to mountains. The highest mountains, according to him, were the most powerful forces. He said: "They are the grand-parents, they have been in the landscape a long time. They see furthest and know most. The mountains are supposed to bring harmony to the home, to the village and the city. But if their command is not obeyed, the mountains punish with rain and frost."

I do not know whether it was a sympathy or a condescension I felt towards the man. I looked forward to getting my money. All at once I began to think of you, Roberto, and Don Carlos. This Indian's faith in ancient stories, handed down from genera-tion to generation, is not so unlike the bond you and Don Carlos have with the Old Testament. One of the three books Don Carlos took with him round the world was the Old Testament. Those ancient stories will certainly be on his desk now, over on the other side of the world. And I dare say you, dear brother, have your leather-bound Bible before you.

Rico never owned a book. When he disappeared he had no more than the clothes he stood up in. Don Carlos, on the other hand, had no problem with money! He could simply write off for it. What does he know about being poor, about being doomed to poverty!

Roberto, if only that English numskull knew that Rico and I had done what many in this city dream of doing, but do not dare. They hide behind reason, and will not acknowledge it as cowardice, pure and simple. But how many fine deeds would there have been had reason ruled all our actions? That is how fearful we are for our own tiny lives!

Dear Roberto, I have not described my present condition clearly. I have said that I live in a tunnel, but not a word about how I earn my living. Possibly I have tried to spare myself from writing the words: I am a beggar. A trade I have despised so heartily that I cannot imagine it as a trade. The number of beggars in the city is increasing. Few have money to spend on letter-writers now.

Our contempt for the beggar is based on our ability to suppress the idea that we might end up in such a wretched condition ourselves. The further

away we trust we have relegate
pect, the more contemptuc
who taught me some of the
Beneath one of the will
Alameda I begged enough
leg I now walk with. B
had to be of sufficient quan.,
gangrene. When months went by u.
letter-client I could not avoid begging.

I learnt a lot about people's ability to smile. Previously, my understanding had been extremely naive. A large number of those who pass by while I am begging either avoid looking at me or pointedly look away. A third group looks down. They seem to be overwhelmed by their feelings. Perhaps they are calling to mind a close relation who has just landed on this frontier of poverty. Their meeting with me is a reminder they have failed to prevent that most shameful of things from occurring to the person in question. For me this group is the easiest prey. With energy and alacrity one must aim a couple of sentences at the ears in the bowed head. The sentences must not be aggressive, making the prospective giver feel even worse than he did when he began his march down the Calle la Alameda and saw my open hand. What is important is that, as he passes the willow

I stand, he should receive a few quite
ary phrases that may ease his sense of guilt.
respect the church has done a vital job that is
th exploiting. My best results have been achieved
nen I have managed to work in some parallel between my own fate and that of Job. It is important
to be quite specific about how the alms will be spent.
When I say the money will go towards a belt to
harness my wooden leg to my knee, my benefactors
adopt a mild expression. Some become almost ec-
static at the thought that the beggar is purposeful
and that his goal is attainable. The ones with the
broadest smiles are the most suspect. Their smiles
often signify that they are well prepared for a meeting with a beggar. Their smiles start long before they
pass. The broadest smilers are those least likely to
give. The smile is a shield. It is there as a decoy. The
beggar is to believe that easy meat is approaching.
When they open their mouths and rap out a nega-
tive answer they hope the beggar will be caught
unawares and overwhelmed. Or that he will realize
at once it would take too long to change their minds.
One of the first things one learns is that the rich are
by no means the surest givers. The poor who still
have jobs are a better bet. They give as if the action
itself were an insurance against finding themselves

in my position, and in gratitude that they have not sunk that far.

The moment is important. Before and after divine service and around festivals is preferable. Roberto, my wooden leg has provided me with much-needed income. Once I had saved enough for the wooden leg and its harness I decided to celebrate at a bar up in Carlos Calvo.

My object was simple: to use up the rest of my money without further ado. It was a long time since I had been there. I recognized some of the customers. I thought of Rico. I missed him. I stood at the bar. I drank beer. I pushed my wooden leg hard down on the earth floor to see if any pain shot up my leg, through my body and into my head. I simply wished to know how well the wooden leg functioned. I felt no pain. Neither carpenter nor saddler had cheated me. I had not drunk more than that when I realized I had made a good buy. I spoke to no one. I was alone with my thoughts and happy with them. The barkeeper tried to strike up a conversation. To divert him I ordered another beer. The door to the bar opened, four men entered. They said nothing. They looked at one another. They looked over at the barkeeper and me. Two of them remained by the door. The other two came towards us. The room fell completely silent.

"Is there anything I can offer you gentlemen?" the barkeeper called amicably.

There was no reply.

"Will you have beer or rum?" the barkeeper asked in a more subdued voice.

Not a word from the people at the tables. I could hear that some of them sat uneasily on their chairs. I gulped. Had I been able to touch my carotid artery I should have felt my pulse hammering. I had been somewhat relieved that this second pair, as they approached the counter, stared at the barkeeper and not me.

The two men were not especially large or powerful. They exuded a brutal authority. Their movements were calm and purposeful. They spoke not a word. It was not many moments before everyone in the bar realized who they were. No one lifted a finger. Those whose hands were on the table dared not to lower them to their thighs. Those whose hands were in their laps could not raise them to the table. Subservience and total submission reigned. At least the steers in the slaughterhouse bellow. I looked into the eyes of the two representatives of the secret police. The two executors of Rosas' will. Their eyes were as expressionless as those of crocodiles. One of them drew out a razor. No one stirred. I have never stood more motionless. I held my breath. With perfect composure he coaxed the blade from out of the handle. It almost seemed this part of the séance was intended to be slow enough for the customers to follow every detail and be in no doubt about what they were witnessing. Each movement seemed like a rehearsed pantomime. The four of them were performing a ritual they knew well. Their individual actions were controlled by a higher authority. The man with the razor struck suddenly, at lightning speed, like a matador giving the coup de grâce.

Roberto. At least a bull may hear tepid or loud applause before everything turns red and black.

My pulse hammered. My heart, that loneliest of all muscles, leapt. The barkeeper's head was decapitated in two quick slashes. The blood spurted over me and his executioner. I was stiff and cold. The heat of the blood startled me into breathing. The head was placed on the counter. The gurgling scream, the eyes, the body falling forward, they knew we would remember every detail. Our rulers cannot control people's dreams. This fills them with vengefulness. I would not have hesitated to barter my ability to dream in exchange for being spared that sight. Our rulers know that the more room nightmares take up in our consciousness, the less space there is left for the good dreams.

Those swine think I am hamstrung. They treated me as if I was not there!

Juan Manuel de Rosas was caudillo of the province of Buenos Ayres from 1829. When Don Carlos met Rosas on the Pampas in 1832, Rosas' title was caudillo, chief. Argentina is made up of ten provinces in all. Rosas played one caudillo off against the other. He is a brilliant schemer. By 1835 Rosas was caudillo of the whole of Argentina. His elegant residence in the quarter of the city known as Palermo was built in pure Versailles style. The buildings, parks and sculptures are all faithful copies. Architects and craftsmen travel like shuttles across the Atlantic to study the originals in Versailles. In contrast to Louis XIV's preoccupation with the sun, Rosas' main employment is studying the moon through his magnificent telescope. The telescope was bought in Paris. One gets no closer to the moon by looking at it. Rosas has recently established a zoological garden in his grounds.

Some days ago he forbade the porteños, the inhabitants of Buenos Ayres, from holding a carnival. He has ordered the porteños to wear a red ribbon on their coats. Red is the federalists' color. Rosas' wife wears scarlet silks and his gauchos, red ponchos. The unitarians are fighting for a stronger central power with Buenos Ayres at its hub. Their platform is the trading license and European ideals of enlightenment. The federalists believe the provinces must be allowed to keep as much autonomy as possible, and depend on support from the landowners. Do you recognize these arguments from home, Roberto?

All official documents from now on must begin "Long live the federation" and "Death to the brutal unitarians." Over the past year I have had a growing suspicion that Rosas, who was originally a federalist, is trying to advance the unitarian cause. His passionate interest in France is typical.

He still has the support of the landowners, the church and the army. One of the laws he will not repeal is that prohibiting the carrying of knives on Sunday. The church extols Rosas for his piety. The usual penalty for transgressing it is to be tied to the stake for a full day. Rumor has it that one Sunday Rosas himself insisted on being bound to the stake for forgetting to take off his knife.

In the army, Rosas has decreed that the soldiers follow the old customs in the selection of their generals. A couple of months ago I witnessed the promotion of a general not far from Baraccas. Twenty wild horses were herded into an enclosure. There were three candidates for the post. They sat on a boom above a gate through which the horses, one by one, were driven out on to the Pampas. The drought had turned the grass a sandy yellow. The sky was infinitely huge and blue. The one who leapt down on to the freedom-hungry horse and, in the shortest time, rode it back to the corral, without saddle or bridle, was appointed. Rosas became a general in the same way.

One of the youngest soldiers who had stood watching jumped up on one of the horses as soon as the selection was over. He managed to keep his horse as it cleared the fence. The horse was trying frenetically to dislodge him. His skin was copper-brown. He looked as if he might have been a half-caste Indian from one of the northern provinces like Tucumán or Salta. A superlative rider. There were several minutes of frantic whinnying, kicking and bucking. From within a cloud of dust, an unspoken pact was forged between horse and rider.

When the youth had ridden the horse back to

the corral he was pulled off his mount. The newly appointed general and his two rivals ran towards the prostrate soldier. He tried to rise. He was kicked in the chest. He curled up. He clutched his diaphragm. The general was carrying a coil of rope. The two others hauled him upright and the general beat him down. Four stakes were driven into the Pampas. The young soldier's legs and arms were tied to the stakes. His body hung, taut, a meter above the ground. When the youth regained consciousness he realized he was stretched out in the same way animal skin is stretched out to dry.

"You damned puppy," shouted the general spitting on the ground.

The youth lay tied up until the sun went down.

In the newspaper, El Telegrafo Mercantil, the police have announced a stricter regime towards beggars. "No longer will any type of criminal activity be tolerated." I believe them. Obituaries and threats are the only truths the newspapers carry. In the streets after dark, or round the corners of houses when people think no witnesses are present, one may hear Rosas' new nickname: the Caligula of Río de la Plata. Caligula had nice table manners, but do not ask what he ate. Some say Rosas has a nice smile.

Roberto, when I wrote to you last, before Rosas took power, there was shooting in the streets. There are still intermittent skirmishes between federalists and unitarians, but these confrontations take place far away from the city. The streets are silent. On such days one can feel too sure of life. At such times melancholy is an important waymark, a guiding thought for my hesitant and halting steps between my hideout and the library. Your Catholic faith, dear brother, has taught you that melancholy and sorrow are sins. For me, necessity and melancholy are the grounds of my existence. The thing Rico has taught me is that I have a muscle I knew nothing of: rebellion's.

Since I lived with the Alborellos in Calle de la Ribera my relations with dogs have been strained. But in the part of the tunnel I inhabit lives a brown mongrel. This creature has annexed the two square yards of Earth I call my own. Rico, who in contrast to me, was fond of dogs, could get no reaction from this cur. Not even when he gave it food or tried to play was there any friendly tail-wagging. The endless rejections never soured Rico's attitude to the miserable creature. Rico stole ever nicer tidbits for it. It paid him no heed. Rico pulled faces and said silly things to try to rouse the spoilt animal's attention. He gave it a name: Bozzo. A name I thought ridiculous. I still use it. I can kick the dog and it will not growl. I can point to where it is to walk, run or sit. The dog obeys. And when I hit the animal it looks at me trustingly. Does it have less fear because it lives without words? Does my irritation spring from a horror of being recognized? Is there something so familiar about me that the beastly creature identifies with it? What if dogs started to walk on their back legs because they no longer wanted to be dogs?

Bozzo? It is perfectly ridiculous this animal should have its own name. The day after Rico disappeared the dog came and stood in front of me. I was trying to write. The candle flame illuminated the sheets of paper. I was listening for suspicious sounds outside. The dog stood there. The dog looked at me. The dog sat down. I had not told it to. The dog held out its paw. Why? The dog held out its paw again. I did not lift a finger. The dog whined. I said nothing. The dog lay down. The dog rolled over on to its side. The dog began to scratch itself. The dog started to wag its tail gently. The dog hung out its tongue. Its jaws were open. Its tongue steamed. Its teeth were white, its gums pink. Saliva trickled from the corners of its mouth and the tip of its tongue. The dog swallowed. The dog swallowed again. It raised each of its paws in turn an inch from the ground. The dog whined, barked, wagged its tail.

"Keep quiet!" I hissed. "Lie down!"

The dog lay down.

I snarled: "What are you lying down for? Why are you looking at me with those pathetic eyes? Why is your tail wagging?"

The dog was silent.

"You want some fresh air, perhaps? Your tongue looks like a flag hanging from your mouth. Why are you drooling? Put your tongue away!"

Dogs are as obedient as condemned prisoners. Trustingly, and with deliberate movements, they turn up in front of the firing squad.

All that fuss to seem good-natured! Even a dog has enough sense not to put on an act.

Not long after I had got to know Rico he asked me to do him a favor. I was to collect some papers from an acquaintance of his. The man's name was Dino Berti. I was apprehensive. He had worked with me at the shipyard. How Berti had got to know Rico I cannot tell. Rico had always spoken of him respectfully. He was an adherent of Voltaire. Dino

Berti had been dismissed from his job as a carpenter at the shipyard. Not long after he had moved to a tiny smallholding with his wife and six children. The "farm" consisted of an eighth of an acre of land, four cows, a few hens and a cock. The Berti family lived on the outskirts of La Boca.

I walked towards La Boca. When I approached the place where I had been told the Bertis lived, I very nearly turned back. I suddenly realized just how dangerous my assignment was.

I stopped. I changed my mind. I walked back the way I had come. Rico had told me that he greatly valued Dino's ability "to keep quiet about this and that." I never asked what he meant.

I turned round again. In La Boca I asked the way to Berti's house. An ox-driver pointed towards a shack.

"There."

He looked thoughtful.

"Thank you," I said, and was about to move on.

"Haven't I seen you before?"

"No," I said quickly, looking past the man. I had recognized him straight away.

"I'm sure I've seen you before!" he cried.

I try at all costs to move about as unobtrusively

223

as possible. Unobtrusively! I, that am so easily recognizable, must do my best to appear as anonymous as a withered leaf. Were I to disappear from street life it would be reported. Our dictatorship has encouraged more and more people in the city to perfect the art of informing. Tips are rewarded, whether they are true or not. Many display a commitment and enthusiasm that must gladden the authorities. Our rulers know all about man's treacherous disposition.

The ox-driver sat calmly on the yoke between his pair of oxen. They were as huge as mountains. He was waiting for an answer. I said nothing.

"You can't have forgotten that letter you wrote for me a couple of years ago."

I was frightened he might bar the way. Running was impossible. I looked down. I thought frantically. I raised my head. I looked at him. I smiled.

"You must be confusing me with someone else."

"Not at all. You were very talkative. You had no scruples about charging a good price for your services!"

He was bald. His eyes appeared to be brown. He was unshaven. The bristles could not hide a scar on his left cheek. I was compelled to look at this face.

"Well, answer!"

He jumped down from the oxen and stood right in front of me. He was taller than me.

"There are two things you should understand," 1 said without knowing exactly how I was going to continue.

There was a silence.

"I have never written letters. I can neither read nor write. Do you want me to call the police?" I said raising my voice.

He departed without a word. I heaved a sigh of relief. I looked in the direction of the Bertis' shack. I waited until the driver on the two enormous oxen was out of sight. There was no sign of life. I was still unsure. I saw smoke coming from the rear of the house. I made my decision and moved closer.

No one could be seen through the ramshackle windows. No sign of life outside the neighboring houses either. The silence drew me round to the back of the shack. I saw a milch cow lying on its side with bile running from its mouth. The flies had begun their meal. It could barely move its tail. There was an awful stench of putrefaction. A bonfire was burning behind the shack. Thick, oily smoke drifted upwards. The ash wafted like sticky, black snow before settling on some blackened skulls, charred ribs and smoldering hooves. From the roof I heard the beating of wings. They flew towards me. I held my hands up to my face. I just managed to glimpse two of the Egyptian vultures, with their bald heads and black feathers, sitting on the roof. I thrashed my arms about, I screamed, I felt the fear contort my face and tighten my throat. I pressed myself back against the wall. The vultures flew up on to the roof again. They were waiting. The dying cow would be their next prey. It looked as if they were waiting to hack at the bloated belly.

I could still see no one about. I was on the point of leaving. I was frightened for my life. I felt I was being watched.

"Run, Giovanni!"

A man appeared in one of the windows. I had no doubt it was Dino Berti. How else could he have known my name?

"But where is your family?" I managed to stammer.

"They took them away and poisoned my animals. Now I'm poisoned, too. My throat and lungs are burning."

I heard a cry and a crash. There was a dead silence, like after the fall of a tree.

Roberto. What do you think I did? I ran away! I

waddled off as only a cripple can. I am a miserable creature, a bastard begotten of perfidy and cowardice. I ran off without trying to help him! Without asking if there was anything I could do! Without trying to ease his pain! Perhaps he did not die immediately? Just think if Rico's papers had been there?

What must Dino Berti have thought of me?
How his last thought has haunted me!

As I was leaving the little farm I caught a glimpse of the cock. He had mounted one of the hens. She was almost invisible. Her wings protruded beneath him. She was sinking into the mud. The cock's thrusts got faster. At last, he fell off the hen. He fell on his side into the mud. The hen flapped her wings, stretched her neck and tripped off aimlessly.

It was beginning to get dark.

I got out of the place. Imagine if every dead creature had a star in the sky. What a light there would be!

It was dark.

After several minutes, at a safe distance from the ghastly scene, my fear was replaced by a dawning realization: I could no longer simply assume the shape of a man.

Each day I can see and feel my miserable body under my restless head.

I knew full well that the incident at Dino Berti's had exposed my fear. My fear of being a man of action.

Roberto. I was not born to please. I was born to be a victim, like most of us. Naturally there are excuses for not doing anything about what goes on around us. That one has lost a leg, has consumption or is starving are all good reasons, naturally.

But now I had had enough! Ora basta!

Rico could focus my action.

I met Rico the next day.

"Well, how did it go?"

"He was dead."

"Thank you for trying," said Rico.

Rico found my interest in books and lengthy visits to the library totally incomprehensible.

Every now and again, I lift my pen from the paper and lay it down. The characters I have just formed merge together and lose my attention. I listen to my breath. I keep my mouth shut. From the moment I realize I am listening to my breath, I draw the air in more deeply and expel it more quickly:

lungs, throat, pharynx, oral cavity, nostrils, until finally it is no longer my breath, but the air of the reading room. It is hot in here.

I look out of the windows. There are the same houses, the same landscape. I have looked out of these windows for several years. The view has become a soothing void I do not see, do not fear, as when the letters on the page in front of me grow indistinct and, at last, invisible.

Sometimes it is an advantage to be alone. To be alone is to keep silence amongst people. One escapes the spontaneous, bewildering chat. I am used to my own words. My voice belongs first to my body, and then to a language. I notice my own breath and my own heartbeat. Was it not father who used to say that the dread within us is the heartbeat of God?

Dear brother, it is not a Utopia I need in order to write, but a face. Yours. It is now more than two years since I last saw Mrs Black. I am no longer her lover. I am alone. Apart from Bozzo and your face, which seems remoter than ever. Your face is more necessary to me now than ever before — from a distance. Are you nursing the hope that in my loneliness, in my humiliating situation and in my fear, I shall seek God? Perhaps, deep down, you have hoped that I would give up and let myself be led, now in my time of greatest need. Perhaps you have thought that soon I would have no words left to say except — God.

Rico was particularly interested in music. He once invited me to a concert near the church of St Ignatius. It was my first concert. One of the pieces played had been written by a Ludwig van Beethoven. I have little knowledge of music, but it seemed to me that what I was listening to was a mixture of thought and experience.

Sometimes words cannot provide the key to everything that happens. I listened to this music. Do not drag the word reason into it! This was a kind of thought, but it had nothing to do with reason. The music reminded of me of a vague pattern of disjointed thoughts.

Even when the choir sang "Alle Menschen werden Brüder" I was spellbound, in spite of the unsophisticated words. Not merely spellbound, but seduced, overwhelmed by a perception outside reason's ken. The more one participates with one's entire being as a listener, the less one can say about the music. Don Carlos would scarcely allow himself to be entranced. I remember when I stood with him in the

Metropolitan Cathedral. I asked him to listen to the choir practicing at the opposite end of the building.

"Isn't that lovely?" I asked enthusiastically.

"I know nothing about music," Don Carlos replied.

Don Carlos' long letter is continually suffused with the belief that it is possible to reconcile religion and science. Folly! He says he cannot understand how the world we see could be the result of chance. Despite his finds and burgeoning new theories, he chooses not to desert the church. Dear brother, no matter what he may unearth, I would stake my life that he never will disown the church. He dare not face up to the full implications of his own discoveries. He transfers the detachment he possesses as a scientist to himself as a man. He does not wish to compromise himself. Not at any price.

Don Carlos writes at considerable length about some coral-reef theories, I shall not bother to repeat them, they would probably mean nothing to you. On second thoughts, they mean nothing to me, either. Don Carlos holds himself in high regard at the moment. When I met him he was more unaffected. I quote what Charles Lyell said to him about his coral-reef theories: "They are quite correct, but do not imagine people will believe you until you are as bald as I."

Lyell is one of Don Carlos' paragons. The young man must be brimming with self-confidence as he sits surrounded by innumerable sheets of notes.

Don Carlos has a 770-page manuscript describing his great voyage. He has 1,383 pages of geology notes and 368 pages on zoology. He has 1,529 creatures preserved in formalin, and according to him, 3,907 skins, bones and dried artifacts. Henslow is helping him catalogue this vast collection. He discusses the geology of South America with Lyell. Lyell speaks so softly that Don Carlos must often ask him to repeat himself. In this way he gets a revision.

Here and there Don Carlos adds a clause about feeling ill or off color. He ascribes this indisposition to his constant seasickness aboard HMS Beagle. He does not mention that there might be something wrong with his own state of mind. That would never occur to him. Don Carlos' countryman, Lord Nelson, suffered from seasickness. But the lord was at sea for most of his life until he fell at the battle of Trafalgar. In the course of his career he lost first his right eye and then his right arm. That was not too bad. After all, one has two of each. But the admiral was never in doubt as to the reason for his nausea. Dread forced its way up his gullet. Nelson had the courage to acknowledge his fear.

Don Carlos was eight when his mother died. But still he maintains he cannot remember her. Will he acknowledge a close relationship with no one at all? It is hardly surprising he has always been frightened of dogs. When he was young his sisters taught him never to take more than one egg from each nest. But at that time he was also a keen hunter who shot more birds than there were eggs. Don Carlos cannot see the paradox.

In England they publish a volume called The Newgate Calendar. It is a chronicle of British criminals. I turned up a copy here in the library some months ago. The story that most fascinated Don Carlos and me in the 1816 edition, was the one about Sawney Beane. Beane had been born in about the year 1600, during the reign of James VI of Scotland. He was the son of a ditcher. He spent his youth near Edinburgh. Beane eventually married and roamed the southwest coast of Scotland with his wife. They discovered a cave that was about a mile deep. At high tide the sea submerged the cave for a distance of some two hundred yards. Some way in, the cave opened out considerably. This chamber became the Beanes' subterranean home. In order to survive, the young pair took to highway robbery. After awhile they realized that their victims might expose their hideout. So they killed them. The robbed became the murdered. Not long after this the couple began to eat them.

Dear brother. There must be a thrilling mutual understanding when missionaries tell cannibals about the Lord's Supper.

The couple had eight sons, six daughters and thirty-two grandchildren born out of incest. The Newgate Calendar estimates that one thousand persons were done away with before the Beane family was eventually arrested. One man had managed to escape after he had been robbed. This was the family's undoing. Their hideout was discovered. The thousand baffling disappearances were at last explained. In the cave they found human flesh in brine and drying. After the family had been arrested, the male members were torn limb from limb and the women burnt.

Don Carlos dare not allow his finds or the things he reads and encounters to trouble his consciousness. Consciousness is the one thing that distinguishes us from animals. Don Carlos fears adversity!

Why was he obsessed with collecting beetles of all things? Such small, impersonal, black creatures. Aboard HMS Beagle Don Carlos was surrounded by twenty-two chronometers where he sat at the end of the table in the chart house and worked with his microscope. Captain Robert FitzRoy paced tensely around shouting commands both short and long. Don Carlos had not one disparaging remark to make about the captain. Do not tell me that Don Carlos' self-restraint will not have side-effects. He is clearly not interested in finding out about them. Don Carlos' sisters got his great love, Fanny Owen, to send him a greeting on the journey. The mere sight of her handwriting would make him wish his circumnavigation of the world was over. Don Carlos made small talk to the captain and obeyed each ludicrous order. He was so seasick that death would have been a release. He got the letter from Fanny. The writing, the lines, the loops, the pressure of the pen in her fingers and hand might have released him. Don Carlos chose nausea instead of passion. He sailed on. His passion suffocated in the stateroom. He sailed on with the vessel that was to inspect and catalogue the South American continent. When Don Carlos set sail in HMS Beagle he took with him Milton's *Paradise Lost* and the first volume of Charles Lyell's *Principles of Geology*. Don Carlos got the second and third volumes in Montevideo and in the Falkland Islands. Don Carlos realized that Lyell's revolutionary views about the history and development of the Earth's crust would have a great influence on his own evolution. The third book that accompanied him when he left Plymouth in '31 was the Bible. But not the usual English edition. It was the Greek version. The Greek! Do not imagine that this young man has ever attempted to fathom the depths of his own vanity.

Outside the window I see quiet streets, agave hedges, olive, peach and willow trees.

The fact that I had never killed a man was a handicap.

Roberto, until early today I harbored a tiny hope that Rico had been sent to Montevideo. Rosas has banished a couple of thousand people already.

From here I can see a clump of trees. Most of them are dead. Just like people. Most of us are dead. Fear, does Don Carlos even know the word? I have never heard him make a single admission. What did he feel on his maiden voyage when HMS Beagle crossed the equator and he was blindfolded prior to the water trial? Not a mention of a pricking in his skin or a racing pulse.

If Rico has not been deported to Montevideo, there are only two other alternatives. Either he has been killed like mine host behind the bar counter, or he is being tortured at this very moment. Why should he not give me away? By supplying my name he would gain temporary relief. Our friendship is new. We have not known each other long. We are not related. Why should he care about me? We became better acquainted in the tunnel, but not so well that I could have any expectations of him. We forged no bonds that might hinder him from sacrificing me for a cup of water.

How can I think such a thing of Rico?

I place my hand over my mouth. I breathe.

How we have laughed together!

All the things we would have done had we been rich: each buy his own coach and four. We would have had two coachmen. Our progress would have made its way to the most expensive outfitters in Buenos Ayres. We would have bought ten suits of clothes apiece and paid double for each. If the assistants had been unable to find costumes that would have graced the court of Louis XIV, they would have had to employ tailors to make good the want. As we emerged from the shop we would have remarked on the coachmen's shabby attire. We would have halted at the best hotel in the city. Pulled up with our retinue outside the main entrance to the Grand and alighted from our coaches. The coachmen would have been ordered to detach one horse each. With an elegant leap each would have mounted his horse and ridden through the reception hall and into the dining room. The horses would each have been given their own trough of fine French wine. Before the terrified waiters and foaming maître d'hôtel had had time to protest they would have been ordered to provide four cases of champagne and two hundredweight of beef for the rest of the entourage outside. And just as the maître d'hôtel was about to call for the police, we would have placed a wad of notes on the damask tablecloth, and he would have smiled the falsest of all smiles!

Out in the streets water-carts are everywhere. The water in the Río de la Plata is not particularly salty. Its taste is abominable. Most water-sellers try to palm off the bad, brackish water from the marshes around the city on to their customers, if they do not take it direct from the Río de la Plata. The water-carts have two enormous wheels. Their diameter is nearly three yards. Two oxen draw the heavy cart. The water-seller sits on a yoke between the horns of the oxen. A wooden barrel is mounted on the cart. A bell warns of the approach of the equipage. "Sole! Sole!" shouts the water-seller. I have never been able to imagine an ox could wear an expression of pain. It is difficult to see their legs in the muddy streets. Their huge heads are even more noticeable because of this. When the enormous animals struggle through the streets of San Telmo, their heads resemble great tubers moving slowly through the intestines of the city. Each cart has its saint fixed to the barrel on a pole. The saint I have observed most frequently in the city is Santa Maria de los Buenos Ayres. This Virgin of the Good Air is the patron saint of seamen. What do the oxen feel as they drag themselves past the beautiful, white brick Post Office with its yellow and green wooden doors on the corner of Carlos Calvo and Reconquista? What do they think when they inadvertently turn their heads towards the Post Office's facade and the whip begins to crack? A second's distraction can overturn the entire load.

Yesterday I followed just such a cart to Parque Argentino, where there was to be a concert. I stopped. I heard the first notes sound from the instruments. My senses were whetted. The repertoire included someone by the name of Haydn and this

Beethoven again. Immediately the concert had started, the conductor had to acknowledge, somewhat unwillingly, that the wind had risen so much that it was causing the musicians problems. The violins noticed the wind first, then the violas and finally the double basses. The rest of the orchestra could certainly have kept going longer. The drums longest of all. The conductor realized, after several glances in the string players' direction, that it was only the wind that was desecrating Haydn. The wind was from the southwest. Everyone in the city, especially the oxen and water-sellers, knows this will cause the water in the Río de la Plata to rise. It usually takes a day or two for the wind to back easterly again. But before that happens, the water level may have risen several yards. The streets and roads become impassable. The conductor urged his audience to return home. Home? The light taps of the baton on the stand and the conductor's forceful appeal made me painfully aware that I had no home, in contrast to the rest of the audience, who were sitting on seats they had paid handsomely for. Like me, the water-seller kept to the fringes of the park so that he could enjoy the concert without paying. I did not recognize any faces amongst the audience. In order to get back to the tunnel unnoticed, I had to take a detour through San Telmo and La Boca. In the harbor lay the schooner Sarandi and the frigates Hercules and 25 de Mayo together with other men-of-war. When I worked at the shipyard I had become acquainted with the strengths and weaknesses of schooners and frigates. The long detour round the city center and the fort with its forty cannons, seven hundred soldiers and two thousand regular militia men, reminded me that my refuge is alarmingly close to the musket muzzles of authority.

Imagine if but one of their lackeys had entertained a suspicion that I had been so close to altering the history and lives of the people of this city!

Soon there will be nothing else for us to inhale but fear.

When I got back, I was met by a fond and highly contented Bozzo. He was clearly replete. I had no wish to speculate more closely on how the animal had managed to satisfy its almost limitless appetite. I have enough problems with my own. My bolt-hole is not damaged by tidal fluctuation. It is also affords me a view of the fort and the churches behind it: San Francisco and San Domingo. I lay down

and looked up at the starry sky: the stars, those se-
ducers that leave certainty so infinitely far away,
while dreams draw near. In a state between sleeping
and waking in which I could either have vanished
into a nightmare or become conscious of my own
body, I heard dogs barking outside the tunnel. I leapt
up. For a moment I thought they had come to arrest me. The dogs were barking because they had
found another of their ilk. Bozzo had been detected.
He returned the barking. But without much enthusiasm. Bozzo was satiated and his master wanted
peace and quiet. This was barked about a good deal.

I have read, unfortunately, that from ancient times
the dog has been regarded as the companion of the
dead and as the messenger between Heaven and
Hell. While Bozzo barked and I tossed and turned
hoping the mangy curs would stop, I tried to recall
other characteristics of the dog. In Norse mythol-
ogy, the entrance to the netherworld is guarded by
the dog, Garm. The dog's faithfulness also induces
it to follow its master after he dies and help him
make himself known to the dead and the divinities
of the netherworld. The notion that I would not be
rid of Bozzo after my death made me think: what
would happen if I died in here? Bozzo would be the
first to discover it. Bozzo would be the first to smell

that I was no longer alive. He would circle me a few times before plucking up courage to prod my foot with his snout. After a few unanswered prods he would approach my head. With his nose, he would first smell and then touch my cheek. The cold skin would stiffen his resolve. A perseverance mixed with a certain piety would make him use his nose, head, mouth and paws to try to raise my head and limbs.

The growing stiffness, caused by the interrupted processes in the muscle tissue, would irritate him. The disfiguring hypostasis would not worry him initially. But decomposition itself? Bozzo would re-act with anger or despair.

I usually lie on my back. The spinal column is probably one of the first parts of the fetus to be formed. And then, a few years later, everything turns dust or ashes and re-enters the world's physical cycle. Special thanks to the flies! Without them we would drown in filth. Think of all the leaves that must be broken down into mold. No, Bozzo! My death is my own. Nor does my death belong to those who murder or execute me. Nor the pain. The pain is my own. No one can take it from me.

Roberto! All our prejudices about death fit us for life. Don Carlos told me of an English philosopher by the name of Jeremy Bentham. In his will he insisted on being dissected. Bentham was dismembered in 1832, when Don Carlos came to Buenos Ayres for the first time. Until Bentham came under the knife, it was only convicts, cripples and prostitutes who were dissected. The rich of Buenos Ayres put locks on their mausoleums in Recoleta. They fear body-snatchers will sell the corpses to the pathologists. It is good that robbers can benefit from the vanity of the rich.

I cannot help being irritated by my continual brooding about whether there was something wrong with the arsenic I stole.

You know the saying about death being a great leveler. It is not true. Death is not equal. As long as one has the least control over one's life, one will have over one's death. Largely thanks to Rico, I have turned my body into an instrument against death and terror. My reward is a sudden death.

In this context suicide is a self-centered vulgarity. A death that weighs no more than a feather, a death to gladden every foolish tyrant.

Those confounded dogs have been here two nights in a row. I lie in my newly purchased suit. It is made of expensive linen. The money Don Carlos forwarded so that I would send him the glyptodont skull was originally intended for a suit, but I did not manage to buy one before the money had gone. Rico paid for this bottle-green suit. You are wondering, naturally, how Rico could afford it?

The blanket I lie on, the small carpenter's bag of letters, and the suit are my only possessions. The suit is my armor. No one, from a distance at any rate, would guess my condition. The suit is generously cut and double-breasted. I have become emaciated. I weigh about eight and a half stone. My height is still five feet eleven. My hair is almost white. My breeches flap about my wooden leg like a fluttering sail. When I take off my suit to assume my begging costume I see how thin I have become. The attire I use in my new profession is identical to my underwear. At night I always sleep in my suit, in case I am taken by surprise. My plan is to play a bewildered Englishman who has lost his way. My English is not perfect but good enough, I hope, to create the confusion that can make the difference between life and death. To keep my breeches pressed I use two planks I found on the shore. So far the driftwood has done its job. Believe me, Roberto, in my suit you could practically take me for a venerable gentleman.

Despite the fact that Rosas is officially a nationalist, he has tried to maintain an amicable facade vis-à-vis the British contingent in the city. Thus far. Over recent months the secret police and soldiers have clearly been given instructions to act with discretion in dealing with Britons. Rosas needs British credit. International relations have come to my rescue! Tyranny's doubt may be my salvation. Do not give me all that nonsense about my being a pessimist by nature! Unlike Don Carlos, I have no anxieties about whether I shall end up in Heaven or Hell. At this moment the fear that causes millions of people such problems, is about as important as an empty closet. In contrast to you, dear brother, I am also relieved of the worry of whether I shall be roasted, boiled, grilled, steamed or smoked in Hell. It may be just as lonely in Heaven as it is on Earth. I do not let myself be fooled by the clear air and white clouds. Just now I am glad I do not share the fears that you and Don Carlos entertain. There are advantages to living unnoticed by God.

In New South Wales in Australia, Don Carlos

came across an ant-lion that caught its prey just as predatory insects in other parts of the world do. For Don Carlos this was the great affirmation. One and the same hand had been active across the entire universe. All things had not been created simultaneously, in the same place. The Creator had indeed needed a rest.

Why is it so important to prove God's existence? Can he really make a difference? I shall not forget Don Carlos' pathetic anxiety about Noah's ark. According to the Bible it was a hundred and sixty yards long, twenty-five wide and fifteen yards high. On board Noah was supposed to have seven pairs of all clean beasts, ruminants and cloven-hoofed animals amongst them, and only one pair of all animals that were not clean, for example hares and badgers. Of the fowls of the air he was to take seven pairs of every sort and just one pair of all creeping things. Was it not so? But nowadays, Roberto, the naturalists know of a thousand species of mammal, six or seven thousand species of bird and fifteen hundred species of reptile. So the new species must presumably have emerged after the Great Flood? Am I giving you these figures in order to shake your faith? Far from it. I am merely declaring that I am spared such anxieties. I hate people's pettiness in being unable to admit that life has its brighter sides too. These godly misgivings are merely a derivative of the greatest of all misgivings: man.

Roberto. Roberto! I am trying to catch a glimpse of you. Do you remember the way mother would preach at us about not looking too closely at prints of Michelangelo Merisi da Caravaggio's paintings? Mother said he was a heretic. I used to think this was because Caravaggio used a drowned prostitute as a model for the dead Virgin Mary. But it was not mere moral indignation, Roberto. Worse was the fact that the picture portrays the Virgin Mary as a woman of the people. She is dressed in the way the poor clothe their dead. The mourners grieve like the poor grieve. When Caravaggio painted the death of Jesus Christ, he painted a corpse. Caravaggio was branded a heretic because he shows us man. The self-same man who can die when he lies down to sleep. I shall not forget how indignant you were when, at some point in our youth, I told you that if one swapped a newly born infant immediately after birth, its mother would not notice. She would suckle the child and bring it up as if it was her own. The maternal instinct, which in this case was supposed to be peculiar to human beings, is of course no stronger in us than in sheep. When Caravaggio painted the Virgin Mary as a human being, he painted her just like any other mammal.

Roberto. Last night I thought I heard Rico's voice in the tunnel. I awoke with a start. I sweated. You think, perhaps, that I am hiding the fact that I have got gangrene again. It would not be surprising if gangrene were to flare up once more. In a fit of sympathy you would hardly ask such delicate questions because they might appear to be tempting providence. A heart attack, on the other hand, is a splendid mechanical defect. To have a condition that aroused sympathy! If only I could have suffered a heart attack! Gangrene and cancer are, by contrast, merely the miserable consumption of bits of the body.

I cough. Gently at first. Then harder. In the end violently. Slowly it subsides. I catch my breath. I breathe normally. Then I begin to cough. Gently at first. Then harder. In the end violently. This cycle repeats itself hour after hour. I notice I grow pale, a state which is then superseded by an intense flush all over my body. It is as if I feel and perceive everything with an extra vividness for the time being. I alternate between euphoria, increased appetite and ardent sexual desire. I am not more of a fool than I realize my flushed skin is caused by fever and my sexual appetite may be a portent of imminent death. You have surely already guessed. I have consumption. I remember the first time I met the poet Esteban de Lucca. I had expected a poet to be a consumptive weighing some six stone. When he turned out to be a powerfully built man, I asked sceptically: "Are you the poet Esteban de Lucca?" I had never met a poet before. I cannot remember if it was just prior to, or just after, my first encounter with Esteban de Lucca that I became persuaded that optimism for the future was meaningless. We human beings have too much influence over it.

I have had no news of Rico. Why have none of our fellow conspirators instructed me on how I should proceed? Are they not frightened I shall betray them?

Roberto! On one occasion I was really surprised at Rico. I had invited him to the barber shop of Alfredo, an old acquaintance of mine. Rico was sceptical. The secret police have infiltrated the majority of barbers' shops. Unlike me, Rico is very careful about his appearance. He almost seems to have constant consideration for the work the undertaker will have to do. He is tall, dark and muscular. His eyes are grey. Most women would consider him a handsome man. I patronize this particular barber shop because the proprietor is pleasant to talk to. Those warm towels about the throat temporarily soothe the neck, throat and head.

I am never reminded of how much I owe.

I wanted to please Rico with a serene and pleasant experience. The previous day I had spoken to Alfredo.

"May I bring along a friend of mine?"

"Of course."

"Can you treat the whole thing with a little circumspection?"

"Yes, don't worry."

I trusted Alfredo.

I managed to persuade a reluctant Rico.

"Alfredo can be trusted," I repeated.

The next day we went to the shop. There was a customer in one chair. Alfredo was not to be seen. It was too late to turn back. A man I had never seen before emerged from behind the curtain. I backed away. Rico sensed my uneasiness.

"Alfredo told me to expect you both."

"Who are you?" I asked.

I cleared my throat. I gulped. I looked round the premises. The razors, shaving brushes, cloths, towels, pomade, powder, perfume, everything in its usual place. Even the small scalpels were there. Minor surgical operations such as the lancing of boils and removal of birthmarks were carried out here at reasonable cost.

"My name is Leopold Carmel. Don't be uneasy. Alfredo had an attack of lumbago early this morning. He asked me to attend to you. As soon as I've finished, I'll lock up the shop."

I looked at Rico. Rico was looking in another direction. He said nothing. He was backing, almost imperceptibly, towards the door.

"How can I trust you?" I said in a voice I did not think sounded desperate.

"I have a letter from Alfredo."

He handed me a letter that confirmed his story. I recognized Alfredo's handwriting. I showed the letter to Rico. I dared not look him in the eyes. I was the one who had got him into this situation. Whether I had done it unwittingly or not was beside the point! It was a matter of life or death. Rico nodded.

"Do me first," said Rico.

"With pleasure," said the man. He locked the door

and hung up Alfredo's handwritten "closed" sign.

Rico seated himself in the chair. He leaned back. He closed his eyes.

Carmel took off Rico's shoes. His feet were placed in a basin of hot water.

"Thank you," said Rico. He did not open his eyes.

I studied his face minutely. He appeared completely composed. The thought that we might nevertheless have been lured into a trap, must have been occupying him as he sat there. He breathed calmly. Was he about to fall asleep? Was he squinting from beneath one eyelid when he was not being observed? Lack of sleep and months of constant danger had not even given him bags under his eyes. He had become thinner, that was all. Our silence unfortunately beguiled the barber into talking too much. He was the type who knew about everything. Leopold Carmel is the kind of representative of his craft who makes one wonder why every country in the world is not ruled by barbers.

Carmel talked and Rico kept his eyes closed. He had a small bump on his left cheek. It was the only irregularity to be seen. Was his apparent calm an expression of resignation? If the shop were surrounded we would have no chance. I looked out. Everything seemed quiet. Just then I realized how hungry I was. I refuse to die of hunger. I had to have food, in my mouth, past my gullet, down my throat, mixed with saliva into my stomach, through my small intestine, and its villi, before the waste is forced out of my rectum. To be able to squeeze out feces is to be alive.

"Shall I remove it for you?" Carmel asked suddenly.

Rico snapped out of his doze as if the barber had shot at him.

Carmel pointed at the little protrusion with one of his smallest scalpels.

"Just one cut and I can rid you of that lump."

"Don't touch it!"

Rico got up from the chair. It looked as if he were about to strangle the barber. Carmel stammered: "It's my specialty."

"Go to hell!" Rico hissed.

I jumped up. I threw myself at Rico. I managed to grasp his right hand, which was trying to get a grip round Carmel's throat. Rico squeezed. The barber's eyes bulged. He could not make a sound. The orifices in the mulatto face struggled to take in air.

Rico bent him over backwards.

He struggled to get out of the hold.

Carmel's arms thrashed about before dangling limp. Rico was in the process of killing him.

I slapped him.

At length he released his grip.

"I can't abide knives," Rico said. He cleared his throat. He panted. With a great effort Carmel got to his feet.

We walked to the door.

"Payment . . . ?" Carmel stuttered, "the boss said . . ."

"Farewell," I said.

Unshaven we walked out into the street. It was the siesta. No one was about. I have not been to that quarter of the city since.

Roberto, I can recall that episode as if it were yesterday. I catch myself smiling!

So Rico did have a weak point. It is possible I feel fear mixed with pleasure. I do not know.

I am still smiling! I am laughing! I am roaring with laughter. I let the laughter well up from my throat. It is a torrent! The muscles of my face are moving. Uncontrollable sounds burst from my mouth. My head tilts backwards. I fall off my chair. What is happening?

I cannot bear to think of Rico now.

Good brother, suppose you and Don Carlos could have kept one secret from God. May one ask what you would have done in that circumstance? But my glee is borne of something else. In contrast to you both, I can keep as many secrets from God as I wish. But religion has its uses: it counteracts suicide. Had there been too much suicide, the act would have resembled a common-or-garden war and thus lost its horror. Although suicide also has its thrilling aspects. A sweetness, a pleasure, an embrace. To slip into the water, sink, get taken by the tide in the Río de la Plata, attempt one last breath, a few seconds and then time seeping slowly out of one's body to remain behind.

I think of Rico. I think of my coming fate. One may stick a pin through a fly without killing it. Then one can lift the pin and study the tiny legs and wings moving. It is Rosas who has me on a pin. That Napoleonic poodle of a despot. His instrument is the secret police. Rosas is aroused only by suspicions. Not facts. Facts may have far worse consequences, but while he continues to entertain a suspicion, it is that, and only that idea he fosters. As soon as a fact corroborates a suspicion he becomes calm. Recently he has been frantically worried about being poisoned. When, one afternoon, it was proved that his soup had been poisoned, the gaucho felt much better. The fact that he had lost one of his favorite dogs during the tasting, affected him not one jot. His suspicion was justified. Harmony was re-established in the dictator's mind. One of the last occasions 1 saw Rosas was on the tribune of honor outside the Cabildo. They were celebrating some anniversary connected with the assumption of power. If one had not been present, it would quickly have been noted. Rosas appeared unmoved by the tribute. Rosas is only forty. I studied the officers standing around him. I noticed one of the very youngest. It was his paleness that caught my attention. He was several years younger than Rosas. He had a weak face. He did not speak. The others appeared to be extolling the dictator's vigor and qualities as a leader. The young officer's wanness and silence suggested great intensity. Something told me Rosas noticed this young man. His qualities might be decisive in a critical situation. If handled correctly, his intensity might unleash resoluteness and energy. I tried to imagine what Rosas was thinking. Rosas spoke as little as this youngest officer. A few days later I discovered his name was Enrique Velasques.

The people standing closest to Rosas looked like

cattle going to the slaughter. They would more than willingly have offered their hearts to Rosas and the nation. The only one out of the fifteen on the tribune who, in common with the young officer, did not look a miserable fool, was General Roca. Roca had been Rosas' right-hand man for several years. One of the older ones appeared to have Indian blood in him. Before the Spaniards arrived, the Tehuelches were the largest Indian tribe in Argentina. Today they are virtually extinct, apart from this bewildered progeny which, for reasons unknown, had ended up on the tribune of honor. The tribune was filled with the highest echelons of the army and the secret police. I was looking at authority. It was a hot day in February. Authority sunbathed in the country's most important plaza. A regime at the top can climb no further. Is the dictator's mistrustfulness his best defense? He has not a single moral scruple when it comes to torture and murder.

Rosas allowed his eyes to alight on the shortest of the officers who strove for his attention. That medal-festooned status seeker possessed a fat head. Gusts of wind revealed that his legs were too thin for his voluminous torso. His gesticulating arms made the strain on his legs worse. Why had Rosas allowed attention to fall on this of all his officers? A vast number of words issued from the officer's mouth. Rosas did not answer. For a moment I thought that Rosas was asleep on his feet, like one of his many horses. Rosas said not a word. Occasionally he blinked, but his glance never wavered from the gesticulating officer. It is possible that the officer's low stature suited Rosas. Lying down and closing his eyes would have attracted an inconveniently large amount of attention from the others on the tribune of honor, not to mention the lifeguards directly below it. By turning his head to this particular officer, he could rest his eyes without closing them. Had he chosen another officer with a higher eye-level, he might have risked seeing a line of distracting eyes in the background, all begging for attention. They would be like dogs' eyes when the butcher appears in his shop doorway with some beef. The short officer tugged continually at his uniform tunic, presumably to reassure himself that the colorful jacket sat properly. The increasingly nervous action eventually began to look like a spasm over which he had no control. It was not the quality of the uniform that was transmitted to the onlookers, but the officer's singular physique. All of a sudden he took a couple of paces backwards. He fell over the balustrade.

A parrot with clipped wings can lose its balance.

Rosas' head did not stir an inch. Enrique Velasques rushed up and got hold of the screeching head's thin legs and hauled him up into a standing position. The short man gawped at Rosas like a sheep with a hammer in its skull. Rosas turned. Without a word he went to the other side of the tribune of honor. He turned his head to the cheering mob. The crowd was so large and far away that he could stand undisturbed with his own thoughts. He scratched his head. The two nearest to him scratched their heads. He smoothed back his hair. The two smoothed their hair.

If Rosas had had the chance to read Don Carlos' description of the prehistoric armadillo, the glyptodont, it might possibly have captured his imagination for a few moments. Rosas would have found it alluring. I shall not pretend that I have not caught myself thinking of the glyptodont in my circumstances. At such moments I feel mildly irritated with myself for getting rid of the glyptodont skull. Don Carlos' sketch of the creature in his letter is more than enough to fantasize over. According to Henslow's and Don Carlos' calculations the glyptodont must have been well over three yards long. Its body armor was in one piece like that of a tortoise. Its tail, which protruded from beneath its armor, was like a spiked mace, a weapon that when swung would have killed a horse or a bull with one blow. The glyptodont was devoid of all thoughts that might delay or disturb its ability to respond. This creature was spared any meditation that might give rise to doubt and afford the enemy a chance to attack. The glyptodont had a perfect body and an ideal level of consciousness: none. Neither morals, religion nor conscience troubled the beast. The first creature to be given a consciousness must truly have understood what it was to be alone. That man would not be the last, but the most lonely individual ever to have lived. Have I at last understood why Rosas has built up a private zoo? Is that where he will plan how to control the human animals in the zoo that is Buenos Ayres?

What joy to be able to witness that man heave his last sigh.

Don Carlos' naïveté disgusts me. The man's folly knows no bounds. One of HMS Beagle's tasks was to return three natives to Tierra del Fuego, the Land of Fire. The previous year Robert FitzRoy had taken York Minster, Jemmy Button and Fuegia Basket to England to learn genteel manners. When the Beagle crew set them ashore again in 1833 they were eager to see how the three would fare. They were dressed like wealthy English youths. In March, 1834, Robert FitzRoy's crew returned to see what had happened. The huts were undamaged and empty. The gardens the crew had laid out had been trampled. In the earth they found the remains of the turnips and potatoes they had planted. So it was possible to grow vegetables in these regions. There was not a soul to be seen. The huts had clearly been empty for several months. Don Carlos and the crew feared the worst. Suddenly three canoes hove into sight. They came from a small island not far off. Through his spyglass, Don Carlos could see two of the natives washing their faces. The others were paddling as fast as they could. There, clearly visible through the glass, was Tommy Button, Jemmy's brother. In the other canoe he saw someone he seemed to know, but could not recognize. It was Jemmy! Not a shred of his English clothing remained. He was wearing some skin about his loins, but apart from that he was as naked as his companions. His hair was long and unkempt. He was thin and red-eyed. Don Carlos got Jemmy to come below deck. Their reunion was cordial. After Jemmy had been given some clothes to wear, he and Don Carlos had dinner in the stateroom. Jemmy ate with a knife and fork. Don Carlos asked Jemmy why they did not first eat their dogs before consuming human flesh.

"Could Grandma catch sea otters?"

Jemmy spoke English like a gentleman. He was particularly pleased to be reunited with Mr Bynoe and James Bennett. It was strange and tragic as far as Don Carlos was concerned that Jemmy would not change his way of life. Jemmy would not leave with the Beagle, and he certainly would not dress as an Englishman again. York and Fuegia were still nowhere to be seen. Captain Robert FitzRoy's social experiment had been a failure. For Don Carlos, the entire story of the three natives is a riddle.

Jemmy had lived by hunting and fishing with his tribal kinsmen using Stone Age implements. Then Robert FitzRoy sent him to an English boarding school for a year, before he was returned to his relations. A year later the Englishmen returned. Jemmy adjusted once again to their language and table manners.

Jemmy Button is no phenomenon. He is a typical human being. In the course of his five-year voyage round the world, Don Carlos has adjusted time and again in order to be accepted in ever-changing groups and communities. He adapts in any way required.

Roberto, I should know what I am talking about. Chance determines whether we are born in the Land of Fire, Varazze or Shrewsbury. The people about us dictate whether we eat with our hands or use a knife and fork. This human trait is understood by all military leaders. Any peace-loving person with no arms' training can make himself kill and pillage. Man is the most flexible of all mammals. Man's ability to adjust is limitless. Is it not so?

Has man the right to make himself superior? Why should we occupy a unique position above all others?

Have you never asked yourself why people are so fond of young children, especially babies? One might imagine their appeal lies in their beauty, smiles, laughter and trustfulness. Anything to avoid speaking the honest truth! Babies are particularly liked because they cannot contradict. That is why we talk to them. We can ascribe to them all the dreams and human characteristics we like. Dogs can satisfy some of these needs. The mere thought that Bozzo . . . No.

★ ★

Roberto! The day before yesterday as I walked through the streets on my way to the library I had an uncomfortable feeling. I had the growing sense that as soon as I got within those august doors I would be stunned by something I would see or hear. Do not ask me why. Despite this unpleasant feeling I walked resolutely towards the library. The more I pondered it, the more the presentiment in my consciousness became a certainty. After several minutes' cogitation there was not the slightest doubt.

I tried to feel happy that I can still walk with a wooden leg. I repeated to myself that I weigh just over eight stone and am five feet eleven inches in height. The distribution of my flesh and bones is what makes me a human being. The juxtaposition of my internal organs emphasizes my constitution. According to the physicians, pigs and men have surprisingly similar kidneys. But the ability to be tortured by one's consciousness is man's alone.

What I see about me is enforced silence.

The dictatorship has brought a hush to the streets. It reminds me of the plague. I deeply mistrust this silence. Just at the times when it is difficult to imagine a greater quiet, the noise of the city and its people is something being stored up. Silence possesses an inherent noise which one does not hear at first, in the same way winter's cold tries, year by year, to suppress our notion of the buds' ability to blossom.

Who has faith in the jacaranda tree's buds when autumn winds chill the air? Who has faith in the jacaranda tree's blue buds when the leaves rustle and the colors of the city have faded? Who has faith in the jacaranda tree's buds when all color has been swept away without a smidgen of piety or respect? I walked, without a single detour, in the direction of the library.

The afternoon closed in monotonously around me. Grey clouds scurried over the city, without bringing rain. Suddenly I no longer knew where to direct my thoughts. I stopped walking because I stopped walking. Not far from Calle San Nicolás I heard a plaintive song. An Indian was singing without looking at the passersby. His gaze was fixed on a lamppost. It was a beautiful lamppost of wrought ironwork right up to the globe. Those who stopped seemed to show a moment's interest in ascertaining whether the man was blind or not. Once they had registered the fact he could see, they assumed an unsympathetic look. The singer seemed to want to address the whole of mankind, on behalf of an extinct race or a forgotten language. Suddenly his song ceased. It seemed as if the Indian had spotted an abnormal eddy in the human sea around him. He had patently seen something that frightened him. Everything happened in a split second. I saw four hands reach out for him. There was a stir in the surrounding crowd. The two men who were trying to grab him were dressed in civilian clothes. Their attempts to reach out for their prey caused two ripples in the crowd. A whispered word everyone understood sounded like the crack of a whip: mazorca. The secret police. The lone singer had detected their way of watching and moving, just like a small fish notices the shadow of a shark. He fled with the couple at his heels, and even though he had several yards' start, I knew how it would end.

It is not always spring.

Suddenly the sun began to shine. I did not feel inclined to enjoy it. The sky above the harbor seemed to be cloudless.

I had been standing still during the entire incident. I started to walk towards the library as soon as the three had disappeared from sight. My feet steered me as purposefully as my heart opened and closed. My steps were as methodical as the empire-building of the world's leading nations.

It takes little to make me feel happy and content as a rule. I recall that I found myself smiling almost immediately after this episode. Sometimes I feel I must greet people I think I recognize. As I pass I see it is some cabinet minister in everyday clothes. I just manage to prevent myself from committing a blunder. Fortunately, I do not have to walk many yards before I realize that my presence is necessary to allay suspicion. Anonymity is a prerequisite of survival.

A face passed by. Who was that? I had seen him before, but when? Ah yes, it was the man who had recently taken over the bar in San Telmo whose owner had been executed right before my eyes. Well, well, so this was the man who had got the vacant job. They say he is married, where and with whom I have no idea. His surname is Fontana. He has three children, he never asks questions. There was a situation vacant, he got the job. He neither gambles nor drinks. He serves quickly and accurately. Perhaps he takes his family on a Sunday outing to La Plata, but he would never dream of traveling to Córdoba. And he would quite definitely never venture outside Buenos Ayres province. It takes quite a lot of intelligence to practice monotony at an advanced level. Each time he reaches across the counter or serves at the small tables, he does it with a friendliness I take for self-righteousness. I must suppress this thought. This man, I must say to myself, is simply a more intelligent man than I. He is a more perfect practitioner of classical, human monotony. Boredom is not planned. It is based on chance and coincidence. Monotony is something one can only achieve through planning or control, or fear.

Adaptation is a product of intelligence. Those who possess nothing more than the ability to be bored will ask what point there is to monotony. There is no reason to fret over these people's foolishness. They have a need for rational explanations about everything in life. What on earth do they need a consciousness for?

Fontana's ability to adapt to a monotonous life enables him to be a man. The ideal city-dweller, as if made to serve the dictatorship. A man who knows how to use his consciousness in such a way must have a highly developed intelligence. He fashions such a stereotyped existence that a common-or-garden fight in Carlos Calvo seems like a boxing match with all of the South American continent's greatest boxers in the ring at once.

That is the way to do it!

An intelligent man has just passed me by.

I have sunk into a sentimental reverie. Viewed in isolation, there is nothing wrong with this kind of thought. Definitely not. I stood in need of any soothing thought precisely because I knew what was in store for me at the library.

But I lack the ability to take pleasure in sentimental thoughts. To show you that I have tried, I shall give an example: I pretended it was Sunday. A tranquil Sunday. I tried to pretend it was one big Sunday inside me. I heard church bells. I let my heart go to church, Roberto. With quick, light steps my heart walked out to church. But, and this was where my thought stranded, my heart did not know where the church was.

In the harbor quarter near the Richuelo and La Boca, it is considerably quieter than in the city center. In the afternoon the wharfs on the Río de la Plata are as devoid of life as straight, bare branches in autumn.

Roberto.

Reason has imposed a lonely thought upon us: the consciousness of being conscious. We are not able to ask ourselves if consciousness has any meaning. Soon the seasons will be the only things that have meaning for me. The changes and the renewals. The seasons are life. The weather, the flowers and the trees are the seasons' signatures. Take the trees: the jacaranda's flowering in both autumn and spring. This has given it a special status here in the city. The palo baracha, the cotton-tree, flowers in late summer in February. The garabato tree, with its clusters of beautiful yellow flowers, blooms right after the jacaranda in parks and gardens. The alagrop tree with its yellow flowers and the paraiso tree's lilac blooms do not, perhaps, dominate the city scene like the other trees, but they are present and give character to the city, and since the city will soon be the only thing my eyes will be capable of seeing, they give me my own identity.

The umbu, that giant amongst trees, with the largest branches I have ever seen. The eucalyptus which los indios often used to cure fever. This green provides the relief for the sky, the walls of the houses, the cobbles and the muddy roads all year round. Even in winter the umbu is green.

The flowers, I must not forget to mention the flowers: the roses are open for much of the year. And autumn's flower, the gladiolus, violet, pink and yellow. The azaleas, white, blue and red. The red, I prefer the red, the flower of summer; and the marguerites with their yellow pupils and the violets, white, blue, yellow, red, violet, mauve, pink, pale red, indigo and orange. Why have I forgotten the lavender? Almost every two-story house in San Telmo has a lavender on its balcony.

The city has its wild flowers, too. Here I can see creepers with light blue, white-eyed flowers. And that is not all, the plant also produces a yellow fruit that resembles a melon. And there is the lovely ceiba, a red wild flower which, like the cardo, is bushier and has thorns. The cardo's flowers are mauve, but this plant also manages to bear a yellow fruit that is eaten by the Indians.

The trees, the flowers and their fragrances, their colors, their sounds, all is change and renewal within my horizon. These impressions, tabulated by consciousness every year, remind me that some things around me can be beautiful.

In Calle Bolívar I was irritated by the people walking about with an expression of dumb contentment. Why do they not dare display anything else? I was immediately pacified by the sight of people going to mass at the church of St Ignatius at the intersection of Alsina and Bolívar.

Not far off stood a greengrocer next to a barrowful of cabbage heads. They were unwashed. He wore a gaping expression. He looked at me. I looked at him. He looked away. I looked at him. He looked at me again. I looked at him. He looked away. He fixed his gaze on the dirty cabbages. I looked at him. He looked at me again. I looked at him. He cast his eyes down. Not before time. What drove him to this offensive molestation? Had he never seen a man with a wooden leg? It was not that. The elegant suit? It was not that. Deserving though it was of anyone's notice. Did he recognize me from the shipyard, the night life in La Boca, or had he been in the bar that ghastly evening? Had he some notion of what would greet me in a few minutes' time?

His black hair and beard seemed to cover a pale, immature face in its mid-thirties. The face told me that his greatest talent was informing. The clumsy movements, the hesitant grasp on the cabbages, all spoke to me of a man who had placed himself in Calle Bolívar from quite other motives than to sell cabbages.

I halted. I crossed over to him. I felt my heart pounding. I saw he was surprised. I saw he was frightened. I was about to open my mouth. I noticed he took a small, almost imperceptible step back.

I asked: "Do you know what the word sarcasm means?"

"No," he answered.

"It means biting scorn."

273

"What?" he said.

"Sarcasm comes from the Greek word sarkazein," I said.

"I see," he said.

"Sarkazein means to tear flesh or grind one's teeth," I said. "And I feel a growing desire to cast a sarcasm in your face."

He took two steps back.

"But now I've changed my mind," I said.

He watched me with listless brown eyes. If I had had some caustic solution to hand I would have rubbed it straight into them.

"What is it you want?" he asked. I noticed he was looking about for help.

"I just want you to hold up one of your cabbages so that I can decide whether to buy it."

Hesitantly, he lifted one of them, wiping it awkwardly. I studied the filthy cabbage thoroughly. He turned it a couple of times. I asked, trying all the while to prevent myself from striking him: "May I feel it?"

He looked about him once more. I rejoiced in his discomfiture. Reluctantly he handed over the dirty cabbage. Slowly, I drew two eyes, a nose and a line for a mouth on it.

"I must say I'm relieved," I said to the greengrocer.

"Why?" he asked.

"For a moment I wasn't sure if it was cabbage heads or heads of something else you had in your barrow."

He looked down. I was content. My recklessness had grown as I studied the miserable creature in front of me, whose accomplices were not close at hand.

Dear Roberto. There is a word I have not used up to now. It is the word contempt. Contempt for one's fellow man was something one was never supposed to have according to our religious upbringing. Today I would say that contempt is a necessary prerequisite for survival. The ass that stood before me was a man who earns money by informing to Rosas' murder squads. As I left him I had an impulse I would ascribe to a desire to live a few days longer. I said: "Thank you for an interesting conversation. Long live Rosas!"

I placed the money for a cabbage in his coat pocket and made off towards the library as fast as I could without looking back. How I should have loved to cast the words: "Look at me just once more! I'm quite capable of murder," into that cowardly, gaping face!

When I realized I had forgotten my cabbage I

simply kept walking doggedly on towards the library. No sooner had I got inside the doors than I felt a pressure at my temples. I thought I could hear a high-pitched, irritating note that pressed against my ears. I raised my hands to my ears and covered them. No, it must have been my imagination. My mouth was dry. I walked slowly upstairs towards my usual seat. My left leg met each step first. I strained to pull up the right so that it would not look like I was dragging it along. Even now, when I knew my life was to alter drastically, I invested thought and energy in my conceit. Folly is insatiable. As soon as I got through the doors of the reading room, I saw it. The newspaper, El Telegrafo Mercantil, lay on one of the tables. Complete silence enveloped me. It was on the front page. I looked round to see if anyone had noted my arrival. Was anyone looking at me? What would have happened if I had rushed across to the table from where the front page of El Telegrafo Mercantil glared at me? I knew instinctively I must pretend to have more important errands in the reading room than gazing at the newspaper. After all, newspapers can be purchased in several places in the city center. I walked deliberately to the part of the room furthest away from the open newspaper. I stared fixedly at the shelves of books and ran my right index finger over the spines within reach, before pulling out the volume right in front of me. It is at moments like these I feel tempted to use those difficult words: here fate played a trick on me.

Roberto, you can tell from the ink smudge that my pen has stopped moving.

The book I took out was about St Peter's Church in Rome. I put the book under my arm and seated myself close to the newspaper without showing any obvious interest in the headline or the sketch beneath the newspaper's title.

I opened the book before me at random. I looked around to make certain I was not observed. The newspaper headline ran: "Arrested After Assassination Attempt on Rosas."

In the middle of the article there was a sketch of Rico. The portrait looked like him. Beneath it was printed Rico's year of birth. 1800. He was still under interrogation. From another part of the article I gathered that the police examination had been thorough on the point of ascertaining who else had conspired in the assassination attempt. It was impossible that he had attempted the crime alone. There was no mention of Rosas' condition.

For the benefit of the others in the reading room

I tried to display a deep interest in St Peter's Church. I noticed that my mouth hung open. My lower jaw had dropped without my realizing it. I felt my tongue lying motionless in my mouth. I felt the skin of my face turn cold. My palms were clammy. I began to sweat from the hairline. Blood was again draining from the body's outermost defense, the skin, and inwards to the main internal organs. My heart was pounding furiously. But still the blood left my head. My brain was receiving too little oxygen. There was a flickering before my eyes. I looked down at the book in front of me, without being able to read a single sentence. The only thing I registered was the elegant dome. The newspaper on the other side of the table was like a dimly defined rectangle in a distant haze.

I forced myself to remain sitting. I pinched my cheek, as discreetly as possible. I took deep breaths.

Roberto!

Is fear what keeps us alive?

Had I jumped up from my seat and dashed out, it would have been noticed immediately. The overseer would first have tried to hush me up and then asked what ailed me. After I had left, he would have tried to reconstruct everything I had done. He would hardly have thought I had suffered some religious scruple from studying the various cupola designs of St Peter's Church. The overseer's genius is to accept his role of loyal civil servant at the bottom of the hierarchy. A promotion might be a possibility after doing the mazorca a service. There is no passion stronger than that of the petty official for his post. He would recall every movement I had made in the room and finally inspect the newspaper's front page to see if I had done anything unusual. I had, at all costs, to remain seated at my place. I opened my carpenter's bag. I took out my papers with a calmness quite at odds with the turmoil inside me. It was a feigned calmness that made my movements slow. I looked around. The fear was still there, but my discreet reconnoitring was of a different character this time. I looked at the shelves, the beautiful books, the view of the umbu trees, the diligent students and researchers at the surrounding tables, even the rigid overseer conjured up something within me, something I would call sadness. I knew full well that shortly I would shut the book on St Peter's Church, put it back in its place and leave the reading room, go down the stairs and out of the doors on the ground floor. I knew that I should never return. I sat in a shaded room with the city outside. I should never return to the library where I had spent so many happy times. My body felt warm all over. My blood was evenly distributed once more. The facility to feel melancholy shower its soft rain on the mind depends on an existence that is free from the daily struggle for survival. Here in the library, with calm and apparent safety round me, I recalled the dejection that had haunted me several years ago. When I had had the chance to ponder the meaning of life. I missed it.

I believe in Utopia. There is nothing like the feeling of melancholy pervading the consciousness. I saw the letter from Don Carlos lying before me. He had written out a chronological list of the places HMS Beagle had dropped anchor before reaching the English coast.

> Cape Colony, 31st May - 18th June.
> St Helena, 8th July - 14th July.
> Ascension, 19th July - 23rd July.
> Bahía, 1st August - 6th August.
> Pernambuco, 12th August - 17th August.
> Cape Verde Islands, 31st August -
>   4th September.
> The Azores, 19th September -
>   25th September.

2nd October, 1836: England in sight.

These dates and places meant nothing to me. To Don Carlos they were stages in scientific discovery he believes will extend man's understanding and make us better people. Don Carlos was presumably the only person on the planet who enjoyed the earthquake in Chile on 20th February, 1835. The young whippersnapper did not witness the earthquake from afar. He was there. The tremor lasted two minutes and caused enormous damage. Don Carlos had just finished reading Charles Lyell's work on the history of the Earth's crust. He managed to keep his feet as he pondered that the thing he was now experiencing might provide him with a theory about how the Andes came into existence. No doubt he also remembered the Shrewsbury of his childhood, and the cold winter he had discovered how the ice could crack. This clinical faculty frightens me. Is it evil or an intelligent kind of monotony?

My meeting with Don Carlos was what caused me to make my first visit to the library. He had goaded me with his depraved stubbornness. I needed knowledge to put him in his place.

I decided to rid myself of the letter from Don

Carlos. I still had some of the money he had sent me.

I marveled at what he had written about his discovery on the Galapagos Islands. There, some birds were reportedly so tame that they did not move if stones were hurled at them. Even here in Buenos Ayres there are people, educated people, so servile and browbeaten that they cannot see the consequences of the cutting of their neighbor's throat.

In the Galapagos Islands, Don Carlos came across some giant land tortoises! Testudo Indicus. He found them, he writes, on higher ground, but also in dry lowland areas. The tortoises were in large numbers. Some specimens might contain six to eight hundredweight of meat. The males were the biggest. What had really excited his curiosity was that the tortoises were of differing shape and appearance. Don Carlos realized fairly quickly that this was associated with the island they inhabited and, even more importantly, how long and arduous their journey to reach water. The ones with the easiest journeys grew biggest. But what really caused the young Englishman problems was why the species, which he had to assume had been created on the Galapagos Islands, was so obviously related to the ones found in America.

There is a small section in Don Carlos' letter that almost smacks of humility! Believe me! He writes that he was dreading Professor Thomas Henslow's minute study of the notes made during the five years he spent sailing round the world in HMS Beagle. I cannot say if he was being coquettish or serious, but he said he feared the learned professor would shake his head. Had he done that, Don Carlos would have given up natural science before natural science gave him up.

I put the book about St Peter's Church neatly back in its place. I folded Don Carlos' letter carefully, before gathering up my own papers. In a fit of self-pity I suddenly wondered what use it was writing a letter I was not certain would ever be read. I imagined you throwing away the envelope behind a bush in the park, before going home to your family. Who is it I am writing to, when I cannot even see your face before me? I placed the letter in my bag, and picked up the letter from Don Carlos in my left hand. I got up and went. I endeavored to walk as if I had all the time in the world. On the stairs down to the main exit, I threw away the letter from Don Carlos. My luggage was lighter. I got out of the building. I turned the corner. I walked a few hundred yards without looking back. I was soon breathless. The breath rushed up and down my windpipe like a trolley in a mine-shaft. I turned. Was it possible?

"No," I said aloud to myself. A little hesitantly but with a certain triumph in my voice. No one was following me.

After a few minutes I began to think about the reference work on St Peter's Church which I should never study again. I recalled the time Father Razio got mother to talk father into taking the family to Rome to see St Peter's Church and the Vatican. Father did not have the money. To avoid offending the priest he saved up for an entire year so that half of us could go. Mother was an obvious choice as the Catholic church's most direct contact in the family. Father was working at the time, so he could not make the journey. But whether you or I was to go was undecided. I was the elder. Do you remember how ill I was? I had never had pneumonia before. You got to go. I was given some pictures of the city's coat of arms showing Romulus and Remus beneath the she-wolf after the two newly born infants had been washed up on the banks of the Tiber, according to the legend you and mother told me. Rome was to stand on the spot where the she-wolf and a shepherd had found the twins. Rome was built round the Palatine hills. The other picture you gave me, I remember, was a drawing of the Pope's lifeguards, the Swiss Guard, in their elegant uniforms. It was the first time I ever saw a drawing by Michelangelo. Were the uniforms yellow, blue and red?

Roberto. Several times you said you wanted to serve in the Pope's lifeguards. We had to disappoint you by saying you had not been born in Switzerland. Have you ever renounced that idea?

The third and final print I got was made up of two pictures. One was of the exterior of St Peter's with its imposing dome, and the other of the interior seen from the High Altar above St Peter's grave, enclosed by the chancel and crowned by the cupola's Heavenly Vault. At the cupola's apex were the words that confirmed St Peter as Christ's successor on Earth, and gave the Popes their guardianship of the gates of Heaven, and thus each individual priest his position and authority. Father Razio was not born yesterday. He knew what he was doing. I shall never forget the words on the cupola's apex:

"Tu es Petrus, et super hanc petram aedificabo Ecclesiam meam, et tibi dabo claves Regni Caelorum." I have not forgotten its meaning. It means: "Thou art Peter, and upon this rock I will build my church, and I will give unto thee the keys of the Kingdom of Heaven."

I walked a few yards further down the street. I halted. I turned cold inside. Had I forgotten to tear off the top portion of the letter where Don Carlos had written my name? If anyone began to ask questions about my last visit to the National Library, all the wastepaper-baskets would be thoroughly examined. They would bring them all in and empty them on a table, sift through every single object and sheet of paper. If they could not find anything of interest on first inspection, they would continue until they did. Let no one tell me that the reading room overseer would not do his utmost to make a discovery, small or large, to please the secret police. Proudly, he would produce the letter from Don Carlos and say: "This is the address of the man who was here less than an hour ago." He would begin to read it aloud in a raucous voice, though no one had asked him to, as if he were on the tribune of honor near the Cabildo in the Plaza de la Victoria on a sunlit Sunday, next to the country's topmost civil servant. After all the obligatory phrases he would shout out my name in his dusty voice: Giovanni Graciani, and then look at Juan Manuel de Rosas with beseeching eyes to see if the master was satisfied with his subject. Next he would trumpet my address like a fanfare across the Fort and the Río de la Plata: Calle de la Ribera 2, La Boca, Buenos Ayres. Roberto? Make no mistake! The bloodhounds would pick up several leads from my old address to my present hideout. Had I torn off my name and address? I had destroyed the envelope many days before. Out of pure despair and distraction I put my right hand into the pocket of my breeches. I felt about with my fingers. There was a piece of rolled up paper! I looked about. The people around seemed to regard me as a perfectly normal porteño on his way home. Carefully I unfolded the paper. It was the top part of the first page of the letter, with my name and address and the date 20th December, 1836. I looked about me again. I tore the scrap in three. I rolled the small pieces up and put them in my mouth. No one saw me. Had I swallowed it all in one go I might have risked a bout of coughing so violent that I would have been rolling about on the ground. People would have huddled in groups. The most helpful amongst them would slap my back and get me to cough up the bits of paper. They would have whispered to each other: "I might have understood it if it had been a piece of bife de chorizo, but pieces of paper! Why hasn't he thrown them away? Is there something on them he doesn't want . . . Ah, I see. Perhaps we ought to get in touch with . . ." I realized I had to swallow one piece at a time. Exerting great self-control I had to let one piece slip down my throat while the other two stayed in my mouth. Neither could I forget that I was in a busy street. Indeed, someone might wish to speak to me. In Calle de la Reconquista there are still some who do that. And worst of all, there are people in this city who have met me before. The first piece went down without problem. It settled, as far as I could ascertain, in the upper regions of my stomach, close to my abdominal cavity, under my diaphragm. I swallowed several times to make sure it had settled in the correct place. I swallowed the other two in the same manner. It was painless and without complications. I was standing in a busy street in Buenos Ayres, with part of my identity in my stomach. Though I no longer live in Calle de la Ribera, you may be certain that the Alborellos would have been more than delighted to help track me down. I was heading towards San Telmo. I had to spend the remainder of my money on a good lantern, a pistol, salted meat and some more paper. I had to be prepared for a long sojourn below ground.

How long would Rico hold out against the torture? If it really was true he was alive, would he not, after so many days' torment start to divulge the places in which we had lived?

Roberto! To be an animal with camouflage! My fear is now tangible at any rate. When I am gripped by anxiety, the object of my fear is not usually clearly defined. I am spared that kind of uncertainty. When freedom grows too great, anxiety becomes even greater.

I constantly find things to take pleasure in. Fear is a survival mechanism. I do not know how much pain I am capable of enduring. When I cut my hand with a knife, the wound first turns white, then red for a good distance round the cut, and finally white again because of a concentration of liquid.

I felt myself breathing. I began to cough, gently at first, then more and more violently. I was feverish. The sun was setting. A long string of donkeys crossed Calle de la Reconquista. Was it not life itself that passed me by there? Our impressions are the only things we own. These impressions and their origins are what we base the reality of our lives on.

The faces coming towards me are like planets looming out of the darkness. They are people of what we call flesh and blood, like a piece of bife de chorizo on fast-moving feet. But there is a soul some-where within the individuals passing by, you may say. I could not glimpse it as, one after another, they inadvertently bumped into me on the pavement.

"Rafael was shot yesterday," I heard a pedestrian behind me say.

That was hardly a sensational statement. But he added: "When I heard the news it came home to me that our old mutual acquaintance, Rafael, had existed. He actually had to die before I could convince myself of it."

I tried to quicken my pace to catch more of the conversation, but the two gentlemen were moving too quickly for me. A few yards further on they passed me. I noticed they were two elderly priests, but could draw no further conclusions from that. My heart began to palpitate. I halted.

I took a deep breath. And another. Perhaps my heart was not palpitating but simply trying to speak. I took yet another deep breath and walked on. If my heart could speak, I would not listen to what it had to say. This is not a world for those who live with heart and head. There is a big difference be-tween fading away like a venerable, old man in con-stant dialogue with depression, and suffering a sudden death. Unless one is fortunate enough to be saved by senility.

My eyes suddenly took in Lezama Park from this part of Calle de la Reconquista. Daniel McKinlay's impressive mansion could be seen almost in its entirety from here. Only parts of the ground floor were hidden. I knew I could see the house from the heights of San Pedro, but not from here. How lovely the whitewashed houses of San Telmo are, with their green shuttered windows, their flowers, their balconies! Everything I experience in this city, happens within me. Everything that ceases in this city, disappears within me. A tree grows, a waiter dies.

It would be dark before I got back to my hideout. The pedestrians were gilded by the sunset. In the south, the last traces of the sun disappeared. Its yellow glow was slowly smothered until it faded into a whitish color which turned blue-green.

The sky's silent landscape spread.

The stink of the streets became noticeable as darkness fell.

What shall my disappearance mean for this city? Nothing. And for me? I am tempted to say: nothing. But as long as I am able to feel fear I must answer: a great deal. I was walking along one of the city's busiest streets and knew that behind my vacuous eyes lay all the dammed-up bitterness of my life like an avalanche.

The gas lamps were being lit. The globes shed a circular pool of light. At the edge of the pool, the light dwindled. Then it turned dark until I walked into a new pool of light. At that moment the gas lamps seemed to me like worldly, wise people who know that each lives his own life, separate from one another.

As I was nearing Plaza Dorrego it struck me that perhaps I ought to pawn my suit. I would get some money for it and the articles I needed for my exile were anything but cheap. I had enough for meat, lantern and paper, but the pistol?

I entered the shop at the lower end of Carlos Calvo. Rico had introduced me to the proprietor some weeks before. Rico had told me how to go about things. I asked if they had any Dutch soap. Unfortunately, it was not the proprietor who stood behind the counter. When I had communicated my errand, I was scrutinised from top to toe by an almost blonde young man with prominent cheekbones and close-set green eyes. Could he actually have been a Dutchman?

"You can come with me to the storeroom."

I was frightened. I glanced towards the door. I was alone in the shop. The assistant opened a red door leading to the storeroom.

"After you sir, please!"

I started at this surprising form of address, which is not common in this part of town. In a gentlemen's outfitters in the city center one might expect such courtesy. But here? No. I hesitated.

"As you wish," he said.

He went in first. I followed. He shut the door behind us. In the dim light I could see no one. All I could make out were stacks of crates. I saw him reach up for something from the topmost crate. I moved backwards trying to shield myself with my hands. I was about to scream for help, for all the good that would have done.

"Take it easy, sir," he said kindly.

The object I had at first been unable to recognize was a bell. He rang it four times. At that, a trap-door opened in the floor and a large, powerful, bearded man appeared. In the dusty half-light I could see nothing of his coloring or features.

"What is it?" he grunted.

"This customer wishes to purchase Dutch soap."

"Does he?"

The patrón studied me carefully.

"Have I seen you before?"

"It's rather dark here," I ventured.

"Ramos, open the door to the shop."

The door was opened a crack so that the light fell on my face. The light illuminated the myriad of motes that drifted about the room. He managed to identify me.

"Oh, my God," he said.

After that it was several moments before he spoke.

"Shut the door Ramos, and get back into the shop!"

After the door had closed, he leant towards me and whispered: "What do you need?"

"A pistol," I said as quietly as I could.

"Keep quiet! Stay here."

He disappeared into the depths and surfaced again after a few minutes.

"It's loaded."

I reached out for the cold pistol. It was heavier than I had imagined.

"I have a problem . . . ," I said haltingly.

"You've got several problems," he put in.

"My problem is that I'm not sure I have enough money. I must buy some other things as well. I can come back . . ."

"For God's sake, take it and don't let me see you here again."

He moved some crates and let me out through a small door that opened out into a narrow alley behind the shop.

I walked back to Calle de la Reconquista. I was able to purchase a lantern, paper and salt meat around the Plaza Dorrego. I had to get back to my hiding place. My false identity card in the name of Enrico Hernandez FitzRoy were so professionally done that it would be a pleasure to show them. But the pistol? A pistol is a pistol. My suit and somewhat helpless gait had possibly been the reason why I had not been asked to prove my identity. I tried to walk faster. I felt my fever increase with the frequency of my coughing fits. My body told me that it was still too soon. Do not misunderstand. Life is long enough. I felt pain. I lived.

I do not own my body. That belongs to the maggots and the earth. I only possess my own experience of it.

I fought to survive. Defiance is also life. I begrudged Rosas' city of terror my body without a fight. I felt as clear-sighted as a frosty day.

I walked past the last street lamps before reaching the pitch black on the outskirts of San Telmo. The lamps were islands in a river of darkness.

Beneath the last street lamp a man lay sleeping on a bench. His hat was under the seat. The man wore the classical gaucho costume. The gaucho is concerned with modes of speech and etiquette. He can slit the throat of a steer or a man with style. The first time I saw a gaucho in all his trappings I thought he was a gypsy.

The gaucho was sleeping with a peaceful expression on his face. He was bald. His head was as tranquil as a stone. I stopped. I went nearer. In the darkness I heard a horse whinny. I started. His horse was tethered to a fence. The gaucho leapt up and grasped the knife in his belt.

"I'm sorry, I didn't mean to disturb you." My appearance disarmed him. He looked at me for a moment and replaced the knife.

"Thank you for your consideration in waking me."

Snakes are lovable if one belongs to the same poisonous group.

He picked up his hat from beneath the bench and walked resolutely over to his horse which he led along in front of me on the illuminated pave-

ment for the last few hundred yards before the darkness would swallow us up. I attempted to stammer
my apologies.

I heard him mutter: "Bungler, city idiot, cripple,
fool" and a number of words I immediately chose
to forget. He walked slowly before me. He was
drowsy. Where the gas lamps ended, the gaucho and
his horse stopped. A large door stood open. A small
slaughterhouse was in full swing. The light spilt out
into the street. Two men were in the process of
slaughtering a steer. A black leather mask was attached to the animal's horns. The steer could see
nothing. A night had fallen before the steer's eyes.
It was unwilling to move. Two ropes attached to its
horns were used to pull it towards the pallet on which
it was to be slaughtered. The mask ensured it would
not be able to twist its head away from the bolt that
was smashed through its forehead. Its legs gave way.
Its body fell like a collapsing house. No wall could
have held its body up. This was real force. One of
the men slit its throat. Blood flooded across the floor.
It looked like a rebel's shirt before it suddenly resembled nothing at all. The steer's pink nostrils still
twitched. Its eyes stared without seeing. Its tongue
lolled out of the left corner of its mouth. Its tongue
was cut out. Steam rose from its head. The knife

was in its throat. The skin round its horns was flayed. Its belly was cut open and the entrails poured out. The blood on the floor was the color of the rose before it has opened. The gaucho disappeared. At length, I arrived at the tunnel. Bozzo's delight at seeing me again was excessive. I stroked him out of pure distraction. Bozzo was unused to being stroked, and immediately regarded my action as an invitation. He began to rub up against me. I booted him away. He thought I was playing. I kicked him again. I got the lantern to light. Top quality. I found some hiding places for the meat, paper and pistol. I wanted to try to sleep. The light revealed a large cobweb on the roof of the tunnel. The good light enabled me to view my hideout for the first time. Spiders are fascinating. Some months ago I read about spiders in one of the reference works in the National Library. It said that webs are not merely traps. They are also used in communication, transport, mating, nest-building and care of the young. I also found Francisco Javier Muniz' name on the loan ticket.

I was about to push my hand into the web. I stopped and raised the lantern. I tried to work out how it had been built. The circular strands were attached to a number of radii that had been stretched out from a stick in the roof. The spider must have made a spiral of temporary threads between the radii. The temporary ones would have been devoured as a new spiral of thread was produced. The spider ended up in the middle of the completed web. I raised the lamp right up to the spider. It had eight legs. At the rear of its body were three spinnerets. Each of its eight legs had a small claw to grasp the web and a small gland that produced a fluid which enabled it to move quickly back and forth on the skein.

The spider had managed to catch a fly whose helpless legs were still moving.

My hand writes. The Earth turns, with its cities, its wars, its peoples, its animals, in all its haste. There are those who never discover this before they fall off.

Soon I shall no longer be able to live in unity with my skeleton.

The lamp I have bought is sufficient to illuminate my world.

A fly circles the light. When I turn the flame down, it will end up in the spider's web. I extinguished the lamp. I lay down fully dressed. I started awake. I still had money! Was I going to risk arrest without having used up every last patacón first? It was barely ten o'clock. I do not know why I did it, but I allowed Bozzo to come too. I walked back to San Telmo. Over the past few months I have visited various bars. I passed La Tasca in Carlos Calvo. Light shone from the windows of the colonial style house. It is the residence of Sergeant Oliden. His daughter, Margarita, is married to Colonel Cuitiño. Cuitiño is the official head of the mazorca. His foremost characteristic is that he never hesitates. It is a trait he displays in his private life as well. Margarita fell in love with another officer at a ball. Cuitiño caught them unawares. He shot the admirer three times and took Margarita home.

What are Sergeant Oliden and his wife saying in the lighted rooms? They could have brought Margarita up differently? Would Cuitiño blame his wife's parents? What could they do to pacify their dynamic son-in-law?

I felt relieved these questions had not the slightest relevance to me. I had fabricated them inside myself. I thought them of no small concern to the people within those illuminated rooms. Far from it. I wished they might go to the Devil with them.

I went to a bar in San Lorenzo. I knew that Esteban Echeverria used to patronize it before he went to Paris. Esteban is a customs' officer and an author. His parents are Basques. Some people have told me he fled to Montevideo. Echeverria was not to be seen. There was one face I knew: Esteban de Lucca. He had just come from Avellaneda. He looked tired and worn. We seated ourselves at the same table. I tried to look discreetly about me. I found repose of a sort.

"Will you permit me to pay for the drinks?" I asked.

"Of course, I'm not stingy," replied the poet.

We drank two rounds of rum before the conversation got going properly. I attempted to show concern by commenting on how tired he looked. He brushed it aside. I tried again. He banged his glass down hard on the table. I took this as an intimation that he would quit the place immediately if I did not change the subject.

"I don't know if you'll take the hint, but please note that I haven't inquired why you look so haggard. Nor have I once asked whether you're acquainted with that ridiculous dog you kicked out of the door."

"I'm sorry," I said.

"You see, young man, one asks but little these days."

"Is there anything you like talking about?" I asked.

"What about ordering more rum?"

I ordered it. Esteban looked about him and spoke quietly.

"At present I'm interested in all things French. Their gardens, architecture, painting and literature are one thing. But after the revolution France has become so absorbed with the word equality."

Esteban de Lucca cleared his throat.

"I don't understand," I said.

"I quite understand," he said kindly.

"Equality, what does the word mean?" I asked.

"In addition to equality, they are very preoccupied with the words liberty and fraternity."

"Aren't many others as well?"

"Quite so. What's new is that they have got the industrial revolution to develop apace with the social."

"I still don't understand."

"Can't you just keep your mouth shut for a minute or two? I promise not to interrupt should you wish to order. Can you keep quiet for three minutes?"

"Yes," I said loud enough to make the heads at neighboring tables turn in our direction.

"The Tuileries were stormed by an armed mob. I

believe it was 10th August, 1792. Louis XVI had fled from the palace. The royal household and retainers stayed behind. During the storming, the revolutionaries discovered the Princesse de Lamballe, one of Marie Antoinette's favorites. She was torn to pieces. One of the revolutionary leaders insisted on eating her heart. He took the heart in his right hand and visited his favorite restaurant where he got the chef to prepare it after the manner the French serve pigs' hearts."

I yawned.

"I'm coming to the point."

"What?"

"After this incident, Josef Ignace Guillotin realized — and you must remember he was a child of the Enlightenment — that executions by the sword weren't humane enough. He wanted execution to be the same for all. Guillotin managed to persuade the Assembly to ask Dr Antoine Louis to construct a mechanism for execution that would be democratic in every sense. Dr Louis was a surgeon by trade. He went to work in a manner which would have pleased any employer. For several months he tried out his execution method at the Bicetre hospital. He executed sheep. The guillotine principle was quick and effective. The only problem that the sheep trials threw up was that the blade became blunt after execution. But provided one had a supply of sharp blades in the vicinity of the guillotine, the executions could continue at great speed and with humane precision.

"Dr Antoine Louis died before the year was out. His head severed from his body by a fast and precise blow from the revolutionaries," said Esteban.

Roberto. As soon as we begin to reduce man to something general, we threaten our own existence. For every animal species we bring to extinction, the closer we come to man's, and for every race we exterminate, the closer we come to our own. Lost races will wreak their revenge. Man must be protected from himself, but by whom? I made as if to leave. The sun had gone. The sky was black. Esteban wrote some words rapidly on a piece of paper. It seemed quite natural that he did not look at me at all. The man is a poet. Inspiration comes suddenly, if not always at the most convenient moment.

"If I hadn't been so skint it would have been my round. I hope I'll be able to buy you one another time," he said. He took a quick look round and, as our eyes met, he pushed the paper across the table towards me as discreetly as possible. I started. His eyes signaled that I should look down immediately and read the note. I read: "Get out! Don't go back to your hideout. Razzia in progress. Rico has begun to talk."

He retrieved the note in a flash and crushed it in his hand.

"Farewell, farewell," were his final words.

I was quickly out in the street. How could he have known I would stop off there? Where should I go? I had not used up all my money. I was reminded that I am not capable of running. I walk with great pain. I move in a manner reminiscent of a human being.

I had to return to my hideout. I had no alternative. Perhaps they had found nothing suspicious. Unless they were waiting for me? I had to take the chance.

I must think faster, more fiendishly and more flexibly than the enemy. Can I do it?

Why did Rico involve me in this hell and what was his resistance group doing about getting him to commit suicide? Was Esteban one of them? I stood on a street in Buenos Ayres thinking that my friend should take his own life. I was reproaching him and his confederates because he was not dead! When, in the cold, clear night, I realized the consequences of my thoughts, I kicked Bozzo. The animal began to whine, as if recalling that, notwithstanding, it had been Rico and not I that had shown it care and compassion. Miserable creature! I was a man of sand. The sand would cascade at the slightest movement. If I breathed the sand would begin to run. I dared not cough. Even my thoughts were as shifting as sand. I could not see my enemies, neither did I know where potential friends might appear from. Friends! Their grins are like pearl-strings of guile!

What would the secret police do? If only I had the sovereign's blind strength or the simpleton's unfaltering Utopia! Why should I make a fool of myself!

Two women came towards me. An unusual sight so late in the evening. One resembled Mrs Black. She came closer. I had never seen her before. A lady and her elderly maid. The elder wore a rebozo of thicker material over her dress. Her mistress had a red mantilla over her elegant black dress, which appeared to be made of silk. They walked arm in arm, laughing. Although they were elaborately made-up, there was no doubt they were beautiful. Women, women! Have I loved any woman, or was what I loved the impressions of my own mind? One cannot love a body; flesh, fat, blood, water and bones cannot be loved. A soul, or a personality, can one love that? Hear how hollow it sounds, Roberto. What of the sexual act: the mucous membranes' touch and friction, the flesh of the lips, the veins, the fat, the tissue, the hair, the secretions? The women's laughter possessed an innocence I envied. I studied them minutely as they walked with quick, resolute steps. Their eyes, their hips, the way they held each other and the thought of the scent that would greet me as they passed, put all my senses on full alert.

Even a gold brooch with Rosas' initials pinned to the lady's breast did not dampen my enthusiasm. It was as if these initials displayed to the outside world a self-confidence, a poise in the way she walked, that seemed to suit her.

The women passed. I stood still. I was a table of empty glasses.

I had to press on. Esteban's silent message had perhaps signaled his fear that a razzia might take place on the other side of the street, where we had been sitting.

The mazorca would hardly expect me to go to

Recoleta. To that part of town where the really large mansions are. The quarter is inhabited almost exclusively by Rosas supporters. Outwardly they do everything to pacify the gaucho. Before going there, I would make a detour to the bordello in Calle San Nicolás. I was obsessed by the idea of using up the last of my money. For some reason I was certain they would find neither salt meat, lantern nor unused sheets of paper. Particularly as Bozzo was not there. The silly creature would presumably have stood by the hideout and begun to growl.

My pistol, identity card, the last bit of money and my letter to you I carry on my person. They will not believe it possible to live in that part of the tunnel. Bozzo barked. What had intervened to make me bring him along? Do not bring God into it, Roberto. He is decidedly absent from this city though his name has never been invoked so much. The Devil is not in Hell. He is here. Just imagine if Christ climbed down from the cross this Easter. The priests in Buenos Ayres, Shrewsbury and Varazze would fly like petrified bats with Father Razio at their head. Banks and palaces would have their golden bowels eviscerated. Cannons and pistols would melt. The trappings of pride would be trampled into the gutter.

Roberto, you know this will never happen!

I managed to get to the brothel unnoticed. I asked for Elvira. It was more than two years since I had been there.

"Doesn't your dog want to come in ?" the madam asked.

"Boot it out!" I said as calmly as I could.

"But isn't it your dog?"

"Get rid of it," I said without answering her question.

I looked at Lala.

"You're wearing well," I said.

"You're most generous," she replied.

She closed the door in Bozzo's face with an affectedly coquettish expression.

"How are things with you?" she asked.

"I'm not interested in answering that most philosophical of all questions. I'm interested in meeting Elvira as quickly as possible!"

"I didn't mean to be impertinent."

I looked at her face. The marked features and Spanish cast made me think she could only have been born in that most Spanish of cities, Toledo. She crossed suddenly to one of the high windows and looked through a chink in the curtain. She peered in the direction of Calle de Empedrado.

"What is it?" I said.

"I thought I heard a shot."

She smiled.

"No, I must have been mistaken," she said, before making sure the curtain was properly closed.

"Isn't Elvira here?" I asked impatiently.

"She's with a client."

The apartments I found myself in were considerably shabbier than on my last visit. It is a poorly kept secret that the apartments are a covert brothel. Each room has its picture of the Virgin Mary and a crucifix with a suffering Jesus.

Elvira came at last. She recognized me. She patted my cheek. I was emotionally unprepared. I backed away a step. She noticed this. For some considerable time I had been used to contemplating women from a distance.

"Has it been a long time?"

I blushed, I was alive.

"Yes."

"What a smart suit you're wearing."

"I'm pleased you think so."

"Shall we stop talking?" she said kindly.

"Yes."

"Come with me!"

I followed her to the room with the largest crucifix. Lala gave conscientiously to the church. It was known that the bordello was almost never raided by the police. A couple of stones' throws away was the Fort and the police station. I had not been asked to put my money on the table before I went off with Elvira. Could this be a trap? Or did they have so few customers that they had to content themselves with what they could get?

Elvira asked me to stand in front of her, upright and completely still. Elvira was blonde. She came originally from Normandy.

"Do me a favor. Relax completely."

"All right. Is it that obvious?"

She cut me off: "Look into my eyes!"

Her eyes were brown. I laughed. My laughter was strained.

"Stand still," she said and took my hands and laid them on her shoulders.

I was obedient.

I trembled.

"Take off your clothes!"

I obeyed. She passed no comment on my wooden leg. She undressed. I am so thankful I do not labor under the Pope's constraints!

She took pity on me. For several seconds at a time

I managed to think of things other than those that would fill my entire consciousness as soon as I left the room. There is a strange intensity about something one does for the last time.

I left my last patacóns on her bedside table. I dressed and left the premises as quickly as I could. Bozzo followed me down the front steps. Lala and Elvira called after us: "Goodbye. God be with you. A Dios." They did not say "Until we meet again."

I came out into the clear night air. I saw no one in the street. I stood still. Bozzo sat at my feet. I savored the second that I stood outside the door of the large, two-story house. I savored the next second and the one after that. I added them together until they made more than a minute.

I had made my decision. I would visit my former mistress, Mrs Black, one last time. What had I to lose? I would do something I should otherwise never have dared, something I could not know the outcome of. I was drunk with recklessness. I wished to balance on the knife-edge of life.

Roberto, you need not think I was pricked by jealousy of her husband. I have my vices, but that is not one of them. Jealousy would make us believe it has something to do with love and lust. What rot! Jealousy is the desire to possess. If one loves someone, one allows them to be free.

Of course I have been jealous, mortally jealous. When I was young I believed I had to possess in order to find love. In maturer years that is no excuse.

It is worst when the need to possess expresses itself as lust. Then one may call it seduction. Lust, more than anything, is lust for the other's lust.

I had to make several detours to avoid the sentries round the Plaza de la Victoria and the Fort. I got to Recoleta without being stopped. The city's streets were still. The civil war has taken on a new meaning. One side in the war has gained such ascendancy that the other lies on the wrack or makes itself invisible. Each knows that today's victims will be tomorrow's murderers.

Lights still shone from the Blacks' house. I walked round the house to make sure no one was keeping watch. The last time I had seen Mrs Black she was wearing a costume that made her look like a native. With all the smacks and kicks I had given Bozzo he had gradually turned into a well-trained, urban lapdog. Our sojourn in the city center had cemented the master-dog relationship. He understood the words "Come here!" "Go away!" "Sit!" and "Stop!" I went up to the front door. Three steps led up to it.

The house was enclosed by a garden and tall poplars. A soft breeze rustled the leaves in the tall, dark trees which looked like a huge fence around the Black family's idyll. I crouched over Bozzo: "Sit!"

He sat. I mounted the steps. I could feel the pistol in my inner pocket. I tried the door. It was locked. It would have been too much to hope it might have been otherwise. I pulled out an awl I had in my left inside pocket. The lock's mechanism was simple. The Black family lived in the vicinity of San Telmo when I cultivated my intimate liaison with the mistress of the house. Since then her husband's printing business had clearly prospered. I had no knowledge of this house. Before I entered I again said "Ssh!" and "Sit!" to Bozzo who was already seated at the bottom of the steps.

The servants had gone to bed. The hall inside the front door was in darkness. I could just make out the stairs leading up to the first floor. Two tall doors directly before me led to the drawing room.

I heard a voice from within. Someone sang in English. A woman. I saw light coming through the two keyholes in front of me. I took a couple of deep breaths. I closed the front door carefully. No one had heard me. The singer was Mrs Black. I had never heard the songs before. Don Carlos had never sung or told me about English ballads. I assumed this was what she was singing. I peeped through the left keyhole. She was just as lovely! She wore a red flower in her dark hair to please her husband. She was standing opposite me on the far side of the drawing room. She was laughing. She was straining to emphasize a point in the song. I hesitated. Once again I listened out for any suspicious sounds. I opened the door and walked in. They jumped. She screamed: "Help!" before I even had the door fully open.

Mr Black cried: "What is the meaning of this?"

"I beg your pardon, I tried to attract attention as I stood at the front door, but no one heard me, and as I gathered the servants had gone to bed, I tried the door."

I looked at her. Why did I not address her directly? I did not remember her being so beautiful. I could of course, as if by chance, as if in absentminded gesture, have placed a hand on her shoulder, conveying the impression that old men do not plan their physical contact.

"I'm sorry I interrupted. Perhaps Mrs Black would care to sing a couple more songs? It would give me pleasure."

"What are you doing here?" said Mr Black.

His wife had seated herself in a red plush chair.

She looked no less gorgeous with her head framed by chair-wings.

"I confess I have arrived at a somewhat unusual time. I have also forgotten something. I have not introduced myself. My name is Hernandez FitzRoy."

My host started. I remembered the downy hair on her neck.

"You are not, by any chance, a relation of Captain Robert FitzRoy?"

Mrs Black ventured to look at me.

"You are not the first to ask," I replied. I was speaking English, a tongue I had not practiced since Don Carlos had been in the city.

I continued: "Not so long ago I received a letter from Charles Darwin. Which, by the by, cost me a small fortune to reclaim at the Post Office. Both FitzRoy and Darwin have apparently returned safely home to England. What was it he wrote about the captain? No, perhaps I shouldn't divulge it . . ."

Here I paused for a moment to see if I had my listeners' attention.

"You divulge it here, surely?" asked Mr Black.

"Oh, very well. I do not wish to be unreasonable. Especially as your doors have been open to me."

"Well, out with it, man," said Mr Black.

"Robert FitzRoy is in the process of writing a book

about his voyage round the world in HMS Beagle. What is piquant in this context is that Darwin is doing the same."

"Wasn't this Darwin a sailor or something of the sort aboard the Beagle? If so, it's hardly loyal of Darwin, is it? He's a good deal younger, too . . ."

At this point in the conversation I had the urge to defend Don Carlos. An unexpected impulse in itself. I said nothing. I looked at the woman in the wing chair.

"You are so quiet, madam, do you not recognize me?"

This was a little tasteless and abrupt. She tried to feign an air of indifference.

"Well, one must be permitted a small joke," I said. I smiled. "Are you sure you won't sing another song while I am here and my eyes not yet closed for the last time?"

Sentimentality is like slipping in a dog turd. Her husband was taken aback for a moment. I heard some quick, padding footsteps behind me. I felt the hammer of the pistol against my chest. I was still wearing my cloak. Could they tell it concealed a pistol? I turned. I chuckled. An animal, one could hardly call it an insect, shuffled across the floor. The small creature ambled calmly over the parquet of inlaid natural wood towards Mrs Black. Its claws scraped against the wood. It was a house pet. Its eyes were hidden beneath a fountain of hair that was parted down its back. Its hair reached to the floor. I was glad Bozzo was not there. It would have been difficult to pick up the conversation after Bozzo had eaten the tiny creature. I did not restrain myself. I looked at her without averting my gaze more than absolutely necessary. I recognized the movements she made as she bent to pick up the fawning bundle. Even her perfume was as I remembered it. She made no sign of looking at me.

I said: "It must be useful to have a pincushion that follows one about. Is it a dog?"

Her husband did not intervene. He wanted to find out more about the relationship between her and me. I had not been threatening. My attire and my convincing story about FitzRoy and Don Carlos had made him continue the conversation. I shot a quick glance in her direction. She noticed it. With a rapid movement of her hand she pulled a scarlet silk kerchief from the neckline of her white dress. She smiled. I froze. My mouth went dry.

"Where do you get the FitzRoy name from?" Mr Black asked. He had not seen his wife's maneuver. I looked towards the door. I could scarcely pretend I had not heard the question.

"Pardon me, but you have not introduced your-self yet," I said quickly.

"Anthony Black."

"And your wife?"

"Sylvia Black," he said without waiting to see if she wanted to answer.

Until now he had not looked at his wife. I had formed a sentimental attachment to him I had been unprepared for. I had destroyed their idyll. He had never done me any harm. He had not thrown me out. It would have been warranted. He needed me in order to find out more about his wife. Was that why I was still in that beautiful house, able to contemplate his wife's lovely silhouette? Had he noticed that I never wearied of letting my eyes caress her figure, up and down, until I had to gulp? Was he wondering how he might get his wife to talk? She had chosen to close up completely, in the hope that this would convince her husband that I had nothing whatever to do with her. The silk kerchief was meant to frighten me and remind me I was in enemy territory. What a mistake it is to underestimate one who has nothing to lose, Mrs Black! Three years ago she discarded me as a lover. She saw that in the long-run our relationship was impossible. A day laborer from the shipyard was a poor match. What was hardest for me to realize was that she was not even emotionally attached to me. So I did not even have that hold on her. Her infatuation evaporated, before mine. What made me blush as I stood watching her, was that I could not recall when my obsession had died. She looked away demonstratively. I screened my face from her husband. If he saw my blushes he would draw conclusions I did not wish him to. She was not likely to witness my confusion as her absorption with the curtains was still intense.

"What lovely curtains you have," I said.

"Oh thank you, they're from England. My wife chose them herself."

"In England?" I inquired.

"No she picked them out of a catalogue," said Mr Black.

She let the silk kerchief lie in her lap.

So, he had no desire to ask his wife the question that for the past few minutes must have been branded in letters of fire on his brain. I decided to ask it. I looked at her. I blushed. I could not tell myself that my passion had died. Its flames burnt in my face. I felt a wholly unexpected infatuation sweep over me, but one with an unusual feature. I felt no physical desire, merely a satisfaction in admiring her from a distance. I looked at her. All my thoughts were directed towards former experiences and associations connected with her body and manner.

I forced myself to say: "Mr Black, doesn't it surprise you that your wife has not said a word?"

"It's against her principles to talk to casual intruders. Especially after midnight."

Did I detect a self-satisfied air during his gentle tirade?

"That was gallantly put. Because of the way this conversation has turned out, I am forced to alter my plans. And I will readily admit that this is because you, Mr Black, have created an unexpectedly favorable impression."

"Perhaps you are a little disappointed that she does not express a keener interest in you?"

I tried to appear unmoved. The prisoner of my gaze sat with her head well protected by the soft chair-wings. For a moment she took her eyes off the curtains. She looked at me: the flowing black hair, the green eyes, the almost imperceptible freckles, some of which adorned her face. I tried to remember if the scent in the room was the same as on those occasions when my nostrils were met with benevolence and courtesy. Previously she had wished my nostrils to mix the scent of her perfume with that of herself. I tried to inhale quickly through my nose a couple of times to capture a few more particles of the perfume that had strayed in my direction. Enough of the scent was in my nostrils for my mind to work: a plant, a floral fragrance. Yes, I recognized it! It was the scent of acacia. Once I had identified the smell, a new chain of association began, only to be interrupted by the master of the house who had gone on the offensive and was now asking: "Did you hear what I said? What am I to make of this?"

He added triumphantly: "If you have any questions to ask my wife, I suggest you ask them now."

They looked at me.

"Well, what have you to say?"

I did not blush. More probably I was turning white. I began feverishly to think about how I could get out of the house. How could I placate this couple who had now reached some kind of pact whose scope I could not guess at?

"Well, can you explain the circumstances in which you met my wife? She must obviously be the reason for your visit."

I was silent. They should not see my steadily rising fear.

"Hernandez FitzRoy, is there any shame in the fact that you think my wife beautiful?"

He took the three paces that separated us. He stood right in front of me. She sat in her chair. She stroked the four-legged pincushion, which once during my visit had been referred to as Poppy. I had to say something. To show he was master of the situation he laid his right hand on my left shoulder.

This contact filled me with disgust, but it also gave me new energy. I raised my left hand and calmly removed his hand from my shoulder.

"Your conduct so far has made me feel a certain degree of sympathy. Try to keep it so. The reason I came was that I wished to say goodbye to your wife. The last time I left her she neglected to say it. That I have lived with. It is not my habit not to say goodbye. Regrettably, I was unable to come earlier this evening. Unforeseen things happen in this city."

I sounded like a flustered and rejected suitor.

"Well, well, was there any other news in the letter from England?" he asked mildly.

"Don't try to change the subject!"

I reflected. "It said there was something new they call a railway, a machine that travels on rails, and that a census for the whole of Great Britain will reveal more than fifteen million inhabitants and that the country is in the grip of a typhoid epidemic."

I tried to go on the offensive: "Your wife is frightened of saying goodbye to me. She thinks it may seem like an admission."

I glanced at her. She was stroking the red silk with one finger.

She turned her head away and put down the animal.

"Perhaps you and your wife will continue the concert after I have left. For, no matter what you both might wish, I am quite determined to leave this beautiful house, but perhaps you could convey a small wish to your wife after the door has closed behind me?"

"What wish?"

"I am sure you can imagine, Anthony Black. Farewell!"

He tried to grasp my left arm.

I had been about to say that I wished my corpse to be burnt and that she should spread the ashes of my sexual organ in the Río de la Plata. That would at least bring an increase to the fish population and be a far more dignified exit than for example that of Georges Jacques Danton, who cursed and swore before the guillotine fell. His last wish was: "Be sure to show the people my head — it's well worth a look."

"Leave at once!" shouted Mr Black.

I drew out my pistol. I aimed at the four-legged midget. Mrs Black screamed. I fired. I missed. Mrs Black threw herself over the terrified animal. I shook. I aimed at Mr Black. He looked at me. He was calm.

"You have forgotten that you must re-load."

"What?"

"Get out. I'll let you go! Get out."

I coughed.

I screamed.

I tried to run. No one followed me.

I opened the doors and pulled them to behind me. I walked quickly through the hall. I found the front door and got down the stairs. Bozzo was waiting. I disappeared into the darkness while the lights burnt in the living rooms. Why had he let me go? Only Bozzo followed me. The sky was black. The moon was an eye that peeped through a hole in a locked chest. I was still clutching my pistol. I loaded it. I wished to approach my hideout with caution. I had to go round the city center and south to the river Richuelo at Baraccas.

The stars shone. I could no longer steer by the

lights in the houses. Bozzo ran ahead alive to every danger. My right leg got heavier and heavier to drag along. I was exhausted. I realized that if the secret police were waiting for me I would not stand a chance. I should be able to fire one shot with my pistol before they overpowered me. Nevertheless, I was propelled towards the tunnel. I wished for a resolution. I had to sleep or die.

I halted.

I felt my larynx. I did everything to stop myself thinking about Mrs Black. I coughed. I tried to breathe deeply. I tried to tell myself that I left the Blacks with my honor intact. I reminded myself that I must forget all thoughts of Mr and Mrs Black. I felt my larynx while I coughed. I took another deep breath. I tried to think of the air I was drawing down my windpipe, through my alveolar ducts into the alveoli that make the effective internal area of the lungs considerably greater than their external volume. I thought of how my ability to breathe still enabled me to divide the air between my right and left lungs and lower lobes. When I breathed too deeply the cold air irritated the bottom of my lungs. Coughing barred my progress. I had to try to breathe more shallowly.

Roberto, do you remember the lovely picture you

gave me after your trip to Rome? With the motif that Mother was not to see? The picture you bought with your own money because you wished to comfort me? You bought it without mother's knowledge as it would have shocked her. I struggled to the Richuelo by the aid of the stars. I stopped. I closed my eyes. I turned my head up to the night sky and saw all the quiet colors of Michelangelo's fantastic fresco in the Sistine Chapel: the Last Judgement. Mother was not indignant about the motif, or the Christ who bore more than a passing resemblance to Michelangelo's flame, the nobleman Tommasco de Cavaliere. What she did not like was all the naked bodies. She criticized Father Razio for not warning her. Death's ferryman, Charon, lifts his oar and chases the damned out on to the far bank of the River Styx, down to hell with its snakes, monsters, devils and flames. On the left, I remember, the righteous ascend towards a pure and clear blue sky where Christ sits on his throne of clouds. Heaven in the background was painted with that beautiful blue, lapis lazuli.

★ ★ ★

Dear Roberto! After I lost my fear of Hell, I lost

my faith. I cannot say I miss it. Roberto, have you asked yourself whether God has any conscience? Why has he given us a mind we cannot even understand ourselves with?

Why has he given us the ability to build expectations? Why has he given us just one heart and one frail skeleton? Ankles, knees and teeth are such poor pieces of craftsmanship, after all.

What will you do when you come face to face with God and between you there lies a flesh and blood-colored book? Will you say that it is we who have written it, while He answers that He was the one who was dictating? Why has God given man a gland that can lubricate all conscience with hate and betrayal?

When there is no one left to turn to, I shall become what I was before I was given a name and a faith. I regret, dear brother, that at the moment God is not causing me great problems. My fear runs deeper, to mankind, to you and me and the acts of tyranny we perpetrate on one another.

Here on the west bank of the Río de la Plata, the war between the federalists and unitarians cannot be heard. Nearer to Belgrano it is so quiet that one cannot even hear a bird sing. But the civil war is raging round me. The factions in the war have realized that man has said all he has to say.

If I should panic, the condition would at least have a prospective logic in that panic is fear's road to death and the fire that cannot warm. When I see all the beautiful obituaries in El Telegrafo Mercantil it strikes me that death must be the best thing that happens to us. I read certain death announcements with pleasure.

As I walked homeward I was grateful to the colonial architecture and city planners. It was in colonial days the city got its rectangular blocks which are about one hundred yards square. These orderly blocks made it easy to find the way. Amongst my workmates at the shipyard were many who could navigate by the stars. My talents in that direction are very undeveloped. Most had learnt the art at sea. I only know one constellation: Orion. Don Carlos pointed it out to me some years ago. But it is not enough to navigate by.

A black wagon drawn by two horses raced past, not far from the Plaza de la Paz. I just managed to throw myself against the wall. Bozzo stood petrified next to me, his hindquarters turned towards the clattering wheels and galloping horses. When, in the early hours, I arrived at the Richuelo, Bozzo and I drank the acrid water voraciously. Bozzo had not let himself be distracted by the barking dogs of the neighborhood. It seemed he had adopted my shyness.

I approached my hideout. I approached a reckoning. Even an albatross must land.

I saw strange footprints. The sun grew from the mirror of the Río de la Plata. I glanced at the blood-red chasm. It would be a hot day. The police had been here a couple of hours earlier. Was I relieved? Maybe. They had not found the place where I had hidden my things. Bozzo sniffed eagerly. He was afraid his secret bone store had been discovered. Bozzo scurried about. Was he sniffing for Rico? I lay down immediately and fell asleep. I must have slept for several hours. I could see the flag on the Cabildo. Río de la Plata still lay like glass. The pain in my right leg increased. I shared some of the meat with Bozzo. He looked suspicious. He circled round the small piece of meat before jabbing it with his right paw. He had never experienced such generosity from his master before. Was my scornful treatment of Bozzo an indication that I was still trying to cling to my own dignity? Was my behavior an attempt to demonstrate that man is superior to the beasts? That I dislike and always have disliked dogs, is one thing, but where people are concerned, I have bowed and traded banalities with even the worst types. I gave Bozzo another piece.

Is one to put up with everything? Is that not precisely what I am doing in these dark and damp surroundings? What am I not able to adjust to! I remembered the story Alfredo, my old barber from down in Calle Bolívar, told me. Before he became a barber he had worked as an attendant at the hospital. He had met Francisco Javier Muniz there on several occasions without feeling the need to address him. Alfredo did not realize Muniz was Argentina's leading paleontologist and passionately interested in prehistoric animals. Alfredo was an attendant in a department where they carried out postmortems. A child had died a peaceful death. Consumption. Alfredo's job was to open the body and remove the organs before the doctors arrived to draw their conclusions. The corpse was placed with its head stretched backwards. The bloody lungs and stomach lay on the table's white marble top. The intestines were spread across the surface between two large pools of blood. The consultant cut open the right lung to see whether their diagnosis had been correct and if they could learn any more about the organs of the human body. The three doctors and Alfredo surrounded the remains of the small corpse. There is nothing more intimate than pathology, nothing more ubiquitous.

The door of the room burst open with a crash. A tall, powerful man with a black beard stormed towards them: "What are you doing?"

He was a carpenter. He had been going to the mortuary to find out when the deceased could be shrouded. He had lost his way and ended up in the postmortem room.

The consultant picked up the scalpel and glanced towards the door. "Get that man out of here," he shouted as he wiped his wrist with a rag.

After a moment, it dawned on Alfredo that it was his duty to carry out the order.

"What are you doing!" screamed the man, as if it were not patently obvious. Alfredo managed to get him out with the help of the two assistant physicians. The intruder began to scream for the police. He hammered on the door, which had been locked.

"What have you done to my daughter! What have you done to my daughter!" he repeated, weeping outside the door.

Don Carlos, or some other lackey of reason, might

well say postmortems are necessary for the advancement of human kind. But they would never be able to dissect the meaning of that despairing carpenter's tears. It was no God he wept or cried out for. He wept because he could not bear the doctors' aloofness and frigidity.

Roberto. James Watt was a Scottish physicist and engineer who died almost twenty years ago. He invented the steam engine. Here, in this city, he is a hero of the liberal bourgeoisie. One of his sayings which I often hear repeated as a sentiment of genius is: "We may conquer nature if we can but find its weak point."

You have reason to wonder how I became acquainted with Rico Trappatoni. In my last letter I told of the time I went hunting with Rico and his brother in the direction of Córdoba. Neither did I neglect to mention that on our return the brothers robbed me of my share of the kill. I had been about to kill Rico. I changed my mind when I realized I would not be able to shoot both the brothers before one of them overpowered me.

I met him again a couple of years later. We met, as is usual in this city, in a bar. When I caught sight of him, I immediately began to plan my revenge. Before I had reached any decision, he was seated beside me:

"I saw you. I think I know what's on your mind. I'm unarmed. Fellow countryman, I hope you can accept an apology."

I looked up and gazed around. Rico stared calmly into my eyes: "No, my brother isn't here. He was killed by a bullet from Rosas' troops near Floresta."

We shared a bottle of brandy. He told me of his childhood in Rome. The dream of his youth was to become a sailor. Rico had been at sea for ten years before he settled down in Baraccas in Buenos Ayres. Is it not strange how all these young landlubbers want to be sailors? Do they hanker for some memories of the sea so they can go to sleep easier at night? At any rate, they turn into the keenest tavern storytellers the world over! Rico was one of them. First he began to philosophize about why the Arabs say "sea desert" when they look on the ocean, though I was unable to grasp his point. After that came the usual yarns about the time he was setting the sails in lashing rain and hurricane, the time one of the youngest sailors fell overboard and all hands knew it was impossible to stop the ship and try to rescue the popular lad from Naples, and the time off

Gibraltar when the mate forced him to go aloft during a storm even though it was not his watch, and so on.

In brief, Roberto, the same stories we had heard a thousand times in Varazze before we were fifteen. And tales about women. Those too. What I found appealing was his ability to make an admission without being forced to. He really did amaze me. I was curious to see if this meeting would lead to anything else. The fact that he had a sense of humor was undoubtedly an asset, but not decisive. He also knew Esteban de Lucca. Rico introduced me to him that evening. The priest in the oldest part of Rome where the Trappatonis lived, had taught him to read. Rico was, in other words, one of the promising the church had taken in hand. The priest presumably hoped that this strong, well-built lad would become a choir boy and, perhaps, ultimately a learned man.

He is — here my pen stops, I do not know if I should write is or was. What was it Rico used to say when we sat outside drinking? "I'm suspicious of camels and everything else that can go without drink for a week."

I groped my way along to the spot deeper in the tunnel where we had hidden the liquor. I drank. I was depressed. My movements became slow and sluggish. It is a good thing I am a pessimist. It is not pessimists who commit suicide, but disillusioned optimists. I slapped both my cheeks with my hand. Bozzo cavorted in front of me, round and round in a circle. He whimpered and whined, his tail wagging and hanging down limply by turns. Bozzo had never seen me do anything like that.

I shouted: "I will not live like a victim!"

Bozzo began to wag his tail hesitantly.

Bozzo's tail wagged furiously. I drank rum.

"Jesus died for our sins." Why should we insult the martyr by not committing any? At this moment you are probably going to the park for a walk with your children and your wife and, from there, down to the breakwater in the harbor. You have all been to church and subscribed to the collection with hard cash, and will soon sit down for Sunday dinner. And you will sit in the bosom of your family. Your conscience is clean because you never use it.

I began to think about my meeting with Elvira. My awkwardness, my blushes and surprise at the chaotic thoughts that welled up inside me when she touched me. I pictured her. Naked, her head turned to the left. She was wearing a string of white pearls. My eyes feasted on her neck, hair, brow, eyelashes, nose and mouth. Her chin was partially obscured by her left shoulder. She did not speak. She had turned her head to the side, sat with open eyes: a look alert to my movements. I saw the gentle curve of the small of her back, the two dimples at the top of her buttocks. Her thighs rested on her shins and feet. Her sexual organs were so visible that I could see her labia. He who is a master of his passions is a slave to reason!

She bent forward. The string of pearls dangled.

If only I could meet Elvira just once more. I would have liked to talk to her.

I want to forget my visit to the Blacks'. Roberto! Mrs Black causes my thoughts to soar on gossamer wings that shimmer so conceitedly they think they are glorious sunshine, until another thought devours them all. When my thoughts turn somber I try to remind myself that living is such an astonishing thing in itself that one ought not to worry.

If only one had another brain.

I try to grasp at any thought that will enable me to forget Mrs Black. Do you remember Chiara Tarditi, my first sweetheart? When she sat in the chair looking in every direction but mine, must she not at least have been thinking about me? By looking away she surrendered her body to my unfettered gaze. There is something absurd about all infatuation. A mutual obsession requires that two people should overflow with one single, quiescent thought in their consciousness: that they can decay. Is it death one is really infatuated with? The abyss has its own simplicity. Death liberates us from the fear of non-existence. Either one abandons oneself to the absurd infatuation or one does not. There is no middle way. One overwhelms and is overwhelmed. Infatuation is like necessity. She could at least have touched me with her finger! It need not have meant anything, just an accidental contact. Does she think of me in a tiny little part of her being? The monologues of the infatuated are never contradicted by the objects of their passion.

Outside it is Sunday!

I should have laid her on her back, stretched her arms back on the bed, heard her love-sighing breath, I should have covered her with kisses until we had melted into each other and become one, with one tongue, one head, four arms, four hands and four legs.

She once gave me a silk scarf. Is it possible to feel tenderness for a silk scarf? "I love you." How much we want to hear these impossible words! My language, my protestations of love are a skin. I want to speak to her. I want to rub the skin of my love against hers. The heart and the penis are the organs of desire. They expand, throb, pump, and shrink. They are all that is not intellect.

She did not want to speak to me! She looked away.

The spider's web on the roof was still intact after the search. I lit the oil lamp to see if there was more in the web. There were two flies now. One lay right in front of the spider, the other an inch away.

I met Rico a couple of days after Rosas had tightened the restrictions on begging. The police and the army would often ignore the increasing numbers of beggars in the city. Presumably because they were uncertain of the consequences of a total ban on the activity. Would the beggars organize? Roberto, you might as well hear it from me as from someone else: I started to steal. And as if that were not enough: my conscience did not deny me. Far from it. I developed a certain skill in opening locked doors. My old trade came to my assistance. There is a lot one can do with an awl, some wire and a stick. I stole to keep starvation at bay. To die of hunger must be the worst kind of death. Roberto, I have not eaten a single person.

I must confess I am not nearly as noble as one of my colleagues who had originally come to Buenos Ayres from Río de Janeiro to get a carpenter's job at the shipyard. Unlike me, he was never able to display his talents as a craftsman. The war with Brazil did not make things any easier for the man. His name was Vincenzo Allemao. His dark, almost black skin was like an enemy flag waved in the faces of the city's burghers. A gaunt and marked man after a couple of years in this elegant, hostile city. He went about in a filthy tunic and bare feet begging for a few meager coins in a charitable cause. The beard and long hair made him look as if he had climbed down from the cross earlier in the day to get a little food before continuing his atonement. The money he managed to collect he spent on small gifts. A flower, a beautiful button or a fruit would be given to someone he thought deserved it. It might be the suffering face of a passerby, a good deed he had witnessed, or a driver on the ox's back in front of a water-cart. Allemao might decide that the driver needed some recognition because he had checked himself while beating the half-ton heavy animals through the streets. I find it hard to believe his benefactors really imagined he would use the trifling sums on those other than himself. They gave on the principle of giving alms to all beggars, including ungifted liars. As you will appreciate, he did not become rich. I choose to believe this was not the only reason he was accepted by the rest of us. We saw that he really did make small gifts to bewildered recipients who either took them quickly and disappeared or pushed him away, fearing they were being lured into a trap. They were frightened of being robbed. On first acquaintance I felt certain there was something he was hiding. I thought him a particularly sophisticated beggar with a secret method of procuring money. All my conspiratorial thoughts were in vain. What he said was true. I spent just as long pondering why he did it. He always was given a little food by someone else in our fraternity, after he had parted with a small gift. "The Small Gift" was his nickname amongst his colleagues. For a time I wondered if he was senile. Was he one of these happy people who have cheated old age? As I got to know him better, I was more inclined to a different explanation. The mind, unfortunately, often has a preference for simple solutions. There is nothing that dulls it more than its unwillingness to grapple with complicated thoughts. Vincenzo was a man who demonstrated that such a simple idea is not always correct. There was nothing about him that pestered or irritated. It was possible he was faultless. That is suspicious in itself. At the moment of presenting his small gift, he might come out with something like: "Noble sir, I hope you will accept this small gift here in gratitude for your indulgence towards your donkey, which must be having a bad day. Thank you for not whipping the poor animal even harder, and please accept this tiny token." If the passerby ventured to halt and glance at the gift, it was not unusual for him to take the button from Vincenzo's outstretched palm and cry: "A button! What the devil do I want with a button!" and toss it in the dirt and leave.

Our colleague seemed to ignore the comments. His action can only be understood as a desire to receive thanks, or a smile, or a quick nod. An affirmation that he had not troubled his fellow men during his time on Earth. The presentations were in themselves small, good moments. He could have made things easier for himself by giving the confounded buttons to some child, but it seemed he did not believe children counted in this context. He had to have the confirmation of a grown man. Otherwise it would not count. I wish him refuge in madness.

I am sitting cross-legged on the ground with the

lamp at my side. Each time I rise I am as stiff as a piece of driftwood. I rage at my skeleton. It helps. My wooden leg follows me unwillingly.

I well remember the day that sealed my fate: I had just spoken to Vincenzo outside a watchmaker's shop. I glanced through the window. The watchmaker sat bending over a small table, studying pieces of a watch through a loupe. When I turned, Vincenzo was out of sight. I was about to leave. Someone touched my shoulder. I turned. I was looking into Rico's eyes.

"How are you?" he said quickly.

"And you?" He looked at me. He was about to say something. The words had caught in his throat. He looked at me again.

"Well, what is it?" I asked impatiently.

"Ah . . ."

He had clearly made up his mind to speak. He took a deep breath, as if frightened of the consequences of what he was about to say.

"I know you have a special aptitude for forcing locks."

"How do you know that?"

"Vincenzo told me."

"I see," I said attempting to conceal my terror.

"And another thing, too. I know you're a keen

reader and often go to the National Library."

I could not deny it. Nor did I get the chance to ask him how he came to know Vincenzo.

"Is it against the law to go to the library?"

"Of course not!"

"What do you want?" I said.

He swallowed. Asking questions can cost one one's life in this city. He studied me again and took a deep breath. He lowered his eyes. He hesitated before looking at me again, as he said: "People who visit the library in this city are generally opponents of Rosas."

He looked me in the eyes. There was no hesitation as he continued: "I haven't been there myself, but that's the rumor. They say there are many books there inspired by the French ideals of liberty."

The conversation continued at a nearby bar. We spoke softly.

He began to tell me some stories about Rosas. He was testing me. On the way across he asked: "Do you know what Rosas tells his soldiers when they're pulling down statues of the former governor, Balcarce?"

"No?" I said.

"'When you pull down the statues, leave the pedestals!'"

"Why does he say that?" I asked.

"What else would Rosas stand on?"

He continued: "Do you know what Rosas said to his wife at the height of the civil war in Buenos Ayres?"

"No?"

" 'If I lose this war, I'll start a new one in your name.' "

We sat in the bar a long time. It was on this evening that Rico involved me in his plans. We went to bathe in the Río de la Plata almost up at La Boca. Darkness had fallen. It had been a very hot day. We undressed. I laid down my crutch. Rico stared at me when I took off my wooden leg and limped across to the water's edge. The dust and my burning skin would soon meet the cool water. Our naked bodies glowed a little until we got out into the river. The black water swallowed us. We swam out some yards before deciding to turn back. I looked at Rico who was puffing and panting. He had learnt to swim a month before. A few minutes earlier he had involved me in some plans that were mortally dangerous and might be decisive for the country. I had been flattered by the fact that he had placed confidence in me. My vanity was still intact. I looked at him and thought how frail a human neck is. If

Rico had been given a quick, and not very hard, blow on the neck, the vertebrae there would have fractured, he would have swallowed quantities of water and sunk like a stone.

We clambered back up the bank. Our teeth chattered. Water ran down our naked bodies. My penis looked like a frightened pet crouching before the scrotum's two, frozen hamster cheeks.

I want to be dressed when I am arrested. What is the reason for this vanity? That the body is so helpless and insignificant compared with death? The following day I wish to be cremated, so that all traces of my crippled body are erased. Occasionally a bull may be applauded by the audience after the matador has thrust for the last time. Why? Everyone knows what their own, and the bull's, fate will be. We clap because the bull meets it with dignity. It honors life and death. I want to stand at the place of execution hardly able to smell that my rectum has passed a motion. I want to be alone with the fear and ask myself if I am the very essence of mankind, as if I were the first human being.

We stood on the bank. We tried to dry our naked bodies with our clothes.

"You know Lefebré," he said.

"How did you know that?" I asked in alarm.

"Through Don Carlos," he said smiling.

"How in Heaven's . . . ?"

"Don't ask so many questions. You know where he lives?"

"Yes," I said.

"Get hold of as much arsenic as you can by midday the day after tomorrow. Meet me tomorrow at six o'clock outside the watchmaker's. Is that all right?"

"Very well," I replied.

I was sold. I had sold myself. No. I had made a gift of myself. I wanted to be swallowed up by one united thought and action.

Evening was approaching. The red tinge on the watchmaker's white wall gradually faded. Rico was talking. Someone we did not know walked past.

Plainclothes police turn up when one least expects it. I tried to force my eyes to enjoy the wall's ever changing tints of red. Suddenly, we were interrupted by a man driving five frisky donkeys before him. Do donkeys spend their entire lives pleasing their oppressors? The alley we were in was so narrow that the donkeys pressed us up against the wall opposite the watchmaker's. We heard angry cries. It was impossible to get a glimpse of their driver. The red hue on the wall disappeared. The color of the donkeys blended with the wall. We got mixed up with the animals. They stopped. Their driver hurled a couple of words of abuse at them. They stood still. They rubbed up against us. Two of them lowered their heads and wanted to push us through the wall. One got a good grip of the lining of Rico's jacket. The driver seemed flustered. He was tall and thin. His head was bound in a grey kerchief. He was bleeding from a wound beneath his left eye. His left eye was hidden by the kerchief. He had lost control. When he saw the donkey attack Rico, he leapt forward and let fly at the animal with a stick.

I remained calm.

A little way off sat a vendor on the cobbles. He was surrounded by black gaucho hats in innumerable different sizes. He could reach them all from where he sat. The passersby looked questioningly at the vendor, he nodded, they picked up a hat, held it in their hands, talked for a long time, asked questions, the vendor answered, laughed, shook his head; the vendor told the story of his life, the customer spoke of the world, no sale, they nodded to one another; the vendor sat alone again amongst his hats, wearing an expression that looked like relief at not having to part with a single one of his treasures.

The donkeys' stench poisoned the air. Finally, they allowed themselves to be driven away after they had decided they were bored. The donkey nearest the patient vendor galloped in his direction. The others followed with the driver a short distance behind. After they had stormed past the vendor, I craned my neck to see what had happened to the gaucho hats. Not one of them had so much as a dent. The unruly horde had kept just to the outside of the island of hats in the middle of the alleyway.

I did not ask Rico for a couple of hours extra in which to procure the arsenic. My objections had been forced right down to my ankles. I had made up my mind.

Roberto, you may think triumphantly that you have heard this before. First it was belief I devoured skin, bones and all, then came my curiosity and fascination with Don Carlos and science, and now politics. Yes. Rico had never disguised the fact that he supported the French ideas of liberty, equality and fraternity. I will not maintain that I am unaffected by the same thoughts, but it was as much his eyes that drew me into it. He gazed calmly at me as I spoke of something I can no longer remember, before steering the conversation towards the reality about us and the duty we faced. I looked at him. Did I blink? I breathed rapidly. Distracting thoughts evaporated. I was ready to kill.

Rico could tell the most grimly humorous stories at the strangest times. When the story was about Rosas, and it usually was, he would consistently call him Caligula. I used to glance uncomfortably at the faces of the passersby. He would carry on talking without lowering his voice. My anxious face would make him smile.

Suddenly I noticed Cico Balbo. He had taken his stand outside the watchmaker's shop. The old, blind beggar who puts on a little show each time he is given a coin: a patacón is put into his hand, he lifts it quickly to his lips, everyone expects him to pop the coin quickly into his mouth to check if it is real or counterfeit. This is quite a daring maneuver in itself, because it can embarrass the giver. His patrons are often astonished that the beggar is audacious enough to check if the coin is genuine. They halt. Balbo chews, allowing the coin to revolve in his mouth as his tongue lifts it to his palate, then almost to the back of his throat, before brushing it against his gums, and repeating the process all over again. I have several times amused myself watching the giver's uncertainty and curiosity. Most of them go half way. They stand hesitating long enough to see that the coin does not return as quickly as when one buys goods in the market or at the shops. It can take a full minute before the coin re-emerges, covered in spit. But those with patience witness the force with which the coin is blown out of the old body. When the examination is finished and sufficient revolutions completed, he tilts back his head, breathes in and blows the coin out of his mouth, past his lips and makes it fly through the air while the spit falls to the ground, before the coin finally lands on his outstretched palm a couple of feet in front of his sightless eyes. He places the money in a little purse which he wears close to his body beneath his shirt.

Rico was schooled in political thought, not I. He asked me to purchase a suit.

"You need one. It's a sort of camouflage."

"You know perfectly well I haven't any money!"

"I know," he said calmly.

He looked about.

"Here," he said pushing an envelope into my right

hand. It was more than enough for a suit. I took it.
I was uncertain. Was I being seduced by evil? No. I
was convinced his commitment was sincere. I acted
out of necessity. Roberto, I thought of evil and asked
myself: If God really is omniscient he must know
about evil, and if he is omnipotent he must be able
to do away with it. And finally: if his goodness is
absolute, why does he do nothing about devilry?

I can forgive God, even though his sins are greater
than mine.

Rico said several times that he was a sincere Catholic. It was possibly one of the reasons I did not believe him to be driven by evil intent. Perhaps I
thought of you? I said yes, without being forced to
by anyone other than myself. I had all the freedom
in the world to say no. Did I doubt? I might fail at
the decisive moment. God could make no difference either way. I stood there like a man naked,
without a single purpose in life. I had been asked. I
had been chosen. I knew I had been selected to steal
the arsenic from Lefebré's because of my ability to
pick locks. In addition I had a first class awl. But I
also felt chosen in another way. They trusted in me.
I would do the job. Rico had not told me what the
arsenic was to be used for. I did not ask. I did not
wish to think about it. I had the power to choose

and I had safeguarded it, unlike the donkeys which were now trotting round the streets of Buenos Ayres. The power to choose what we wish to do with our lives sets us apart from vertebrates that also have four limbs and toes on each foot or paw. Our fetuses develop through stages that correspond to various forms of lower life. As Alfredo had taught me: the adult body retains vestiges of such lower life. Feel your coccyx, Roberto. Our digestive system and blood is like that of other mammals.

Next morning I bought the suit and committed the perfect burglary. I handed the arsenic over to Rico at the appointed time and place. He was satisfied. He said so. I liked that.

Do you remember, Roberto, how glad father was when anyone praised him? He must have passed that characteristic on to me congenitally, the way chicks in the nest start making fly-catching movements before they have ever seen a fly. Rico asked if I wanted to help assassinate Rosas. I had already stolen what was needed to kill him.

When animals of the same species fight, they do it to get food. Mankind has enough for all, but lets the majority starve. We are like doves. Those peaceful creatures. Some exhibit them, some wash and tend them, some give them food and wish more than anything for a white dove they can keep indoors.

I forgot to tell Don Carlos the story of one of the most pious and lovable people I have met in this city: Father Massimo Crippa. Some years ago he bought two tranquil doves in the market close to the Plaza de la Victoria. He also bought an elegant birdcage. He carried the cage and the two boxes of cooing doves home. He entered the hallway and informed his housekeeper. He led her into the living room. She was a freed black slave and well advanced in years like himself. The cage was placed on the living room table. After considerable effort the doves were maneuvered into the cage. They took up position, one on each side of it. The priest and his housekeeper looked at one another and smiled. They were anticipating the cage's delights over the coming months. A minute passed. Then another. The doves that had apparently not registered each other's presence, flapped their wings, as if some kind of signal had been given. They fell upon one another. The priest and his housekeeper watched quietly as the furious doves pecked each other to death.

"What did that episode teach you?" I asked the pious padre.

"Nothing. Human beings would never have done anything like that," was the man's answer.

Roberto. Is it really that I court danger in order to extend my consciousness of death? If so, what does it profit me? Does preparation make one any stronger? Am I trying to show that my body is capable of more than surviving?

Rico had borrowed some dispensing scales from one of his fellow partisans. We weighed the arsenic. The scales stopped at four hundred and fifty grains. A grown man may be poisoned by a fifth to one grain. Somewhere between one and a half and three grains is lethal. We had enough to kill between one hundred and fifty and three hundred men. Shortly after the poison was digested the victim would experience cramps, vomiting, diarrhea and dehydration before his respiratory system would become paralyzed and death finally ensue. Rico had a plan which he had not divulged to me. Though he had discussed it with the leaders of the resistance movement. Rico said that he and his friends had considered it too dangerous to let me know the details beforehand. It was a highly risky undertaking. It was mortally dangerous. That was all he had permission to tell me.

Roberto, perhaps it might gratify your sentiments if I wrote that I suffered moral torment. I want to tell the truth: I wished the dictator dead with all my heart. This feeling has grown within me each time I have seen him on the tribune of honor. Not even the strongest bola about my neck could tear me away from this thought. But, your conscience, I hear you say. Exactly! My conscience told me that this man should draw his last breath as soon as possible. Dictators often look fine until they fall. Rico wanted to let me witness the toppling of South America's greatest dictator. I was glad I knew no details. I am unsure of my ability to stand up to torture. Informing on others would have been a greater pain to me than death itself, no matter how barbaric it might have been. Rico's friends had discussed whether my wooden leg and unpredictable cough were an advantage or a drawback. They decided they were an advantage. I was to wear my elegant suit and put on an English accent. Rico was to be my assistant and say as little as possible. Rico's friends provided us with forged papers that stated we were British citizens. Rico was also given a new suit. From what we knew of Rosas' habits it would be catastrophic to administer too much arsenic. Rosas would then witness the reaction of the household pet that had been set to taste the food. He had to be given a dose that would work over time. As we went towards Recoleta to visit Rosas, I was carrying three engravings of zebras. Rico had the arsenic and a letter. Rosas' zoo had enjoyed a steady influx of new species over the previous few months. The apothecary whose scales we had borrowed was to pick us up some five hundred yards from Rosas' residence. We traveled to the house during the siesta. Scouts had confirmed that he was at home. We were stopped a good way from his residence. We showed our identity card while I spoke a quick and disjointed English. We were unarmed. We knew we would be searched. My awkward and labored gait must have convinced them that we could not have had sinister motives. I also took care to have a bad fit of coughing to reinforce the impression of infirmity. When we arrived at the main door, we were again stopped. Our papers were checked once more. The letter we had with us was thoroughly perused. It announced that we represented businesses and factories in England that wished to make Rosas a present of three zebras for his private zoological gardens. Rico and I were introduced as experts on African animals. We were asked to wait. Five minutes passed. Ten minutes passed. I continued to talk. Rico nodded. After a few more minutes a senior officer appeared and said: "Come with me!"

A moment later we stood face to face with the dictator. I was no longer afraid.

"Speak," said Rosas, turning to me.

He had a napkin tucked up at his throat the way a child wears a bib. He stood by the side of the dining table. He had not finished his meal.

After all the civilities that must be observed when visiting a dictator, I asked: "Have you ever seen a zebra?"

"No, I know very little about African animals. I very much want these three zebras."

I pointed to the park.

"Have you any objection to showing me round out there so that I can ascertain where their enclosure should be?"

"Sit!"

I coughed protractedly. He sat down.

"Thank you," I said.

Rosas continued to eat. He ate fast. There was a piece of beef, some salad and bread on his plate. Next to it was a bowl of rich, red tomato and onion soup. He concentrated on his eating.

I walked round the table. I halted at the first chair. I grasped the back of it with my right hand. I pulled out the chair. He was looking down at his food. I had my weight on my left foot. I raised my right leg carefully. My right arm shook. I bent my left knee. He raised his eyes. I bent my hips. I looked at him. I removed my hand from the chair back. I placed both my hands on the table. I felt the pains in my leg. My left leg shifted position. I bent forward. I lowered my body until I was sitting on the chair.

"Are they English?" I asked.

"What?" said Rosas.

"The chairs?"

"Yes."

I coughed.

He raised his head. He put down his cutlery.

He looked at me.

"What sort of zebras are we talking about?"

"What sort?" I answered haltingly.

"Was my question not specific enough for you, perhaps?"

"Certainly not."

"What have you to say?"

I swallowed. I do not know why. I noticed that the tips of the thumb and second finger of my right hand were rubbing together frenetically.

Rosas looked at me and smiled. "I repeat: what sort of zebras are we talking about?"

"There is nothing wrong with the question. Definitely not," I added quickly.

"Why do you hesitate?"

"The subject is extensive and complex. I have a tendency to become somewhat long-winded. I should not wish to detain you."

"Get to the point! Begin! I will tell you if you're taking too much time."

I swallowed twice. I cleared my throat. I pushed my toes forward in my shoes.

Rosas studied me carefully.

"The point is . . ."

I had difficulty in continuing.

A servant brought in a platter with a whole watermelon on it and a long, sharp machete.

"While you ponder the answer, to which I look forward with ever increasing anticipation, I wish to say something about providence and God's goodness."

He raised the machete and tested the blade.

"It looks sharp," I said.

"Very sharp. Providence, or God's benevolence towards man, has made the sun rise for us, the stars shine for seamen and the watermelon a shape that's easy to cut."

He was standing with his back to the table. He

spun round abruptly. With power and precision he sliced the watermelon in two. The machete did not touch the dish the watermelon stood on. Quickly, he cut the two halves into sixteen pieces.

"Would you care for one?"

He handed me one before I was able to reply.

"You think, perhaps, I've forgotten what we were talking about?"

The place was crawling with guards.

"The zebra is, in fact, an African species of horse."

I stopped.

I could hear I was not speaking.

I looked out of the window.

I looked at the sky.

There are days when I do not see the sky, but only sense it, because I live in a city and not on the Pampas.

There were a very few white clouds in the sky. They were moving rapidly. Following a little way behind were heavy, grey-black clouds. Some were completely black with a few off-white flecks. Despite the strong wind they appeared almost motionless.

Green vases of poplars bent silently so that even more of the sky came into view. I looked at the clouds: I am the distance between what I am and what I am not. I am what I dream myself to be and what life has made me. What a difference there is in the size of the clouds! In the sky's play, huge mountains of ice move south to be swallowed by black, eight-footed elephants. The clouds are like me, a vague transition between sky and Earth.

The clouds continued to move past.

I wished I had been in a bar. All I am fit for is listening to the buzz of voices between two sips of rum, and watching time fall like a cloud on to my creased breeches.

"I'm waiting."

It was not my voice. The voice was calm. My eyes stopped at the chair next to Rosas.

The tunic of his dress uniform hung over the back. The tunic was blue. The buttons were of gold. The collar and lapels were red. When he was wearing it, the collar was turned up so that his somewhat weak chin was not visible. He was shorter than me. He looked to be of a robust physique. Rosas was wearing a white shirt and newly pressed uniform trousers. His mouth was small and narrow. His ears small, his eyes large and intense. His hair thick and reddish. His nose large and narrow and hooked halfway down. He was younger than me.

"Can you pull out the chair?" he asked.

"What?" I said.

Rosas shouted to two of his bodyguards in the adjacent room. I began to sweat. I had heard of a new method of execution employed by Rosas' adherents. The victim stands between two soldiers who each raise their swords simultaneously and, on a given signal, run the prisoner through.

I suppressed a scream which might force my mouth agape against my will.

Rosas placed a piece of beef in his mouth.

"You haven't said much about this splendid gift. Perhaps you might stand on the chair so that I can hear what you have to say?"

"I have some difficulty getting on to chairs. I suffer pains . . ."

"I can see how things stand with you. Just do it!"

He laughed.

I had no choice. I had to make an effort. I walked to the chair. My mind worked feverishly at which leg I ought to attempt to raise first. I took a firm grasp of the chair back with my right hand. I had to let my bad leg take my body weight while I lifted the left on to the seat.

Rosas put down his knife and fork, chewed and watched the performance.

As soon as I lifted my left leg I could feel the pain

in my right leg, lower back, neck and head. I went hot and cold by turns. My left foot was on the seat. The most difficult part remained: to shift my weight to my left foot while raising the rest of my body with the help of my right hand on the chair back. The entire upward movement had to be coordinated with the balance of the chair, my wooden leg and the pains in my right thigh. I could only attempt it once.

I raised my right foot. I gasped. The pain was unendurable.

How I shook! I swayed. I stood!

The crown of the dictator's head was almost bald.

Dear Roberto, you see I have indeed experienced the sense of the penultimate moment before.

I saw the color spectrum in the crystal of the chandelier. Outside I saw a drop of blood in the corner of the sky. I looked into Rosas' face.

Thoughts forced their way in without knocking. Some climbed in through one ear and left by the other. Others fretted and lingered.

To love man as he is, is to betray his possibilities.

Can there be anything more lonely than a belief in the good in man?

Roberto, I can grow tired too.

Why do I breathe? Is it conceit? And my heart, is

it from before Newton's time?

Roberto, I know no other world. I am matter.

Rosas' face had feminine features. I cannot recall if that surprised me. Rosas looked at me without speaking. Was he curious to see if I should fall? Or was he crucifying me mentally? I began to think of the boats which, after dark, would sail to Montevideo with refugees at their gunwales, anticipating the journey's metamorphosis.

Rosas cleared his throat.

"Upon my word!" said the dictator.

I cried: "A day comes in each man's life when he must take the bull by the tail and look the situation in the eye!"

Rosas laughed.

I did not understand at first what I had said.

"Very witty. Perhaps you have something to say about zebras too?"

The bodyguards positioned themselves on either side of me. I closed my eyes. I waited for the swords to plunge into me.

I felt my mouth opening. My voice was forming with the help of my lungs, windpipe, larynx, vocal cords and throat. The sound was articulated with the help of the tongue, teeth, soft palate and jaw.

Without a quaver in my voice I said: "One may

divide zebras into three main groups."

"I'm waiting."

"Equus zebra or the mountain zebra from the far south of Africa; Equus grevyi which is as large as a horse and comes from the northern part of Africa, and the one in between, Equus quagga, which lives in the eastern parts."

"Which is the species I'm to get?"

"The largest."

"Good."

"What is it you like about zebras?"

"The stripes."

"All the stripes are different," I said.

"Indeed . . . ?"

"Why do you like the stripes?"

"I think black on white is beautiful."

"They look like bars."

"Precisely!"

"A zebra is an imprisoned horse," I said.

"Each animal . . . ," Rosas looked about him as he continued, "is like a galloping jail on the savanna."

He laughed.

I cannot look at a laughing man without thinking: he wants me to look at him, he believes it will be for the last time.

Roberto, just imagine if I had suffered a major hemorrhage there and then. A violent, uncontrollable fit of coughing could have been enough. One ruptured artery and I should have been a dying fountain of blood. My last glance might have been directed towards Rosas, but the sounds I should have heard would have come from the other side of the house. Three men were laying cobblestones in the square outside. Through the open windows I could hear the sound of hammers on chisels. A duller sound came from a thick wooden log, about five feet high with a crosspiece that served as a handle. This tool, which is called a tamper, pounds the cobblestone into place in between the other, laid, stones.

"Would you be kind enough to accompany me down the stairs and into the garden?"

He looked at me. I met his gaze. He looked about him and drew breath.

He grasped my arm and escorted me.

The commanding officer remained with Rico.

I commented on the grounds. I said that the place was ideal for zebras. I looked at the lawn. I looked at Rosas. I breathed. I turned round.

The commanding officer was still inside with Rico. I had managed to get Rosas outside without much difficulty. He was standing motionless looking at me, just as a bull stands before the matador adjusting itself to the idea that the last thrust will come.

The commanding officer did not budge.

I remarked on the height of the poplars. He made no answer. I asked how large the park was. He answered. I did not listen to what he said. Rosas stared at me.

The commanding officer stood rooted inside in the gloom.

Everyone stood still. I could not run, I could not walk, I could not open my mouth. I must fall. I threw myself forwards. I fell on my right side. I screamed. I shut my eyes. I screamed again. I heard running footsteps on the gravel. I cursed in English. I writhed. I clutched my wooden leg and pulled it into place. I opened my eyes. I saw the commanding officer. Two of his guards stood over me. Rosas and the commanding officer bent over. They squatted down. They breathed into my face. I moaned. After a few minutes I asked them to help me up. With the greatest care and consideration they accompanied me up the steps and into the house. Rico approached us. He asked what had happened. I stopped. I drew a sigh. I shook my head. I looked at

Rosas. He looked away.

"Can I offer you anything, gentlemen?" Rosas asked.

New dishes were brought in. I forced myself not to look at the food.

"No, my assistant and I must hurry on," I said.

I asked Rico if we had done everything. Rico smiled and nodded. I was about to make for the door. Rosas looked at me.

We paid our respects and left the scene of the crime with the well-chosen courtesies the situation required. Everything went to plan. We were picked up and brought to safety. We thought we had succeeded. The idea was that we should get across to Montevideo via Entre Ríos. That same evening we had a visit in our safe house. Rosas was fit and well. The Ministry of Propaganda had chosen not to divulge that Rosas had been the victim of an assassination attempt. They wanted to try to catch us unawares. An informer had saved us on this occasion. We should have to remain in hiding several months before we could attempt the crossing of the Río de la Plata and reach Montevideo.

★ ★ ★ ★

I have been writing feverishly for the last few days. Bozzo stays close by me. He whines.

I stroke the animal.

Roberto. Do not say that men are immutable. Casanova ended his days as a librarian.

We can hear the soldiers not far away. It is raining lightly. The wind is blowing. There can be no doubt. They are coming in this direction. Oh, for the chance to be melancholy a few more days! Imagine having enough money, a bed to rest on, cool, clean sheets, a pillow, a blanket, a foot wash, a shave, or to gaze out over a peaceful Plaza de la Victoria without one anxious thought, just sunlight and me amongst all the others. My only chance of sending you this letter is to ask for extreme unction. Then I shall beg one favor: that the father forward you this letter.

Yesterday night I awoke screaming. The scream was a huge hole I could not swallow. I can still hear the scream. It was like a deep red vein, gushing through my air tissue towards my ear and freezing solid in my brain. I managed to light the lantern and dig up a small piece of mirror Bozzo had buried. Had I screamed because I had felt a suffocating dread? Had my brain reminded me that I was ephemeral? I looked at myself in the mirror. I smiled in order to put off the moment when I had to realize why I had awoken. I studied my face, my wrinkles, the furrows in my flesh. I regarded myself. I let my tongue play over the broken canine. I was in communion with my skeleton, which will outlive me. My tangible posterity.

I shut my eyes. I could not close my ears to the sounds that came from within. I clambered up to my little lookout post from where I can see the Río de la Plata. All was still. The moon was shining. The jet black water was darker than the darkness. I could see small points of light north and south along the river shore. And within the specks of light: the small homes around the lamps. Let it be light before they get here!

Could the cook have discovered something unusual? Did Rico put the arsenic on the wrong plate? I shall never know the answer to these questions.

I looked upward. I missed thoughts about the sky. The moon had placed a black kerchief over my eyes.

I might have needed to carry the thought further. Ignorance surrounded the thought and drowned it.

I could have barked. I was a man. I was here on Earth. I shouted with my head. I shouted with my language.

I shouted with my body, the carapace and catapult of my voice.

I shouted with a voice I assume must have been a
dull sound. A shout that will be heard for centuries
to come.

It got light.

Roberto. It would be better if nothing remained
after a life. That one was simply obliterated for those
who, afterwards, have only a vague inkling of one's
voice. That which is left can sometimes linger like
some unreasonable demand on the living.

Shall I turn my gaze towards the Río de la Plata
when they aim their rifles at me? Does the water
put me in mind of something that will endure?

How vague the future still was in the days when
we lived like insects, and the Earth was still warm.
What possibilities! Not everything can be foreseen.
If all the cobblestones had been eaten up one morn-
ing, Don Carlos would have had an explanation.
His reason is always at the ready.

Some angels are so fat that their wings will not
carry them. The letter from Don Carlos! I tore up
my name and address on the first page, but not the
ones later in the letter! The secret police are no fools.
The overseer has given them the letter. That zealous

jackanapes would have gone through everything in the library's wastepaper-basket at the end of the day and found the letter. His curiosity would hardly have been dampened by the fact it was written in a language he cannot understand. He would have had it translated, discovered my name and address and immediately given them to the police.

Bozzo: a heart severed from its body, which continues to beat, that is true loyalty.

They are right outside. They have not discovered me yet. They know they are close. Something has made them halt. Bozzo creeps close and looks at me. Without a sound. Loyal to the last!

Do animals and men think alike?

How much have I lived without living?
How much have I thought without thinking?
I sit here with all the wounds from battles I have not fought. My body is crippled by its own muscles. I am exhausted by efforts I have not even contemplated making.

I hear footsteps above us. There must be more than a hundred men.

I am flattered.

I hear their voices, fragments of words, parts of

sentences. They know they have come to find me here.

I bury the pistol. If they see me with that they will shoot me, and I shall not have the opportunity of passing this letter on. I must make up some story that will get them to execute me ceremonially, with a last request, extreme unction, a pious padre who will take the letter and post it because he has promised! Perhaps I shall make myself interesting and "inform" on some of their agents? What a fool I have become! The letter will never leave this place. It will never arrive to plague you, Roberto.

I breathe. I breathe calmly. I swallow regularly.

There! Someone shouted exultantly that he has found fresh footprints. Another cries out that he has discovered the opening of a tunnel covered with branches and leaves.

The envelope with your name on it lies before me. I straighten my back. I breathe deeply. The lamp flickers. Never have I noticed the smells about me so intensely. The air is damp and stale. The air is earth, rock, sand, dog, man.

My mouth is dry.

I cough. I cough again. I put my hand over my mouth.

I stifle the sound in my mouth, throat, neck and lungs. Bozzo whimpers.

I am feverish, Roberto.

Some pass away. One never sees them again. But there are more. There are so many more still living.

Your brother Giovanni,
1st March, 1837

GREEN INTEGER
Pataphysics and Pedantry

Douglas Messerli, *Publisher*

Essays, Manifestos, Statements, Speeches, Maxims,
Epistles, Diaristic Notes, Narratives, Natural Histories,
Poems, Plays, Performances, Ramblings, Revelations
and all such ephemera as may appear necessary
to bring society into a slight tremolo of confusion
and fright at least.

*

MASTERWORKS OF FICTION

Masterworks of Fiction is a program of Green Integer
to reprint important works of fiction from all centuries.
We make no claim to any superiority of these fictions
over others in either form or subject, but rather we
contend that these works are highly enjoyable to read
and, more importantly, have challenged the ideas and
language of the times in which they were published,
establishing themselves over the years as among
the outstanding works of their period. By republishing
both well known and lesser recognized titles in this series
we hope to continue our mission bringing our society
into a slight tremolo of confusion and fright at least.

BOOKS IN THIS SERIES

José Donoso *Hell Has No Limits* (1966)

Knut Hamsun *A Wanderer Plays on Muted Strings*
(1909)

Raymond Federman *The Twofold Vibration* (1982)

Gertrude Stein *To Do: A Book of Alphabets
and Birthdays* (1957)

Gérard de Nerval *Aurélia* (1855)

Tereza Albues *Pedra Canga* (1987)

Arno Schmidt *The School for Atheists: A Novella =
Comedy in 6 Acts* (1972)

Sigurd Hoel *Meeting at the Milestone* (1947)

Leslie Scalapino *Defoe* (1994)

Charles Dickens *A Christmas Carol* (1843)

Michael Disend *Stomping the Goyim* (1969)

Anthony Powell *O, How the Wheel Becomes It!* (1983)

Ole Sarvig *The Sea Below My Window* (1960)

Anthony Powell *Venusberg* (1932)

Jean Frémon *Island of the Dead* (1994)

Arthur Schnitzler *Lieutenant Gustl* (1901)

Toby Olson *Utah* (1987)

Andreas Embiricos *Amour Amour* (1960)

Knut Hamsun *The Last Joy* (1912)

Arthur Schnitzler *Dream Story* (1926)

Joseph Conrad *Heart of Darkness* (1902)

Mohammed Dib *L.A. Trip: A Novel in Verse* (2003)

Thomas Mann *Six Early Stories* (1893-1908)

Thorvald Steen *Don Carlos* and *Giovanni* (1993 / 1995)

GREEN INTEGER TITLES

1   Gertrude Stein *History or Messages from History* $5.95
2   Robert Bresson *Notes on the Cinematographer* $8.95
3   Oscar Wilde *The Critic As Artist* $9.95
4   Henri Michaux *Tent Posts* $10.95
5   Edgar Allan Poe *Eureka, A Prose Poem* $10.95
6   Jean Renoir *An Interview* $9.95
7   Marcel Cohen *Mirrors* $12.95
8   Christopher Spranger *The Effort to Fall* $8.95
9   Arno Schmidt *Radio Dialogs I* $12.95
10 Hans Christian Andersen *Travels* $12.95
11 Christopher Middleton *In the Mirror of the Eighth King* $9.95
12 James Joyce *On Ibsen* $8.95
13 Knut Hamsun *A Wanderer Plays on Muted Strings* $10.95
14 Henri Bergson *Laughter: An Essay on the Meaning of the Comic* $11.95
15 Michel Leiris *Operratics* $12.95
16 Sergei Paradjanov *Seven Visions* $12.95
17 Hervé Guibert *Ghost Image* $10.95
18 Louis-Ferdinand Céline *Ballets Without Music, Without Dancers, Without Anything* $10.95
19 Gellu Naum *My Tired Father* $8.95
20 Vicente Huidobro *Manifestos Manifest* $12.95
21 Gérard de Nerval *Aurélia* $11.95
22 Knut Hamsun *On Overgrown Paths* $12.95

23 Martha Ronk *Displeasures of the Table* $9.95
24 Mark Twain *What Is Man?* $10.95
25 Antonio Porta *Metropolis* $10.95
26 Sappho *Poems* $10.95
27 Alexei Kruchenykh *Suicide Circus: Selected Poems* $12.95
28 José Donoso *Hell Has No Limits* $10.95
29 Gertrude Stein *To Do: A Book of Alphabets and Birthdays* $9.95
30 Joshua Haigh [Douglas Messerli] *Letters from Hanusse* $12.95
31 Federico García Lorca *Suites* $12.95
32 Tereza Albues *Pedra Canga* $12.95
33 Rae Armantrout *The Pretext* $9.95
34 Nick Piombino *Theoretical Objects* $10.95
35 Yang Lian *Yi* $14.95
36 Olivier Cadiot *Art Poetic'* $12.95
37 Andrée Chedid *Fugitive Suns: Selected Poetry* $11.95
38 Hsi Muren *Across the Darkness of the River* $9.95
39 Lyn Hejinian *My Life* $10.95
40 Hsu Hui-chih *Book of Reincarnation* $9.95
41 Henry David Thoreau *Civil Disobediance* $6.95
42 Gertrude Stein *Mexico. A Play* $5.95
43 Lee Breuer *La Divina Caricatura: A Fiction* $14.95
44 Régis Bonvicino *Sky-Eclipse: Selected Poems* $9.95
45 Raymond Federman *The Twofold Vibration* $11.95
46 Tom La Farge *Zuntig* $13.95
47 *The Song of Songs: Shir Hashirim* $9.95

48 Rodrigo Toscano *The Disparities* $9.95

49 Else Lasker-Schüler *Selected Poems* $11.95

50 Gertrude Stein *Tender Buttons* $10.95

51 Armand Gatti *Two Plays: The 7 Possibilities for Train 713 Departing from Auschwitz* and *Public Songs Before Two Electric Chairs* $14.95

52 César Vallejo *Aphorisms* $9.95

53 Ascher/Straus *ABC Street* $10.95

54 Djuna Barnes *The Antiphon* $12.95

55 Tiziano Rossi *People on the Run* $12.95

56 Michael Disend *Stomping the Goyim* $12.95

57 Hagiwara Sakutarō *Howling at the Moon: Poems and Prose* $11.95

58 Rainer Maria Rilke *Duino Elegies* $10.95

59 OyamO *The Resurrection of Lady Lester* $8.95

60 Charles Dickens *A Christmas Carol* $8.95

61 Mac Wellman *Crowtet I: Murder of Crow* and *The Hyacinth Macaw* $11.95

62 Mac Wellman *Crowtet II: Second-hand Smoke* and *The Lesser Magoo* $12.95

63 Pedro Pietri *The Masses Are Asses* $8.95

64 Luis Buñuel *The Exterminating Angel* $11.95

65 Paul Snoek *Hercules, Richelieu and Nostradamus* $10.95

66 Eleanor Antin *The Man Without a World: A Screenplay* $10.95

67 Dennis Phillips *Sand* $10.95

68 María Irene Fornes *Abingdon Square* $9.95

69 Anthony Powell *O, How the Wheel Becomes It!*
    $10.95

70 Julio Matas, Carlos Felipe, and Virgilio Piñera *Three
    Masterpieces of Cuban Drama* $12.95

71 Kelly Stuart *Demonology* $9.95

72 Ole Sarvig *The Sea Below My Window* $13.95

73 Vítězslav Nezval *Antilyrik and Other Poems* $10.95

74 Sam Eisenstein *Rectification of Eros* $10.95

75 Arno Schmidt *Radio Dialogs II* $13.95

76 Murat Nemat-Nejat *The Peripheral Space of
    Photography* $9.95

77 Adonis *If Only the Sea Could Sleep: Love Poems*
    $11.95

78 Stephen Ratcliffe *SOUND/(system)* $12.95

79 Dominic Cheung *Drifting* $9.95

80 Gilbert Sorrentino *Gold Fools* $14.95

81 Paul Celan *Romanian Poems* $10.95

82 Elana Greenfield *At the Damascus Gate: Short
    Hallucinations* $10.95

83 Anthony Powell *Venusberg* $10.95

84 Jean Frémon *Island of the Dead* $12.95

85 Arthur Schnitzler *Lieutenant Gustl* $9.95

86 Wilhelm Jensen/Sigmund Freud *Gradiva/Delusion
    and Dream in Wilhelm Jensen's* Gradiva $12.95

87 Andreas Embiricos *Amour Amour* $11.95

88 Eleni Sikelianos *The Monster Lives of Boys and Girls*
    $10.95

89 Kier Peters *A Dog Tries to Kiss the Sky: 7 Short Plays* $12.95

91 Paul Verlaine *The Cursed Poets* $11.95

92 Toby Olson *Utah* $12.95

94 Arthur Schnitzler *Dream Story* $11.95

95 Henrik Nordbrandt *The Hangman's Lament: Poems* $10.95

96 André Breton *Arcanum 17* $12.95

97 Joseph Conrad *Heart of Darkness* $10.95

98 Mohammed Dib *L.A. Trip: A Novel in Verse* $11.95

99 Mario Luzi *Earthly and Heavenly Journey of Simone Martini* $14.95

101 Jiao Tong *Erotic Recipes: A Complete Menu for Male Potency Enhancement* $8.95

103 Chen I-chih *The Mysterious Hualien* $9.95

106 Louis-Ferdinand Céline *The Church* $13.95

107 John O'Keefe *The Deatherians* $10.95

109 Thomas Mann *Six Early Stories* $10.95

116 Oswald Egger *Room of Rumor: Tunings* $9.95

119 Reina María Rodríguez *Violet Island and Other Poems* $12.95

137 Thorvald Steen *Don Carlos* and *Giovanni* $14.95

Green Integer EL-E-PHANT Books (6 x 9 format)

EL-1   *The PIP Anthology of World Poetry of the 20th Century, Volume 1* $15.95

EL-2   *The PIP Anthology of World Poetry of the 20th Century, Volume 2* $15.95

EL-3   *The PIP Anthology of World Poetry of the 20th Century, Volume 3 (Nothing the Sun Could Not Explain — 20 Contemporary Brazilian Poets)* $15.95

EL-4   *The PIP Anthology of World Poetry of the 20th Century, Volume 4* $15.95

EL-51 Larry Eigner *readiness / enough / depends / on* $12.95

EL-52 Martin Nakell *Two Fields That Face and Mirror Each Other* $16.95

EL-53 Arno Schmidt *The School for Atheists: A Novella = Comedy in 6 Acts* $16.95

EL-54 Sigurd Hoel *Meeting at the Milestone* $15.95

EL-55 Leslie Scalapino *Defoe* $14.95